The Carriage House

W. Bennett

iUniverse, Inc.
New York Bloomington

The Carriage House

Copyright © 2009 by W. Bennett

All rights reserved. No part of this book may be used or reproduced by any means, graphic, electronic, or mechanical, including photocopying, recording, taping or by any information storage retrieval system without the written permission of the publisher except in the case of brief quotations embodied in critical articles and reviews.
This is a work of fiction. All of the characters, names, incidents, organizations, and dialogue in this novel are either the products of the author's imagination or are used fictitiously.

iUniverse books may be ordered through booksellers or by contacting:

iUniverse
1663 Liberty Drive
Bloomington, IN 47403
www.iuniverse.com
1-800-Authors (1-800-288-4677)

Because of the dynamic nature of the Internet, any Web addresses or links contained in this book may have changed since publication and may no longer be valid. The views expressed in this work are solely those of the author and do not necessarily reflect the views of the publisher, and the publisher hereby disclaims any responsibility for them.

ISBN: 978-1-4401-1633-9 (sc)
ISBN: 978-1-4401-1634-6 (ebook)

Printed in the United States of America

iUniverse rev. date: 03/20/09

Acknowledgement

With the greatest thanks to Bruce and Jennie Morris,
for giving of their time, their talents, their friendship

For Granddaughter Brianna, a very special young lady.

Chapter 1

"Mister Fraser is expecting you," said the receptionist, her voice sweet and sorrowful, sickeningly sweet thought Shawn Duncan. She pointed down a hallway. "His office is the last door on the left."

Dominic Fraser, owner of Fraser Funeral Homes, stood and offered his hand. "I'm so very sorry for your loss, Shawn." He spoke as though greeting an old family friend although it was the first time the two men had ever met. He pointed to a chair. "Please, have a seat?" Fraser opened the file that was already on his desk and studied it momentarily. Everything about Fraser said, taker-of-the-dead; his dress, his mannerisms, his grooming, his sad basset hound eyes.

Looking up from the file Fraser asked, "Has your Dear Mother ever discussed her final wishes with you, Shawn?"

Duncan shook his head. "Not really. I'm guessing that's what we're about to do right now? She always had this terrible habit of putting things off."

"Actually," smiled Fraser, "I'd have to say that she did a very good job of making her final arrangements. My job would be so much easier if everyone was that thorough."

"Really?" said Duncan. "The world's worst procrastinator."

"Well not this time. In fact this was all taken care of many years ago."

"My God!" Duncan shook his head in disbelief. "Are we talking about the same woman?"

"We are indeed. And are you aware that she didn't want a wake or church service? And no graveside service?"

"Mother never discussed her final wishes in any detail, but it doesn't surprise me that she'd want it that way. She always found those things a bit morbid----and so do I."

"And everything is paid for. In fact it was paid for----let me see now." Fraser again checked the file. "Yes, back in August of 1961."

"Unbelievable!" Duncan gave out a light laugh. "If you had known my mother, you'd know why I find that so hard to believe."

"Well it's true. Her burial plot and internment fees were all taken care of at the same time."

Duncan raised his hand to stop Fraser in mid-sentence. "Her burial plot? There must be some mistake?"

"I beg your pardon?" said Fraser, somewhat confused.

"Are you sure that's my mother's file you have in front of you, Mister Fraser?"

Fraser again glanced down at the file, "Quite sure. Why?"

"Because mother will be buried beside my father in Pleasant Hills Cemetery with the rest of the family members, and those plots were purchased almost a century ago."

Fraser leaned back in his chair and stared at Duncan for a moment. "I see your Dear Mother didn't tell you everything."

"What's there to tell? She'll be buried in Pleasant Hills Cemetery beside her husband. Those plots and the large family headstone were purchased by my grandfather, and if she was talked into buying another burial plot then someone took advantage of her."

Fraser was stung by the remark but remained calm. Rising to his feet in one steady motion, he stood with his hands joined behind his back looking down on Duncan. "Mister Duncan," the sweetness was gone from his voice, "this funeral home was opened by my father back in 1928. It has survived on honesty and trust. Now I know you are quite distraught by the passing of your mother, but I assure you, sir, the arrangements made by your mother were *hers,* and *hers* alone."

Duncan was about to interrupt but Fraser cut him off. "I presume you know of a place north of here called Portage Lake?"

"Portage Lake? What's that place got to do with any of this?"

"Do you know where it is?" repeated the undertaker, his tone quite sharp.

"Of course I know where it is. Our family owns an old summerhouse up there along with a large parcel of land. But how did Portage Lake get into this conversation?"

Fraser ignored the question. "And on the southeast corner of that lake there was once a village by the same name, now an official ghost town I believe. The only remaining structure left is a church; a Lutheran church if memory serves me?" Fraser bent over his desk to glance at the file. "Yes, it is Lutheran."

"Sure, I've seen it dozens of times. When I was a kid I used to spend my summers up there."

"Then you also must have noticed the cemetery beside the church. That's where your mother will be laid to rest."

Duncan slowly rose to his feet. "Like hell she will."

The two men were glaring into each other's eyes.

"Oh I assure you sir, she will. Those are your mother's wishes and they *will* be respected."

"And I assure you, *sir,*" said Shawn Duncan with fight in his voice, "they will not. I don't know what in hell is going on here, but that's never going to happen."

Fraser softened his tone. "Mister Duncan, as a funeral director it is my sworn duty to carry out the wishes of the deceased. Sometimes those wishes are very upsetting to family members, and in this case I can understand your viewpoint. But unless you can get a court order to have them changed I'm afraid there is little you can do about it. And, I wish you'd try to keep in mind, these are *your mother's wishes,* not mine." Fraser handed Duncan a sheet of instructions. "These are her instructions, and if you look at the top of the page you can see the date. She drew this up back in August of 1961."

Snatching the paper from the undertaker's hand Duncan shook his head in disbelief as he read it. "But this is crazy. Why would she request such a thing? She never once mentioned any of this to me. Sure, she had mentioned funeral arrangements a few times and that's how I knew to call you when she died, but she never once said a word about any of this. Not a single word."

"And," added the undertaker, "there will be no headstone. The grave will remain unmarked."

Duncan pressed his fingertips to his temples as though searching for a button to clear his mind. "That was almost forty years ago."

"Thirty-seven to be precise," said Fraser. "Shawn, your mother dealt with my father back then. At the time she also left the clothes she wished to be buried in; a plain white summer dress, a mauve coloured scarf to be tired around her neck, and a small neck chain with a gold cross on it. And no shoes. And, as you can see, this is an official document drawn up by a lawyer." Fraser placed his finger on the law firm's letterhead at the top of the page, then to the lawyer's signature at the bottom of the page.

"What's happening here?" asked Duncan. "This makes no sense whatsoever."

"Perhaps to you and I it makes no sense," replied Fraser calmly, "but it certainly did to your mother. I've had far stranger requests. You can't imagine the number of shocked face I've seen in this office. Have you checked her personal documents for an explanation?"

"No, I haven't done that yet. I'll do it as soon as I get home."

Fraser remained silent while Duncan struggled to understand what he'd just been told. "I know this has come as quite a shock to you," he continued after a lengthy silence, "but since your mother was quite explicit about her internment, and since there will be no church or graveside service, the day and time of the burial is not a pressing matter. If, however, you wish to be present for the internment I'd be glad to choose a day that would be convenient for you----and of course, any other family members who might wish to attend."

Fraser picked up a calendar from his desk and studied it. "This is Wednesday." He tapped his finger on his chin as he thought. "I'll have to make arrangements with someone at Portage Lake to have the grave opened," he said, as though thinking aloud. Another silent spell followed. "Would next Monday be convenient. Say at nine, or ten in the morning?"

"I'll----I'll have to get back to you on that."

"I understand," said Fraser.

Duncan offered an unsteady hand to Fraser. "I'm sorry for what I said about…"

"Perfectly understandable," Fraser replied with his integrity intact.

Shawn Duncan left the funeral home trying desperately to absorb what he had just learned, wondering if he had ever really known the woman he had called Mother for the past forty-three years.

Chapter 2

A FINE TURN-OF-THE-CENTURY HOUSE, it was the only place Shawn Duncan had ever called home. After returning from the funeral parlour he stood for a time on the sidewalk and admired its grandeur, red ivy covering its Tudor walls like a crimson blanket, up to the eaves and around the windows and doors. The landscaping, the leaded diamond windows, the green copper flashings, the lion-head knocker on the oak door, the timber and stucco construction; such a solid and safe haven it had always been. But in the leaf-filter light of the late morning sun the same details which once gave the house its mystical allure didn't seem all that important anymore. It was just another house, on another street, like all the other houses in the area.

"Hello," he called out the minute he entered the house. "Are you here, Fatima?"

The clumping sound of footsteps resonated down from the upstairs. "I'll be right down, Shawn."

"Hello, Fatima. How are you doing?" he said to the weepy-eyed housekeeper as he gave her a hug. The plump little woman of Portuguese descent took a hanky out of her apron pocket and blotted her eyes. Shawn remembered Fatima from the time his mother first employed her, remembered how sinewy and lean she once was, and how attractive. She had raised a large family and always claimed, "Kids will keep a body thin". Obviously she was right; her children were grown and gone and she was no longer thin.

"Oh, Shawn, I still can't believe it."

"It's pretty hard for me to believe too, Fatima."

Still blotting her eyes, she asked, "Do you want me to stay on, Shawn, or am I finished?"

"Fatima, I want you to keep coming to work and looking after the place----at least until I get things sorted out."

She tried to smile. "Thank you, Shawn."

On the foyer table sat Connie Duncan's purse, and beside it the note she had left for Fatima, the last two things his mother ever touched in her lifetime. He picked up the note and read it for the umpteenth time.

> Fatima:
>
> I had to go up to Portage Lake. Something unexpected came up. I'll probably be back in a day or two. If I'm not I'll call. If Shawn is looking for me tell him I'll be staying with Harriet Colburn. Her number is in the address book by the phone.
>
> Connie.

As he glanced down at the slate floor in the foyer an image flashed through his mind, the image of his mother's body lying there, the way she was when he came into the house after Fatima had called him. Again he looked at the note. *What was so damned important that she had to hurry up there? She hadn't been up there in years and suddenly she couldn't wait. Why?*

"Fatima," he asked as he picked up his mother's purse, "do you happen to know if mother kept a spare set of keys to her office?"

Fatima turned quickly and walked down the hallway toward the room in question. Stopping at a hallway table she picked up a small vase, upended it, and the keys fell out. "Here you go," she said, handing him the keys.

Shawn was forced to smile. *Good old mom; keep it simple.* All those years and he never knew where she kept the keys to her private world.

Unlocking the door and stepping into his mother's office he had the strange sensation that he was trespassing. At one time Connie Duncan's office was a storage room, a place where the silverware, linen, extra place settings and other bric-a-brac were kept. He remembered the day he came home from school and she had the room's contents piled in the hallway and was busy sorting through it all, reassigning items to drawers and shelves in other areas of the house. He was commandeered to carry some of the displaced items to the attic.

"What are you doing, Mom?"

"I'm taking over this room. From now on this will be known as Fort Constance, and all intruders beware."

"But why? It doesn't even have a window?"

"And that's the beauty of it. No distractions." Then she laughed. "And I'm putting a gun slit in the door, too."

He remembered laughing. "How about a mote and a drawbridge outside?"

"Good idea. I'll keep that in mind."

They both had a good laugh over it. He remembered kissing his mother's cheek before going into the kitchen to examine the contents of the fridge while she went back to her work. *Strange how I can remember the simple act of kissing her cheek so many years ago?*

Flipping on the lights, he stood for a minute and examined his mother's private world. The room personified Connie Duncan. She was not a good housekeeper and the office reflected that flaw. An antique bookshelf sat along one wall with plenty of space for additional literature, the books lying flat instead of on their edges. A rocker-recliner took up one back corner of the room. A large flattop desk and swivel chair sat central along another wall, an ancient Underwood on the desk with a green blotter pad beneath it. From the twelve-foot ceiling a fan hummed lazily as it preformed its monotonous duty.

Shawn went to the desk and sat. Tilting the swivel chair back he absentmindedly stared at the blank wall in front of him, stared at it until it finally struck him; the wall was bare. Why? Nails protruded from the plaster, nails that once held pictures. He could distinctly remember looking into the room and seeing pictures on the wall, and the one he remembered most of all was a portrait of his mother. It too was gone.

Getting up from the chair he turned on the display light and studied the blank wall. *Where in hell did the pictures go?*

Then he noticed them. They were leaning against the wall by the door. The largest, the portrait of his mother, was facing the wall. In a large shopping bag were six smaller charcoal sketches. After a moment of puzzling thought he hung the portrait back where he remembered it being, on the very nail that was already there to receive it. Sitting back down he studied the painting for a time. *That artist was damn good, whoever he or she was. My God, Mom, but you were one beautiful woman in your day.* He then replaced the six sketches back to where they belonged, where they fitted perfectly. *Why did she take them down?*

It was the signatures on the charcoal sketches that brought him back to his feet. He couldn't believe what he was seeing. *"My God! J. Kane. Could they be the work of thee, Jeremy Kane? If they are, how in the world would mother have gotten her hands on them?* Taking the sketches back down from the wall he examined each one closely as a lifetime spent in the art business kicked into high gear. After examining the backs of the sketches he concluded that they were indeed authentic. Although he had never owned any of the artist's work he had read in one of his many art catalogues that Jeremy Kane always put the date of the work's completion on the back, in the lower left-hand corner. And he always crossed the vertical arms of sevens with a tick, the way that is common in Europe to write the numeral. *But they're not landscapes. He's well known for his landscapes, not portraits.*

One of the sketches was of a freckled-faced boy smiling with a missing front tooth. Another, a nude woman standing in water up to her hips with her back to the artist, her perfectly rounded buttocks ringing the water around her. Another was of a woman on a blanket wearing a light dress with a sunhat covering her face, her shoes on the blanket beside her with a basket and wine bottle on the grass near the blanket. There was one of a man splitting wood, also with his back to the artist, and one of a woman pinning sheets on a clothesline, a fluttering sheet hiding her face. None of the sketches showed a face. *Where would mother have gotten these?*

Shawn carefully hung the sketches back on the wall before going back to studying the large oil portrait of his mother. He instantly noticed that it was not signed. *Artist unknown!* Plopping back down on the swivel chair he was totally enthralled by what he was seeing, fascinated by the fact his mother had somehow obtained six sketches by a famous artist. While staring at the work he absentmindedly toyed with the office keys.

The only visible lock in the room was in the large drawer of the desk. Breathing deeply, he inserted a key into the lock and turned it. Inside the drawer were several bundles of paper, all separated with rubber bands. One stack of papers were mostly certificates and stock receipts, copies of mutual funds, deeds to investment properties and bank statements. Judging from the numbers of certificates and deeds he knew they represented a considerable amount of wealth. He thumbed through the papers looking for Connie Duncan's will, but there was none.

Then he noticed a small metal box on the light stand beside the rocker-recliner. Not a large box, just the right size to hold The Last Will and Testament of Constance Louise Duncan. Stepping over to the recliner he eased down onto it. Setting the box on his lap he was about to try the smallest key on the ring when he discovered it was already unlocked. *My god! She was looking at her will just recently. She had it out and forgot to put it away.*

On opening the box he found his mother's will, and stapled to the corner was the business card of a lawyer, a Milton M. Cossney. Beneath the will, also with an elastic band around them, were papers of a personal nature; marriage license, birth certificates, deed to the family home, a deed to the property at Portage Lake. The final paper in the box was a receipt for a burial plot in the Lutheran cemetery at Portage Lake, purchased in 1961 for the unbelievable sum of twenty-five dollars. There was also a copy of burial instructions, which Dominic Fraser had already shown him. The only thing missing was an explanation, the thing he wanted most of all. The will was a simplistic document leaving all of her earthly belongings to her only child, Cyrus Shawn Duncan.

When he was about to place the papers back into the box he noticed two tuffs of hair in the bottom, both tied with thin red ribbons. He removed the tuffs and studied them. One tuff was his, he guessed; it was the same colour and texture as his own hair. *She must have taken it from me when I was young.* The second tuff, dark and curly, he knew to be his mother's hair. A sinking feeling came over him as he pressed the tuffs between his fingers. And that was it, the life and times of Connie Duncan. The life of an uncomplicated, unpretentious, non-mysterious woman who just that morning had shocked the hell out of him. He was suddenly overwhelmed with a need to cry.

When he was drained of emotion, he stood, went back to the desk and stared at the painting on the wall, stared at the beautiful woman his mother once was. *She was widowed so young, and yet never remarried.* It was the first time in his life he ever really wondered why, why she had never become involved with another man? He knew she had dated men over her lifetime, and had once gone on a cruise with a man, but nothing serious ever came of it. She had plenty of friends, both male and female, yet she remained single. Was the marriage between her and his father so powerful, so strong and deep that she could never forget Cyrus Duncan? But she never mentioned his name. And why would she wish to be buried away from him? And why did she smile so warmly from the canvas? Was there a secret in those beautiful greenish-brown eyes?

When he first entered the office he had set his mother's purse on the desk; it was now time to open it. Finding nothing unusual in the purse, nothing he didn't already expect to find in any woman's purse: lipstick, comb, mirror, car keys, a wallet, and down in the very bottom a small bottle of aspirin tablets. However, in a side compartment he found a prescription that had been issued the very day she died. He slowly pulled it from the purse and studied it. He didn't recognize the name of the drug, but he couldn't help but wonder why his healthy mother had been prescribed anything at all. And what was Coumadin? He thought for a moment before picking up the phone and calling Doctor Raymond Philips, a long-time friend and family physician.

"Hello," said Raymond Philips.

"Hello, Doctor. This is Shawn Duncan."

"Oh yes, Shawn. And how are you today?"

Shawn just said it. "Mother died yesterday."

"My God," he whispered. After a silent moment the doctor said, "Shawn I'm so very sorry."

"Thanks, Doctor. But why I've called is because I was going through some of mother's things and I found a prescription for a drug called Coumadin. It was just made out yesterday----by you. What was the drug for, Doctor?"

"It's a blood thinner. Your mother had had a heart attack."

"She did? When?"

"I'm not sure, when," replied the doctor, "but it's often referred to as a silent heart attack. It strikes women far more often than men. Usually the patient doesn't even know they've had it. She came in to see me last week, said she was experiencing shortness of breath and tightness in the chest. I sent her for blood work. It showed up in her blood work and that's why I prescribed a blood thinner. I told her to get on it right away----to avoid blood clots. In fact, I was just now setting up appointments for her to have additional tests done."

"Well, I'm afraid it's too late for that now," whispered Shawn.

"So sorry," repeated the doctor.

Shawn thanked the doctor and hung up.

Doctor Ray Philips sat quietly and recalled seeing his old friend for the last time.

"Ray, you must be mistaken? I'd've known if I had a heart attack."

"Not necessarily, Connie. What you had is called a silent heart attack. They happen mostly to women. As a rule they don't even know they've had it. But, that being said, it's not the end of the world. You've had a heart attack and now we must deal with it."

Connie Duncan's complexion turned gray and she said, "Then I'm finished."

"Nonsense, Connie," scolded the doctor. "There's no reason why you can't live to be a hundred. Now I don't want you to go and get yourself all worked up over this. I'm going to put you on a blood thinner until I can have some more tests done. I want you to get on it right away."

She hadn't heard a word he said. "I thought I had all the time in the world, Ray, but I don't, do I?"

"Don't be silly, Connie. And stop talking like that. Now, I want you to go home and take it easy." He smiled warmly at her. "And stop worrying."

She looked at him with deep concern. "There's things in life we should never put off, Ray."

Perhaps I should have spent more time with her? Perhaps I shouldn't have let her leave the office in the state she was in? Maybe I should have made her take something right away? Maybe I should have giving her a tranquilizer? Ah, hell! If I go around second-guessing every decision I make I'll go crazy. I can't baby-sit my patients.

Shawn Duncan remained seated for a time and thought about what he had just learned. *So mother, what was so important that you didn't have time to fill the prescription? What's so important at Portage Lake you didn't have time to look after your health?* He held up the unfilled prescription, stared at it for a long time before putting it back in the purse.

When he was finished in the office he locked the door behind him and dropped the keys back into the vase.

"Fatima?"

"Yes?" The voice came from upstairs.

"Could you come down for a minute, please?"

Fatima came down the stairs with a duster in her hand. "Yes, Shawn?"

"Fatima, did mother ever mention to you anything about where she wanted to be buried?"

She shook her head vigorously. "No."

"So, she never discussed anything like that with you?"

"Oh no. I don't like to talk about that kind of stuff."

Shawn put his arm around Fatima's shoulder and squeezed affectionately. "I know mother thought the world of you, Fatima."

The housekeeper began to sob again. "Oh Shawn, I'm going to miss her something awful."

"Fatima, I think you should go home for the day. Take a couple days off." He looked around the house and then added with a smile, "I don't think anyone is going to notice whether you're here or not." He helped her on with her coat, opened the door for her, kissed her cheek and said goodbye.

After Fatima had gone and he was alone again, he drifted from room to room recalling his growing-up years there, remembered his mother, could still hear her voice echoing through the silence of a once happy home.

"Hi, Mom. I'm home."

"Hi, Dear. How was school?"

"Okay. What's there to eat?"

In the home's large living room a bulky chesterfield faced the fireplace and along the back of the chesterfield sat a sofa table, the top of the table and the shelf beneath it literally covered with pictures. Shawn examined the pictures, pictures of himself at different periods of his life. *Too many pictures of me.* And there were pictures of family members back in Cape Breton Island, a place they had visited many times. There was even a picture of a cat they once owned, a cat that had lived for sixteen years and was not replaced when it died.

Where's father's picture? He quickly looked over the entire collection and found none. He had seen a picture of him once, he knew he had, but where had the photo gone. After considerable thought he went to a drawer in the buffet----the junk drawer his mother always called it----and beneath a stack of old photos he found it.

It had no frame and he knew by the whiteness of the paper that it had been put away a long time ago. He studied the photo and tried to look past the age of the man, but it was the image of a stranger, an old man he could not connect with. He could vaguely remember Cyrus Duncan when he was alive, could remember asking him question about schoolwork and receiving blunt and accurate answers, but could never recall being close to him. At that moment he tried to feel something for the man, tried to recall a good moment in time, but couldn't. He replaced the picture, closed the drawer, and felt a pang of guilt for not feeling something for the man who was his father.

Reality suddenly pressed down on him, and the reality was that Connie Duncan, the dearest person in his life, was gone forever. It was as though a great vacuum had sucked the love from the house. He decided there and then that he'd sell the house as soon as possible. He had always believed the house would be his forever and would never part with it, but in an instant it all changed. He found it unsettling how a love-filled haven that was once such a great part of his life could suddenly become nothing. And he needed to go to Portage Lake to see where Connie Duncan would be buried, to try and unravel the mystery of why?

Hurrying upstairs to his bedroom, he threw a change of clothes and shaving kit into an overnight bag and then rushed downstairs and out of the house. Locking the door behind him, he threw his bag onto the back seat of his car and backed out of the driveway. Driving directly to his art gallery he posted a sign on the door, "Closed because of a death in the family". He then headed north.

Chapter 3

THE NOONDAY NEWS CAME on the radio just as he pulled onto highway 400, but Shawn Duncan didn't hear a word. Using his cell phone he called Fraser Funeral Home and said, "Yes, Monday morning at ten would be fine for the burial". The northern flow of traffic was light and moving fast, the October sunshine brilliant, the autumn colours incandescent, but he saw none of it. *Why? Why did she do this?*

So many questions without answers. He could never once remember his mother going to Pleasant Hills Cemetery and visiting her husband's grave. *Probably she had and just never mentioned it.* He wanted to believe that. He then remembered something else. *Good God, I've never visited my father's grave either. I don't have a clue where it is. I even have trouble remembering what he looked like. But how could I? I was only seven when he died. And who were my parents? Did I really know them? I always thought I did, but did I really? And Cyrus Duncan, my father, what was he like? Who were the*

Duncans? He remembered asking his mother those very same questions but she never went into great detail about them. He knew their names, where they came from, how they made their money, but he really knew little else about them. Connie Duncan had a genius for dismissing the questions of a young boy; eventually he just stopped asking.

He suddenly craved answers, wanted to know about his family. His life went by without giving them a second thought, as though they didn't matter, but now he wanted to know. As he drove along unaware of the miles rushing by, another truth crept to the forefront of his thoughts. *I just didn't care enough about the past to find out. It wasn't important enough for me to ask. Dear God, I don't even know who my parents were. I've met many of my relatives, but I never really knew any of them. Jesus, was I that selfish? That spoiled? I'm forty-three years of age, totally alone in the world and I haven't a clue as to who I am.*

Then he remembered another woman in his life. Victoria Picklow, Vicki, the woman he almost married, wanted badly to marry, was madly in love with. The day after proposing to her, she sent back his engagement ring with a note, "I'm sorry, Shawn, but I don't love you, and I can't marry you. Good-bye."

And there was Jean Zouker, a woman he went with for over four years. He didn't love Jean, but he would have married her too, if she had agreed. "I think the world of you, Shawn, but let's not spoil what we have." *I wined, dined, and slept with that woman for more than four years and nothing ever came of it. Why? What's wrong with me? Is the Duncan name cursed? Why am I half way through my life and still alone? I don't want to spend the rest of my life alone.*

"Who in the name of God am I, anyway?"

Chapter 4

SHAWN DUNCAN'S GRANDFATHER, ARCHIBALD Duncan, emigrated from Scotland in May 1896. It was the dream of a quick fortune that brought him to the new land. He had been a bank clerk back in Glasgow, but because of the Duncan family's low social standing he knew the possibility of financial advancement in the old class-regimented country was bleak. Being a man in a hurry he also knew that rank and privilege was not a requirement in other parts of The Empire and a man could become rich through hard work and without a title. At the age of twenty-two he said good-bye to family and friends, took his small savings and purchased passage on a ship to Canada, fully confident good things waited for him on the other side of the Atlantic. He came to Toronto.

He was stunned by the severe contrasts of the place, a dirtier version of what he had left behind. The noises that assaulted his ears could just as well have been Glasgow's noises; squealing iron wheels, horses whinnying, illiterate men cursing, steam whistles shrieked out their messages from textile mills, foundries, and slaughterhouses. Toronto was a place of shacks and grand mansions, of rich and poor, of the plump and lean, of brothels and churches, of sewers and pristine parks. Except for the many foreign accents he was right back in Glasgow.

Archibald took the only job he was qualified to perform, a bank teller, but now the future looked even bleaker than it did when he was back in Scotland. He was alone in a hard land without the support of family or friends, and without the means of returning to the place where life was at least safe and predictable, where sea winds kept the air sweet.

However, good fortune can jump up and say hello when least expected and in Archibald's case it came in the shape of a somewhat plump, round-faced twenty-eight-year-old woman named Muriel McPherson.

Archibald found a measure of comfort amongst his own kind and Muriel McPherson was a second generation of his kind. Their meeting came about when he volunteered to help at a church sponsored charity event to raise money for a new wing on the minister's house. The minister's wife, although pushing forty, was still producing offspring at a steady rate and the family needed additional space. Muriel was the daughter of Cornelius and Hilda McPherson, and when Archibald discovered who the McPhersons were he became extremely interested in their unattractive daughter.

Cornelius was a first-generation Scotsman and like his father before him—the man who laid down the framework for the family fortune—he was stern in makeup, arrogant and pompous in demeanor, brutal in his pursuit of wealth and blindly proud of his Scottish heritage. And, like-father-like-son, he seemed to have but one purpose on earth, to accumulate wealth. He was also a master in the art of hanging onto it. Short, paunchy, always dressed to the nines, he strutted through life aloof of his fellow citizens, lived in one of the city's finest homes, often dined with politicians and businessmen, and didn't give a damn or a dime to the downtrodden of the world. To him the poor were just another commodity to be exploited, their plight being of their own making, their own fault.

Cornelius had his greedy hands in many pots and he seemed to possess a sixth sense when it came to sniffing out a profit. If it was manufacture, grown in fields, ran on rails or floated on water, he made money from it. In his grim way he loudly proclaimed the evils of alcohol, but he saw no conflict with holding shares in several distilleries and a brewery. High moral standards were one thing, a sure profit was something else.

Understanding that daughter Muriel was physically unattractive, Cornelius naturally became suspicious when the going-nowhere Archibald Duncan began taking an interest in her. Alarm bells rang in his cynical old mind. Why would any man take an interest in his daughter? If she were the daughter of a chimneysweep would anyone come courting? Certainly not. He instructed Muriel to have nothing more to do with this man, but Muriel was desperate so for the first time in her life she stood up to her domineering father. "He's a fine and good man, Father, and I'm going to marry him."

Faced with such unexpected resistance, and understanding the desperate situation her poor looks placed her in, he decided to go along with the marriage for her sake. But he couldn't have his only daughter marrying a lowly bank teller. Cornelius held great sway in the banking world and he would do something about it. Before a wedding could take place Cornelius would put the commoner into a higher social standing. Taking his future son-in-law under his wing he taught him the fine art of greed and Archibald took to it with a ravenous zeal; he certainly craved wealth, he just lacked the know-how to obtain it. Cornelius saw to it that Archie----the pet name he was then called around the McPherson household----was promoted to Assistant Bank Manager. The following year Archie was managing his own bank branch and Cornelius had him dabbling in the world of investments. The new son-in-law took to the stock market and investing like an old hand and Cornelius saw great potential in the grasping young man.

But Archie's newfound fortunes did little to change who he was, nor did his new clothes or new house. He was not a handsome man. Far from it. Being somewhat long and gangly with a sallow complexion, tired sad eyes, hollow cheeks, clean-shaven with heavy mutton-chop sideburns, he radiated despair. His life was devoid of self-pampering and humour, but the straight-laced unattractive Muriel, although five years his senior, saw him as a perfect match. No man ever gave her a second look, and certainly would never consider her as a life-long partner, so when Archibald took an interest in her she was overjoyed and liked him just the way he was.

For his part, Archie could easily look past Muriel's plainness and see her for what she truly was; the daughter and only child of Cornelius McPherson who someday would inherit her father's wealth. And, understanding full well that he was no great-looking catch himself----sort of a long and gangly Abe Lincoln look about him----he went for Muriel like a man possessed. It was not Cupid's arrow that had pierced his heart, he had simply become ensnarled in McPherson purse strings. And Cornelius saw to it that the marriage was a wonderful event throwing open the squeaking doors of his bank account to guarantee his daughter's happiness.

Archie loved his bride, as best he understood love, and she respected him, which she believed was all that was really required for a solid relationship. In their unshakable stern ways they were a perfect match and the pieces fitted perfectly. At bedtime they also discovered something else fitted perfectly and he partook of her female warmth at every opportunity. It couldn't be called lovemaking, but she wanted to please her husband and went along with the nightly ritual without complaint. She had been forewarned of what to expect after the nuptials so she decided to accept sex as just part of married life, another chore, like doing the dishes after dinner. But Archie seemed to enjoy it immensely, snorting and snuffing with satisfaction as he thrust in and out of his lifeless bride, but she gladly held open the door to Archie's happiness.

Each night a nine o'clock sharp the light in the bedroom was turned off, and under the security of the covers Muriel hoisted her nightdress and Archie climbed on top of her. The duration of the God-approved act lasted ten minutes, seldom more, seldom less, and was carried out without a single word passing between the participants, only the sounds of Archie giving it his all, like he was straining at some back-breaking task. Once completed, he breathed a deep sigh of satisfaction, immediately rolled off his lifeless bride while she lowered her nightdress. Minutes later the room was filled with snores.

Archie did truly enjoy the nightly ritual, while Muriel, to get through those ten minutes of being thumped against a firm mattress, made mental notes as to what needed to be done around the house the next day. If that was all she had to do for the right to say she was a married woman, to have her own home and to have a man walk her to church each Sunday, then she could tolerate it without complaint. And as much as she told herself that it was her duty, and that it held no pleasure for a woman, she did experience a certain sensation in that area of her body which seemed to interest Archie so greatly. In fact, she soon became very taken with the nightly affair and looked forward to it.

Two years into the agreement they called marriage, and much to Muriel and Archie's surprise, she was pregnant. With overwhelming happiness, in February 1900, she bore a son and they called the child, Cyrus Archibald Duncan.

Archie's life had surpassed anything he could have ever hoped for back in Scotland. He was married to a good and loyal woman, was father of a healthy son, and lived in a comfortable home in a respectable area of the city. Then his life got even better when his father-in-law, Cornelius, started going senile. Archie gladly took over all the old man's business affairs and had Cornelius sign everything over to him before he was too far-gone in the mind. When Cornelius died they sold their modest home and moved into the McPherson mansion. As part of the deal they took care of mother Hilda to the end of her days. For his troubles, Archie was rewarded with the deed to one of the finest homes in Toronto along with unbelievable wealth. He was rich, a pillar of the community, respected and feared, and he was still a young man.

Chapter 5

YOUNG CYRUS DUNCAN PROVED to be the perfect son; obedient, smart, and somewhat better looking than his parents. Archie and Muriel never let the lad forget that he belonged to them; they owned the boy the same way a man owns a dog, and like a good dog Cyrus was trained to do as he was told. Throughout his life he had certain standards drummed into his head: it was his duty to respect the wishes of his parents, the Duncan name must never be smudged, and it was a child's duty to care for his parents regardless what life threw in the way, and no matter what, he must always show respect. His life was regimented, predictable, depressing, unrewarding, and extremely lonely. His father's ways became his ways; he lived by the clock, accumulated wealth, protected the family name, but unlike his father he remained single.

Under Archibald's tutelage Cyrus learned to sniff out opportunity, what to look for when investing, how to balance the books, how to legally cheat the taxman, when to stand strong and when to count your losses. But unlike his father, Cyrus never knew hard times, therefore wealth brought no pleasure with it; it was only money and accumulating it was a job.

During The Great Depression, when other men buckled in despair as their investments swirled down the financial sinkhole, Cyrus prospered simply because making money was in his genes. Each morning he sipped his tea, scanned the financial pages, ate his toast and jam, and never wavered in his belief that good times would return. Throughout those ten miserable years when other men around him moaned in despair, Cyrus Duncan kept on looking for opportunities and pounced on them with the alertness of a cat when they came along. This is not to say that the shrewd man did not experienced losses, he certainly did, it was just that they were seldom and he accepted them as part of doing business.

One of those poor investments made him the owner of a summer home and a thousand acres of land on Portage Lake a four-hour train ride north of the city. He acquired the property through a bankruptcy. Cyrus's world was centered on Bay Street and he didn't particularly care to own a tract of land in the far off reaches of a northern forest, but his instincts sensed opportunity, so how could he pass up so much for so little?

Wallace Anderson, a man in his early forties, was a rising star in the-sky's-the-limit period of the 1920s. If there was something to know about investing Wallace believed he had all the answers. To him money was something to be reinvested, or spent, not salted away like dried cod. Money made money and he was out to make millions. Although he and his lovely young wife owned a fine home in a better part of the city, the summer's heat had a fermenting effect on the discards of city life. Even when a breeze managed to swirl through the city streets it carried with it a ripening stench. For those who could afford to do so, they sought out a more pleasant environment for themselves and their families. Some went to the Muskokas and stayed in grand resorts, or purchased land on an unspoiled lake and had summer homes built. Wallace purchased a stately old Victorian beauty on Portage Lake along with a thousand-acres of pine and hardwood forest.

But something did go terribly wrong in those heady times when nothing-could-go-wrong. October 1929 put an end to it for Wallace and his lovely wife. Countless others who held his same financial beliefs tumbled off their thrones with the Anderson's. Wallace discovered that his investments were suddenly worth ten cents on the dollar----or nothing at all----and when the bankers and lenders started knocking on his stately door they wanted repayment dollar for dollar. Throughout the month of November he tried everything to ward off bankruptcy, but to no avail. His business genius ended in the basement of his home with one end of a rope tied around his neck and the other end around a floor beam. He escaped the shame of bankruptcy and his young widow was left destitute.

But she emerged from the debacle much the wiser. She eventually remarried, but for her second attempt at the good life she chose a widower loaded with old money. He was wealthy, lived in a grand home, and was only weeks away from his seventieth birthday. Six years later, after his death, she was back on top of the world and that time she stayed there. What remained of Wallace's holdings were picked over by his lenders, but few wanted a summer home four hours away, especially with financial gloom and despair hanging over the land. Cyrus Duncan quickly saw the possibility in the property and snapped it up. But as the Depression dragged on he discovered his investment was really a poor one, but as luck would have it, it proved to be a blessing in disguise.

Shortly after acquiring the summer home, Cyrus took his aging parents on a train ride to see the summerhouse on Portage Lake. They both loved it. Archibald said it reminded him somewhat of Scotland, and old Muriel believed the fresh air helped open the congestion in her lungs. Cyrus instantly understood the importance of keeping the place. Both parents would be spending their summers miles away from him and the city. After that discovery he would never consider selling, and each June he shipped his parents off to Portage Lake. They were at the lake and Cyrus had the summers to himself. It was little different from other times of the year for his routine never varied, but at least it was a quiet time for him and he could enjoy the solitude of the rambling family home without always being bombarded with demands of his intolerable mother. The summerhouse on Portage Lake held value far beyond its sticker price.

Archibald died at the lake in 1939 while Muriel lived on for another dozen years and kept going back each summer. Cyrus hired a local woman to stay with her and do the cooking and cleaning; in fact, he hired several women over the years because they kept quitting. No one could tolerate Muriel's demands or her mean disposition. And it was just after his father's death that Cyrus hired a fulltime handyman to keep the place up and running, a handyman named Darrell Colburn.

Women fascinated Cyrus, and he often imagined what it would be like to partake of one's warmth, but that was as far as it ever went. It seemed he was doomed to a life of celibacy and loneliness. His only sexual experience----with someone other than himself----happened shortly before his thirtieth birthday. He had promised himself that he was going to enjoy the pleasure of a female's body before he turned thirty. He had long ago given up on the idea of love and marriage, but just once in his life he wanted to experience lust. It was his surest goal in life and he craved it. Muriel had often warned her son of the destructiveness of lust and of the diseases that would undoubtedly come from it, and of the pending torments of hell and damnation if he should ever indulge. She had trouble with the words but got her point across; keep away from women.

The Duncan family's office was housed in a large red brick building they owned down near the lakefront and Cyrus's life was spent between the office and the family home. First it was business, and then it was looking after his aging parents. The entire lakefront was a grimy collection of warehouses, grain elevators, foundries, ship repair sheds, and a host of lesser manufacturing plants, all crowded in between the main railway lines and the central part of the city, a cheap place to run a business.

Just north of the railway tracks, tucked away in a small area east of the city center was the red light district. Every man knew of its existence. On a brutally cold January afternoon with his thirtieth birthday looming, a day so cold the streets were practically deserted, he made his move. It got dark early that time of the year and he was confident he could get to a whorehouse, fulfill his dream, and get home in time for the evening meal and no one would be the wiser. With his hat pulled low over his face, his overcoat collar high around his head to ward off the stinging wind, like a robber sizing up a bank he skulked around the front door of one of the better brothels. When the coast seemed clear he quickly darted inside.

A bulky Madam asked him in a Cockney accent, "What type ya lookin' fur, Loove?" Cyrus was speechless. He struggled for a reply but nothing came. She instinctively knew that he had never been before. "Oh, I've just the sweet young thing fur-ya, Loove". She handed him a key. "You just pop upstairs to room four and she'll be along smartly."

Taking the key he hurried up the staircase and entered room number four as quickly as possible. Five minutes later a buxom young thing, not more than eighteen years of age, entered the room wearing only a kimono.

"Hello, Love," she said, her voice soft and teasing. She shed her kimono and for the first time in his life he was standing face-to-face with a naked woman. His heart hammered against his ribs and his throat went dry. Throwing herself on the bed she smiled at Cyrus. "Well, come-on, love. You can't do it with your cloths on, now can you?"

Cyrus fumbled out of his clothes all except for his long johns and stockings. He quickly got under the covers before removing his underclothes. The prostitute instantly knew it was his first time and she found the proceeding amusing. Getting under the sheet with him, she began to stroke his erection.

"Well, Love," she teased, "now aren't you just the shy one?"

At that very moment the worst possible thing happened; Cyrus ejaculated into the whore's hand.

"My, my," she laughed, "Hasn't that gun got a touchy trigger?"

Cyrus sprang from the bed and frantically began dressing, his face scarlet, his erection quickly wilting away.

"Oh, come now, love," she laughed, "don't leave. You come back and lay close to Dora and I'll have 'im back in fightin' order in no time at all."

Cyrus threw an assortment of bills on the bed and without once looking at the whore he bolted for the door, his shirttail hanging out, both sides of his suspenders over one shoulder. As he raced from the brothel he could hear the young woman laughing at the top of her lungs; he would hear that laughter for the rest of his life. Down King Street he hurried, his teeth chattering with the cold, his socks and long johns still under the sheets on the whore's bed. He never again attempted union with a prostitute, and never again would he tolerate humour at his expense.

Cyrus's short venture into the brothel was the extent of eroticism in his life. After that pitiful night he went back to being the obedient son and running the family business. For the following nineteen years he stayed on the straight and narrow. In fact, he accepted the glaring reality of his situation, that he would be a celibate bachelor until the end of his days. That knowledge caused him the greatest pain of all. He would die and so would the family name. Like the dinosaurs, the Duncan name was doomed to extinction.

It would be honest to say that Cyrus Duncan's second life began when his mother's ended. Muriel Duncan was five months past her eightieth-second birthday when she went on to her eternal rest. There were no choruses of laments at the news of her passing, not a single tear was shed, not even by her only child. "Never been sick a day in my life", she always claimed. "I've the constitution of a mule", and people whispered that she also had the looks to go along with it. But the brutal winter of 1951 proved to be extremely hard on the old mule. She picked up a flu-bug, went downhill quickly, and expired shortly afterwards.

Her wake was an expensive affair. Muriel wanted to be missed and believed that money could buy grief, but very few came to say goodbye. As Cyrus sat alone in the quiet of the funeral parlor, his mother's cold remains his only company, his mind fleshing out what the future held for him; the prognosis was grim. So there he sat, alone, a pathetic sight to see.

A young woman came into the funeral parlor, introduced herself as an employee and offered her condolences. He guessed her to be about thirty years of age, impeccably dressed, attractive, but wearing a wedding ring, and very professional in her mannerisms. Her husband was one of the owners of the funeral home and she felt a certain pity for the man when she witnessed him going through the mourning process with no one to comfort him. She sat beside Cyrus, took one of his hands in hers and talked warmly to him. She knew how to say all the right things; that Muriel lived a good long life, that she didn't suffer a long illness, etcetera.

Cyrus Duncan didn't hear a word the woman said. The fact that he was sitting next to an attractive young woman, could feel her warm hands in his, could smell her perfume, could feel her radiant heat did something wonderful to him. She didn't stay long but it had a powerful effect on him. He then looked up at his mother's cold face, and even with her eyes stitched shut, and even though her corpse was facing the ceiling, he sensed she was glaring at him. But it was the very moment that an epiphany lighted the dismal existence; his roadblock to happiness would soon be under the ground. There was still a chance of experiencing love, marriage, having a child and giving immortality to his meaningless existence, saving the family name from oblivion. Perhaps his life's greatest dread could be avoided after all.

Over the following year he thought more and more about that young woman who held his hand, and he began noticing other women. He noticed them when he passed them on the street, noticed the way their hips swayed, noticed their dress, noticed their shapes, understood they were baby machines.

There was one glaring problem, however; if he wanted a namesake then he would need a wife, one of those strange creatures he knew nothing about. Not only was he sent to an all-boys' school in Toronto during his grade school years, he was also sent to a parochial all-boys' school in Scotland for his teen years. His father had purposely selected that school because of its strict religious teachings and uncompromising discipline. Cyrus was told it was to temper him against the meanness of life and to discover his heritage, but it was really to keep him single and obedient. He grew up with absolutely no idea as to how one walked along the bridal path, and to make matters worse, he knew his genetic hourglass was running out of sand.

Chapter 6

THE DUNCAN INVESTMENT COMPANY had only one employee, Helen Borden. Other than old Muriel she was the only woman allowed into Cyrus's life. Company secretary and bookkeeper, she was married to a railway worker and was the mother of six children. Certainly no raving beauty, and certainly not someone a man would seek out for an affair, but she was female and Cyrus had an unusual liking for the woman. Quite large in stature, her well-padded frame gave her a clumping way of walking, her heavy hips waddling somewhat as she moved about. Being well experienced in the field of motherhood she often used that expertise to mother Cyrus.

Shortly after hiring Helen, Cyrus came to work on a raw February morning suffering from a stiff neck. Helen insisted on messaging it for him. He instantly forgot about his pain; the feel of the woman's soft hands on his neck was heaven to him. Over the years he often asked her to perform the duty. And Helen understood the reason behind the massages, but she pitied the man and didn't mind. If he demanded nothing more than a little human contact occasionally then that would be their little secret and she could live with it. She needed the job and Cyrus Duncan needed Helen.

But as Helen grew older so did her weight. And with the weight came health problems. The office was housed in an old structure, deep and narrow with a tall set of stairs leading to the upper level where the business files were kept. Those steps needed climbing many times a day. Helen's knees and hips began to give out on her and walking became painful. If Cyprus's coldhearted father was dealing with the situation he would have just replaced Helen, but Cyrus liked the jolly woman. He needed her in his life. She was the only one who could cheer him, the only one who ever attempted to bring him out of his fits of melancholy, the only one who seemed to care. And she made the perfect cup of tea.

It was not long after Muriel died that Helen came into Cyrus's office and informed him that she'd have to leave because of her health; she could no longer climb the high stairs. The second woman in his life was about to leave him and he couldn't allow it. He would hire Helen an assistant. Just minutes before closing time on a warm afternoon in May, a young woman, Constance Louise Lawson came into The Duncan Investments office and he hired her on the spot. Cyrus Duncan's life took on new meaning that very afternoon.

She was a fisherman's daughter. The sea winds could take credit for the ruddy glow in her cheeks, put there from years spent in the harsh weather of The Gulf. With greenish-brown eyes, a slender nose, hair dark and thick, the veins on her slender neck and strong arms showing lightly through weather-tinted skin, when she stepped into Cyrus Duncan's office she was a creature from his dreams, a fulfillment of his dreams. Surely she was sent to him by a Higher Power.

Connie Lawson was the ninth child in a family of eleven children----three boys and eight girls----all born into the hard life that was The Maritimes. A survivor by nature, she accepted her position in the world without complaint but was always on the lookout for something better. Her father, Fergus Lawson, never wanted to see his children entrapped in the slavery he and his forefathers had endured, and so he encouraged them to leave Nova Scotia and find a better life elsewhere. He saw to it that each child completed high school, and as the years slipped by and the number of faces around the dinner table diminished, he and his good wife Johanna knew that they were doing what was best for their offspring.

Connie came to Toronto in March 1950 two full years after completing high school. As a rule the Lawson children left home shortly after completing high school, but Fergus Lawson broke his leg when a wharf piling slipped and fell on him. Connie, being the eldest still at home at the time, stayed behind to help out. She remained on Cape Breton until the last boy, Carl, was about finished school and she was no longer needed. Her first employment was at the large Eaton's store on Queen Street. She worked in the Order Department preparing and shipping catalogue orders. It paid for her room and board and little else, and so while she worked she kept looking for something better. There seemed to be plenty of jobs for young women, but like all women's positions the pay was small. The Second World War had ended five years previous and most all the single women had quit their wartime jobs, had gotten married, and were then mothers.

Each day while eating her lunch Connie went through the routine of circling the want ads in the newspapers. One day she casually circled the add placed there by Cyrus Duncan, "For a young woman to assist in the mailing department of an small investment company." That afternoon, after her shift had finished, she quickly left Eaton's and walked down to the lakeshore, to the street number given in the paper. She located the office of Duncan Investments just minutes before Helen Borden locked up.

"May I help you, Miss?" said Helen Borden.

"I came about the advertisement in the paper."

Helen looked at the wall clock. "We're just closing for the day," she said, sounding tired.

"Well, can you tell me if the position has been filled?"

"There's been several interviews, but I don't know if Mister Duncan has chosen a girl or not."

"Oh, all right then. Well thank you for your time," she said politely and turned to leave.

Cyrus Duncan was coming down the high staircase with a thick sheath of papers in his hands. He looked at the young woman and couldn't take his eyes from her.

"Hello," he said, with a slight nod of the head.

Connie smiled and returned the greeting.

Helen Borden quickly put in, "I've just told this young lady that it's quite late and job interviews are finished for the day, Mister Duncan."

"Oh I'm sure I have time for one more, Mrs. Borden." Cyrus hurried down the stairs, set the papers on the counter, and held his office door open for the young woman. "Please, come in?"

He asked her four questions: Her name? Was she now employed? How much Eaton's paid her? When could she start? He offered her twenty-five cents an hour more than Eaton's were paying, and she would start work the following Monday. She was warmly assured she had nothing to worry about, that Helen Borden would teach her everything she needed to know. That was the day the bland life of Cyrus Duncan was infused with a heavy dose of sweetness. Helen Borden saw the change in him almost at once, and it wasn't long before she pointed out the change to her new assistant.

"He has an eye for you," she told Connie one day while they were eating their lunch.

"Don't be silly. What in the world would he see in me?"

Helen gave her a wry wink. Then she whispered, "And he's wealthy----very wealthy."

Six months after hiring Connie Lawson, on a late afternoon in early December, Cyrus asked Helen Borden if she'd mind staying a few minutes late. "I'd like to discuss something with you," he said, when Connie was out of earshot.

Thinking that her job was about to be terminated because she was now doing so little around the office, Helen expected the worst.

"Helen," he began, after Connie was gone and the office door was locked, "I wish to ask for your guidance on a delicate matter, and this discussion must remain confidential."

Feeling an instant reprieve from the executioner, she answered, "Of course, Mister Duncan. Everything in this office remains confidential with me. Always has, always will."

"I know it does, Helen. I know it does."

Cyrus began to pace in a tight circle. "Do you see me as an old man, Helen?"

She paused and thought a moment. He was certainly not strikingly handsome, but then he was not unattractive either. He had developed a slight paunch, but he struggled to keep it in. The little hint of white hair just above his ears did more to improve his looks than to detract from them. "Mature, yes----old, no," she answered. She had an inkling as to where the discussion was heading and was careful to take her time and say the right thing. "Of course you're not old!" she proclaimed loudly.

"Do you…?" He cleared his throat. "Do you think Miss Lawson----Connie---- would find me old?"

"That's hard to say, but I know that she likes you. She has often said what a good employer you are."

Cyrus smiled at that bit of positive information. "But, what do you think she'd say----if I---you know----asked her…?"

"Out on a date?" Helen completed the difficult question.

Again he cleared his throat. "Yes."

Another pause. What if she encouraged him and Connie turned him down? What if she turned him down and then she quit her job because of it. She was in a tight spot and she wasn't sure what to say. "Let me think about this for a moment, Mister Duncan."

With every passing second Duncan became more flustered and embarrassed. "Let's just forget it. She'd probably find me too old and pathetic, and might even laugh at…" the memory of the whore's laughter flooded into his mind. "Of course she'd turn me down, and who could blame her?"

"Nonsense, Mister Duncan." She had an idea. "I just had a thought. Seeing as Christmas is drawing near, perhaps you could take us both out for dinner some evening----as a Christmas gesture? Bosses often take their secretaries out for a Christmas meal." Up until that point he had never taken Helen out for so much as a sandwich. "There's nothing disrespectful in that. And if you asked both of us, it would seem quite respectable."

"Go on," he said, cautiously.

"And suppose I had to leave early and you could see that Connie was escorted home?" Duncan nodded. He liked it. "But better still, suppose you ask us both out for dinner *and* a movie? And after dinner I announce that I'm unable to go to the movie----I'll come up with a valid excuse----and you two could spend an evening together at the movie and see how things go. That much couldn't hurt, could it?"

Cyrus smiled broadly. "I knew I could count on you, Helen." Duncan unlocked the office door and helped her on with her coat. It was the first time he ever performed the gentlemanly duty. "Does this seem----well----foolish of me, Helen?"

"Miss Lawson is a lovely young woman and you're a mature handsome man. I think it is a most natural thing in the world. If you don't try, then you'll never know what might have been."

"Good night, Helen," he said, with a warm smile. "And thank you."

"Good night, Sir."

As was the plan, the next morning Cyrus asked the two women if they'd be free for dinner on the following Thursday evening? He apologized for not making the arrangements earlier so it could have been on a Friday evening and they wouldn't have to go to work the following day, but the weekends at The Royal York Hotel were already booked for Christmas get-togethers. His planned soirée had to happen in the city's finest establishment. He had to impress. The two women accepted instantly, both very excited about dining at the city's most prestigious hotel. And then a movie at a downtown theater afterwards was just too much to comprehend. They were both giddy with anticipation.

Just a week after employing Connie, Cyrus happened to look in the window of the General Motors dealership, the same one he drove past every night on his way back to his empty house. A new blood red 1950 Cadillac was in the show window. Never in his life had he done anything in a spontaneous way, especially when it came to money, but on that evening he drove around the block, came back to the dealership, traded in the old black family Packard sedan and purchased the Cadillac. He wrote out the cheque without giving it a second thought.

That Thursday night he picked up the women in the Cadillac, held doors for them, helped them on and off with their coats, was a perfect gentleman throughout the entire evening. In fact, after the evening was over and he had time to reflect back on his performance, and seeing as he had had no previous experience, he was justifiably proud of himself.

True to her word, and just as planned, after dinner Helen Borden announced that she was unable to attend the movie, "I don't believe I'd be able to sit through it. Those little seats have a tendency to cause me no end of discomfort. I'd be fidgeting through the entire movie and probably ruin the evening for the both of you."

"That is a shame, Misses Borden," said Cyrus, sounding sincere. "There's plenty of time before the movie starts so I'll drive you home."

"Oh, don't be silly. I'll take a streetcar."

The proper gentleman informed her, "You'll do no such a thing. I'll deliver you to your doorstep, madam---
-safe and sound."

And Cyrus Duncan was very impressed with the young woman he so admired. She conducted herself with grace and style throughout the entire evening, a proper lady to say the least, as good as any young lady who had been educated in a fine finishing school. What he didn't know was, after she accepted his invitation she went straight to the library and took out a book on dining etiquette, studied it thoroughly and was well prepared to enter the foreign world of the dining elite. During the meal, as Helen Borden hesitated with each spoon and fork, she discreetly guided the elderly woman though it as though she was an old hand in the art.

After the movie ended Cyrus escorted Connie to the front door of her little apartment. It was nearing midnight. "Well, goodnight Connie," he said with satisfaction, but sad to see it end. "I hope you enjoyed yourself?"

"Oh, very much, Mister Duncan. And thank you."

He began to fidget. "Mister Duncan sounds so formal," he said, trying to keep things going. "People who know me----my friends that is----call me Cy." In truth, he had very few friends. In fact there was no one he could really call a good friend.

"Well then, on this special night, I'll say thank you so much, *Cy*." Then she smiled, "But tomorrow morning it'll be back to Mister Duncan." She then kissed him on the cheek and thanked him again. She was about to go into her apartment when he suddenly took her by the hand.

"Aw----Connie," he kept his eyes to the ground as he spoke. "I was wondering if perhaps---- you and I could do this again sometime? You know, go out for dinner? Take in a movie----or something in that order?"

Her face contorted into a smile. "You know something, Cyrus Duncan, I didn't buy that feeble excuse of Helen's. She sits at her desk all day and it doesn't seem to bother her. Do I detect a conspiracy here?"

Cyrus blushed like a schoolboy. "Miss Lawson, you seem to have caught me with my hand in the cookie jar."

She laughed aloud. "I thought as much. Yes. I'd like that very much," and again she kissed his cheek.

When Cyrus Duncan drove away that night he went straight through the first stop sign he came to. He was a man in love and the world was wonderful. She had kissed him, not once, but twice.

In the following three months Cyrus smothered Connie with expensive gifts, things she could continue to expect if she would say, "I do". He taught her to drive, took her to the finest dining establishments and entertained her in the Duncan mansion. The spectacular home would have knocked any struggling woman off her feet with its wide staircase, rosewood paneled library, thick carpets, a maid, a chef, and a dining room that was seldom used but always set for twelve. Cyrus Duncan used the same tactic to hook young Connie Lawson as her father used to hook cod; he jigged with shiny bait.

In April 1951, after only a four-month courtship, twenty-one year old Constance Louise Lawson wed the fifty-one year old Cyrus Archibald Duncan.

Helen Borden's job was secure for as long as she wanted it.

Chapter 7

It was three o'clock in the afternoon when Shawn Duncan pulled up in front of the old Lutheran church at Portage Lake. Remaining in his car for a time he studied the forgotten little building and marveled at how little it had changed since he was a boy. The afternoon sunlight filtering through the giant pines that surrounded the church gave it a look of sanctity. It was the first time he ever really looked at the building, at the details in the woodwork, at the weathered patterns in the aging lumber, at the ornate cross atop the stubby steeple. He wondered how many artists must have put the little church down on canvas over the years. There was a rustic beauty about the structure, its setting in the forest, its weathered façade, and its look of peacefulness. Slender gothic windows pointed to the heavens, windows glazed in clear ripple glass with narrow coloured glass panes as a border. Off to the left-hand side of the church, still standing after so many years, the old hitching rails poked up through the grass, the place where the parishioners once tied their horses, rails he once used as balancing beams so many years ago.

Constructed entirely of wood in board and batten style, the exterior of the church had never been painted and time had darkened the wood to a gray-black while under the overhanging eaves the wood was a lighter orange-brown. Directly above the door was the open belfry of the steeple. Shawn noticed the bell was gone. When he was a youngster he would throw stones at the bell to make it ring. Someone had stolen the bell. *Who steals from a church*?

On the opposite side of the church, in a tangle of vines, weeds, and grasses and closed in by a collapsing fence, was the cemetery, a place of dread, the place where his mother would be laid to rest. Peeking above the vegetation, close to the church, was a row of white headstones, markers for a people long gone. Someone had erected a plaque beside the road----or more precisely, a sign----telling of the church's history. Shawn rightly guessed few people ever stopped to read it. The sign was housed in a wooden box and protected from the weather by a sheet of glass. Printed in black lettering on a white background it had obviously been put there by someone who cared about the past.

Stepping from his car he walked over to the plaque and read the inscription. For the first time in his life, and after years of knowing of the building's existence, he learned when the church was built, and why. In 1884 mica and iron ore deposits were discovered in the area and a group of people----mostly German immigrants----had settled there to work the mines and to log the giant white pines that once blanketed the land. They built homes and cleared the rolling hills for farming. Over the years the mines ran out, the white pines were depleted, and the soil proved too sandy for farming. The people began moving away until none remained. The plaque also gave a short history of the village called Portage Lake, a village that was no more. The little weathered church was all that was left standing of a once bustling community.

The road in front of the church was gravel and seldom used; it continued on for a few hundred feet before terminating at a locked gate, the gate to the Duncan property. Behind the gate the roadway continued on down the hill toward Portage Lake, to the Duncan summerhouse.

A heavy lock had been installed on the church's front door, but someone had kicked the door in shattering the doorjamb. Shawn pushed hard against the door and the reluctant hinges gave way with loud protest. When he was a boy all the pews were still inside, along with a small lectern, but now the lectern was gone, as were two rows of the pews. Again he wondered, *who steals from a church?* But the windows were still intact; every single pane of glass was there, none broken, none cracked. And it was amazingly clean inside considering the length of abandonment the church had endured. The white-plastered walls were still quite bright after many decades of neglect, and except for dust webs high in the arched ceiling, the building had weathered the passing years amazingly well.

Taking his handkerchief he dusted off a spot on one of the remaining pews and sat for a while and listened to the silence. He recalled the last time he was ever in the little church. *How old was I then? Six? I couldn't have been more than seven, if that. And I was with Caroline Colburn. Yes, I was with Caroline.* It was as though by entering the church an entire chapter from his past instantly reopened. *Funny I should remember that day, and so clearly. All those years and I never once thought about it again. I was here with Caroline and we sat here on a pew.* They had entered the church because a violent summer storm had suddenly come up and they couldn't make it back to the summerhouse. *We were both wet and afraid.* He smiled as he remembered the time. *We sat here on a pew with our arms around each other with the rain pelting the building and the thunder exploding all around us.* He almost laughed aloud. *I was her knight in shining armour and I was more frightened than she was.*

Strangely, for a moment he could actually feel her presence beside him. He could feel her in his arms. They were just children and yet he remembered it so clearly, could sense the warmth of her body next to his, could actually smell the wetness of her clothes and hair. The memory of that day flooded back to him with remarkable clarity. *I wonder why I never came back here? Mother and I never came back up here after that year. Why? We both loved it so much and yet we never came back. What happened that summer to change things? And yes, that was the year before my father died. It must have been 1960. That must have been it. That had to be the reason, because the place reminded her of father. It had to be that? But if that's so, why is she not being buried beside him?*

Shawn remained in the church for the better part of an hour, a place that seemed to bring him a measure of peace. And as the afternoon light waned and splotches of colours slowly moved along the muted walls, a deeper sadness began intruding on his thoughts. Because he was in a church, he asked, *what's this all about, God? Help me understand this?*

The sun was a perfect orange disc hanging close to the rim of the western horizon when he stepped out of the church. It was time to visit Harriet Colburn, Caroline's mother.

Chapter 8

He hadn't seen his childhood friend since they were thirteen year-olds, but he recognized her the instant she opened the door. Her body was slim and firm, her eyes dark and sharp, her cheekbones somewhat pronounced, her smile warm; the building blocks of attractiveness were certainly there, but badly neglected. Her hair was lightly laced with strands of gray and above her forehead, like a lopsided tiara, was a splotch of solid white, like she had touched her head on a freshly painted ceiling. He found it odd that she never tried to hide it.

"My God! Shawn Duncan. Is it you?"

"Hello, Caroline."

They automatically embraced. "How long has it been, Shawn?"

"It's gotta to be at least twenty-five years," he guessed.

She held the door wide open. "Well for God sakes, come in?"

"How have you been, Caroline?" he asked as he stepped inside the tidy bungalow.

"As good as time allows. And yourself?"

"Not so good."

Her smile vanished. "What's wrong?"

"I'm on a mission, and I don't really know where to start----or even what I'm looking for. You see, mother died yesterday."

"Oh, dear heavens. I'm so sorry." She took his hands and held them. "I'm so very sorry, Shawn."

He choked slightly when he thanked her.

After a slight pause Caroline gave him a puzzled look. "Isn't that the strangest thing?"

"What is, Caroline?"

"Your mother----she called me yesterday morning."

"Mother? She called you? Yesterday?"

"Yes she did. She was looking for mother."

Shawn reached into his jacket pocket and produced the note his mother had left for her housekeeper, Fatima. "And do you want to hear something really strange? She wants to be buried up here----in the old cemetery across the lake."

"My God!"

"Yes, and that's why I'm here----to try and find out what this is all about. I was wondering if your mother would know why she'd request such a thing? Is she around?"

"Mother hasn't lived with me in years. She moved into a senior's unit in Meedsville.

Caroline started toward the telephone then stopped. "I can't give her that news over the phone. I know they haven't spoken in years, but still. We'll have to drive in and see her. It's less than an hour's drive from here."

"I hate to put you out like this, Caroline, but…"

"Don't be silly. It's no trouble at all." Caroline grabbed her jacket and headed out the door.

On the drive into Meedsville the two caught up on their years apart. Shawn told about his art business and studio, that he had never married but had come close to it once. Caroline revealed a little about her married life, about her late husband, Peter, that she had no children, that she was still operating the marina on Georgian Bay, the marina where Peter was working when he was killed. The trip seemed to take only minutes as the two caught up on years of being apart.

"What are your plans for tonight?" asked Caroline, after stopping in front of her mother's apartment.

"I want to go over to the old summerhouse in the morning and see what kind of shape it's in, so I'll just get a motel room somewhere around the area for the night."

"You'll not be staying in any motel room, Shawn Duncan. My house has two empty bedrooms and you can have your pick."

"Oh thanks, Caroline, but I couldn't impose."

She laughed. "Impose! Don't be foolish. I'd love to have the company. Besides, this is not the time in one's life to be alone. And I owe your family many nights of lodging, and many great meals."

"You do? And how do you figure that?"

"Can you still remember when we were little? I stayed at the summerhouse lots of times."

Shawn thought for a moment. "You and I used to play together all the time. Yes, I remember you often slept over at the summerhouse and we shared that big brass bed."

Caroline laughed. "Watch who you say that too."

He caught the meaning and laughed. "You're right. And I'll never forget the night we were blowing bubble gum in bed. You blew this gigantic bubble and it burst and you got it all through your hair. Do you remember that?"

"How could I forget? It was torture getting it out."

The sun was well below the horizon when they stopped in front of Harriet Colburn's apartment. Shawn asked Caroline, "Why did your mother move into here? Why didn't she just stay with you?"

"Actually, we tried living together after Peter died but it didn't work out. Mother and I just don't see eye-to-eye on most things. We never did. She was going to put the house on the market so I just bought it from her. I've always loved that little house and I could never part with it. Besides, she's better off in town with her friends." Then she added with a smile, "In fact, when she's with her friends, we're both better off."

"Caroline! And for heaven's sake, is it----Shawn Duncan? What in the world…?" said wide-eyed Harriet Colburn when she opened the door.

Sixty-eight year old Harriet Colburn carried herself with an elegant grace. Because of her slimness and correct posture she appeared taller than her five-foot-six. She always dressed well, kept her hair coloured, and looked younger than her years. But what her demeanor hid, her coarseness exposed. She was of humble beginnings and it came out in her speech and mannerisms.

"Hi, Mom."

"Hello, Harriet," said Shawn. The two shook hands politely.

"What in the world…?" she repeated as the two entered her apartment.

"I'm afraid this is not a good visit, Mother."

Shawn broke the news. "Harriet, mother died yesterday."

Harriet's hand flew to her mouth. "Oh my God," she whispered. After the magnitude of the news settled on her, she hurried to the bathroom.

Caroline followed her and tapped lightly on the door. "Are you all right, Mother?"

She eventually heard the weak response. "Yes, I'm fine. Just give me a minute."

Caroline went to the kitchen and fixed tea; she instinctively knew her mother would want tea.

When Harriet finally returned to the living room she walked up to Shawn and embraced him stiffly. "I'm so very sorry, Shawn," she whispered. "We haven't kept in touch for some time, but at one time we were the best of friends."

"Yes, I know you were," said Shawn.

Caroline brought in the teapot and cups and set them on the coffee table. The tea was poured and an uncomfortable silence followed with only light clinking of china filling the void.

"Mother." Caroline said, breaking the silence, "something has come up and Shawn was wondering if you'd know the answer to it?"

"Yes?" Harriet replied cautiously.

"It's about mother's funeral arrangements?" said Shawn.

"What about them?"

After telling her about the funeral arrangements made by his mother, Harriet's facial expression showed surprise, but not great surprise.

"Harriet, what do you know that I don't?" he asked.

"What do you mean?" she said, a hint of indignation in her tone.

"Because you don't seem all that surprised at the news. It knocked me for a loop, but not you. Why?"

Without answering Harriet rose stiffly and walked to her bedroom closing the door behind her. Caroline and Shawn sat and looked at each other in bewilderment.

"She knows something about it," said Shawn.

"Perhaps," said Caroline, 'but you never know about mother."

Harriet stayed in her bedroom for several minutes, but when she did come out she seemed to be back in charge of herself. She sat on the sofa and waited for the questions.

"Why, Harriet? Why's she doing this?" asked Shawn. "Why is she not being buried beside my father?"

"Because it's her right, and it's not for you to question."

The sharpness in Harriet's answer brought an instant response from Caroline. "Mother! You have no right to speak to Shawn in that tone of voice."

Shawn knew it was not their first confrontation.

Harriet's head dropped. "Yes, I'm afraid I was a bit blunt. I'm sorry, Shawn, but what your mother chose was her affair, and hers alone. I just don't know of any other way to say it."

"But she phoned you just yesterday. She must have said something."

"Where did you ever get an idea like that?" said Harriet defensively. "I have no idea what you're talking about. I haven't spoken to Connie Duncan in many years."

"Mother," put in Caroline, "she phoned me yesterday morning wanting your phone number and address, and I gave it to her. You must have talked to her."

"For your information " she snapped, "I was out yesterday for most of the day. She may very well have called, but I wasn't here. I did not speak to her. And as you know perfectly well, I don't have an answering machine."

After a quiet spell Shawn said, "It's okay, Harriet. It's okay. But just off the top of your head, would you have any idea why she'd make such a request?"

"Shawn, you're a grown man, so I shouldn't have to tell you that marriages go sour. Maybe Connie's did, maybe it didn't. Maybe your father was dead for so long that time took away the memory of him. Who knows? I don't know why she chose to do this, and that's all there is to it. That's it! There's nothing more to be said on the matter. She always loved it up here and probably just wanted to be buried here. In fact, I can distinctly remember her saying that very thing. But it was a long time ago, and when you're young who really thinks about such things?"

Shawn tried to look into Harriet's eyes but she refused eye contact. "And that's it?" he said. "No hidden meaning?"

"None that I know of," she answered calmly. "Shawn, don't read things into this that aren't really there. Let your mother rest in peace and be thankful you had her for a mother. And please, keep in mind, I hadn't heard from her in years. The last time I saw her you were just a boy. I have no idea why Connie chose what she did. And for that matter, I have no idea why you came here in the first place. What's any of this got to do with me?"

Shawn produced the note his mother had left for Fatima. "Then why would she have left this note for our housekeeper? Do you have any idea why she suddenly needed to see you?"

Harriet took the note and read it. When she was finished reading she rose stiffly and began walking toward her bedroom. "I have absolutely no idea, Shawn. She never contacted me so I don't know what any of this is about. It's a shame I missed her call."

When Harriet was gone from the room Shawn looked at Caroline and shrugged.

Caroline went to her mother's bedroom door and spoke through it. "Are you going to be all right, Mother?"

"Yes, I'll be fine."

"Shawn and I are going back to my place now----unless you want us to stay longer?"

The door instantly flew open. "You're going back to your place? The two of you?"

"Of course. Shawn is going to spend the night with me and leave in the morning. Why?"

"He can stay here with me tonight if he wishes----or go to a motel. He shouldn't be staying alone with you."

Caroline was taken aback by the statement. "*I beg your pardon*?"

"You heard me."

"Oh, I heard you all right, and probably Shawn did, too. Who do you think you're talking to, Mother, a child?"

"Caroline, you are a single woman and he's a single man. What would people say about such a carry-on?"

"*Carry-on? Carry-on*? And if by chance there was any *carrying-on,* it would still be none of your business. Honest to God, Mother, I swear you're getting worse every year."

Caroline turned and walked away.

"Don't you dare talk to me like that, Miss."

Caroline kept on walking and didn't respond. She went back to the living room, snatched her jacket from the back of a chair and beckoned for Shawn to follow. They left the apartment immediately.

Shawn did indeed hear the confrontation. On their drive back to Portage Lake he remarked, "I seemed to have caused some turbulence between you and you mother. I'm sorry Caroline, I'll just get a motel room."

Caroline waved it off. "Don't be silly. That *turbulence* as you called it, has been going on for as long as I can remember. We never got along and never will."

"That's a shame."

"But my dad and I were very close," she added with sadness.

"Oh yes, Darrell. I can vaguely remember him. He was a good guy though, wasn't he? I remember he was very quiet, but very interesting. Quite clever with his hands, too, if I recall."

"I was only sixteen when he died, and I still miss him," said Caroline. She remained silent for the remainder of the trip home as she thought about her father.

Just as Caroline pulled into the her driveway, she asked, "Shawn, are you satisfied with mother's answer?"

"I have to accept something, Caroline. What else can I do? And when you think about it, it does make a lot of sense. I can't remember mother ever talking about my father. I guess everyone wants to believe their parents were happily married, and maybe mine were not."

"And you're okay with that?"

"To be quite honest, now I feel a bit foolish about everything----you know, coming up here looking for answers. I should have been able to figure it out for myself. But I guess I needed to come up here and see where she'll be buried."

"I can understand that," said Caroline. "And when will the funeral take place?"

"Monday morning at ten. But there won't be a funeral, as we know the meaning of the word. She wanted no wake, no church service, no graveside service. She always thought those things were morbid.

"So you're all right with everything, then?"

"It's all very strange, but I have to accept it."

"Good." She undid her seatbelt and opened the car door. "So grab your overnight case and come on inside. I'm starved."

Chapter 9

SHAWN SAT ON THE sofa and tried to watch the TV evening news as Caroline busied herself in the kitchen. However, with the day's happenings' tumbling through his mind, and Caroline busy preparing the evening meal he didn't hear a word the anchorman said. Besides, his mind was tired of it all; he didn't need to hear of the world's doom and gloom. He shifted his attention toward the kitchen. "You sure I can't give you a hand?"

"No thanks. Everything is under control."

He liked watching Caroline, her effortless moves, the way she showed muscle most women didn't possess. He found her physical strength almost sensual. He could easily imagine the woman running her own business and making every move count.

Less than an hour after entering her house the meal was on the table. "Come and get it," she said in a light-hearted way. "It would have been better if I had more time."

"Looks great," Shawn said, taking his place at the table.

In a short space of time she had baked two large chicken breasts, broiled potato wedges, peeled and boiled carrots, and started it all off with a large tossed salad served with a glass of red wine. She even remembered a candle for the middle of the table.

"Are you sure you weren't expecting company? It would have taken me all day to put a meal like this together."

She smiled at the complement.

When the meal was over Caroline washed the dishes and Shawn insisted on drying, the two standing by the sink chatting away, old friends again. After the dishes were put away they retired to the family room and sat on the sofa and watched the fire through the glass doors of the wood stove. Caroline served cookies and coffee.

"Are you going back to Toronto tomorrow morning?" she asked.

"It'll probably be early afternoon before I start back. But like I said, I want to go over to the summerhouse while I'm up here and see what kind of condition it's in. I haven't been there in----let me think now." He paused a moment. "I drove mother up a couple times, but that was years ago----twenty or more, I believe."

"I suppose you'll be selling it soon?" she said, sadness very evident in her voice.

"To tell the truth, I haven't given it any thought. I always believed mother would be around for many more years to come, and she'd never sell it, and I have no idea why she insisted on keeping the old place. Different developer's approached her about buying it, but no way would she sell it. She told me I could do as I pleased with it when she was gone, but as long as she was alive it stays in the Duncan name."

"Wouldn't it be a shame though," said Caroline.

"What's that?"

"Selling to a developer. It would certainly change the character of the lake."

Shawn thought for a moment. "Yes, I suppose it would, and it probably wouldn't be for the better, either."

Caroline then realized that she had crossed a line. "I'm sorry, Shawn. I have no right to question what you do with you own property. It's none of my business. I'm sorry."

Shawn waved her concern away. "There's no law that says a person can't have an opinion. And I can certainly understand your concern." He looked out the patio doors at the darkness, but in his mind's eye he could see the unspoiled scenery beyond. "Yes, I can understand your concern very well."

They sat in the cozy little family room until close to midnight with easy-listening CDs playing in the background and talked about anything that happened to pop into their heads. Most of the conversation was of bygone times, happy times.

When it was time for bed Shawn stood and embraced Caroline, embraced her longer than could be considered a thank-you. She didn't seem to mind.

Caroline came to the kitchen in the morning and found Shawn standing in front of the patio doors looking out over the lake and countryside.

"Good morning," she said. "Did you sleep well?"

"Like the proverbial log."

A sliver of the sun had just cleared the horizon and the frost-coated landscape was alive with reflected light. The hardwoods reminded him of a Monet painting, brilliant splashes of colour spotting the deep richness of the evergreen forest. A pink mist lay motionless over the lake surface and Shawn instinctively viewed it through an impressionist's eye. "I never saw anything like it in my life. I had forgotten how beautiful it is up in this country." Caroline came and stood silent beside him. "And I can see why you'd never leave this place."

As the sun climbed above the eastern hills the pink mist quickly darkened into a vivid red. "We'd better enjoy it while we can," said Caroline.

"Oh? Why's that?"

"Red sky in the morning," she answered.

Shawn filled in the missing half. "Sailor take warning."

"I suppose you're in a hurry to get going?" said Caroline. "That red sky is beautiful, but I'm afraid there's a drastic weather change on the way."

"Actually, I'm in no hurry to leave at all, but I guess it's going to come to that, isn't it?"

Caroline placed a hand on his shoulder. "I'll get breakfast started."

"After that meal last night I don't know if I can handle breakfast."

"If you're planning to spend the morning over at the summerhouse, you'll need it. There are no fast-food joints up here in the boonies," she reminded him with a smile.

He reached over and took her hand. "Thanks again for everything, Caroline."

She squeezed his hand and held it for a long moment before going to the kitchen.

Chapter 10

LEAVING HIS CAR PARKED at the property entrance by the heavy locked gate, Shawn walked the quarter mile into the summerhouse. Taking his time, he removed fallen limbs from the roadway as he strolled along, a roadway that was little more than a path after so many years of neglect. *It all looks so different now. So much sadder than when I was a kid. Almost unrecognizable.* The heavy growth of underbrush and the girth of the trees lining the road reminded him of just how many years had slipped by since he had last walked the road.

When the house came into view he stopped walking and studied it for a time. It was clearly in the early stages of dilapidation. Visible sag lines ran along the length of the wrap-around veranda. Roof valleys were packed with dead leaves, the shingles green with moss, the eave troughs sagging from the weight of the accumulation in them, a weight that was tearing them from the building. Wild berry canes had taken root close to the foundation walls and were thriving in dense clumps their swaying canes scratching the clapboards in fan-shaped swatches. Lawns, once mowed and lush, were now weed-choked and browned with a thick thatch of dead leaves and pine needles.

Walking to the opposite side of the house, to the terraced patio, he recalled the summer barbeques, could still smell the wood smoke, could remember how good everything tasted when it was eaten outdoors. The patio had been excavated into the side of an earthen bank just off the kitchen and then bricked in to form a 'U' shaped terrace. At each corner of the patio colonial lights were mounted on tall iron posts, but the lights were gone, apparently hacked off and stolen. The stone chimney of the barbeque pit was still there but in very poor condition, the iron grates a mass of rusting metal. Flagstone flooring on the patio was heaved and blistered from years of winter frost and from small shoots that had forced their way up through the grouted seams.

It required a firm shoulder-push on the front door to open it, and when Shawn stepped inside the house his nostrils were greeted with the strong odor of abandonment; of pine wood, paper, tattered rugs, and furnishings that had developed their own scent. He had entered the world of the dust mite, the meadow mouse, the carpenter ant. The white of his breath highlighted minute dust particles that floated thick in the dead air, particles that had suddenly taken flight after years of remaining undisturbed. Squeaks and complaints rose up from the floorboards as he moved about, his body's weight forcing dormant boards to flex.

There was little of value left in the house. Years earlier his mother had the furniture, cutlery, dishes, paintings, and knickknacks moved out for safekeeping----or sold. "No sense inviting thieves," she said at the time. All that remained were odds-and-ends, items of little value. A faded wall tapestry still hung on the wall opposite the fireplace. A wicker loveseat, its cushions flattened from years of usage, still faced the fireplace as though waiting for someone to come by and warm himself in front of the long ago extinguished fire. A matching wicker chair, its strands broken and stretched, sat undisturbed beside the wood box where it had always sat. The braided rug covering the center of the floor was still there but its only value was to the mice who used it for nesting material. A fishing pole and two canoe paddles leaned forgotten in the corner beside the fireplace.

Over the fireplace the Duncan coat-of-arms remained imbedded in the stonework and it was the first time in his life that Shawn ever really studied the crest. Archibald Duncan, his grandfather, had it installed, but other than the Scottish thistle he had no idea what the symbols represented. As he stood in the middle of the room he tried to recall the last time he had been in the old house. *So many years ago. How many years was it, anyway? Twenty? Twenty-five? More?*

The hallway leading from the family room to the kitchen was even darker than he had remembered it, the varnished pine wallboards showing no feature, no reflection of light, like walking down an unlit tunnel. But the kitchen was still quite bright, its white wall tiles bouncing light even after years of accumulated grime. Suddenly he could smell baked beans and fresh bread buns. *Yes, baked beans and Harriet Colburn's fresh baked buns. Funny I should remember that.* He could actually remember how good they tasted. He remembered back to when Harriet and Darrell Colburn worked at the summerhouse and of how good the kitchen always smelled.

Two sets of stairs serviced the upper level of the house; one ascended off the kitchen, the other at the main entrance. He went up by way of the stairs off the kitchen.

A single pain of glass was broken out of a window in the master bedroom and birds had discovered the opening. A nest had been built on a window casing and the bedroom floor was littered with nesting material and dried droppings, little pellets that crunched under foot as he walked about the room.

Forcing open the swing-out floor length windows that faced the lake, he stepped out onto the widow's walk and was momentarily stunned by the view. He had forgotten how it looked, and for the first time in his life he truly appreciated just how spectacular the setting was. Little children were not capable of appreciating such splendor. The unblemished lake surface reflected the sunlight as would a large mirror, and its beauty forced him to stand for a time and soak it all in. In that moment-in-time he was a boy again. He could hear little Caroline Colburn running up the stairs calling his name, could hear the sounds from the kitchen below, could smell the cooking, could hear his mother's voice.

The upstairs only bathroom was in a niche at the end of the hallway. White ceramic tiles surrounded a cast iron claw-footed bathtub, a pull-chain toilet, a pedestal sink and a wooden towel rack. He smiled when he thought how those very ancient fixtures were now back in fashion. Walking slowly through the upstairs rooms and hallway, he thought, *yes, it was once a Victorian beauty, and still could be.* Although sadly outdated the building itself was still plum and square and the setting, priceless. *No wonder Mom never wanted to sell it. I'm glad she didn't.*

Walking down by the lakeshore he found little remained of the dock he once caught sunfish from. Years of winter ice had torn it to pieces. Only the wood cribbing protruded from the pristine water with rusted spikes sticking from the rotting logs like brown twigs, the stones that once anchored the cribbing in place sitting on the bottom in rounded heaps. The boathouse had long ago been torn down by Darrell Colburn. But the lake had remained the same, still as pristine as a swimming pool. And he could see the mica flakes spotting the sandy lake-bottom, polished little mirrors of mineral twinkling in the sunlight like diamonds.

As he turned and walked back toward the house he suddenly stopped in mid-stride. It was the carriage house. Its roofline peeked above the tops of the cedars, trees that had been planted years earlier in an attempt to hide the building, its two dormer windows staring at him like arched eyebrows. The building had been erected at the same time as the summerhouse, back when the horse was king, before the automobile made its début. Constructed in the same style as the summerhouse it sat about four hundred feet back from the house on a slight rise of land, put well back to keep the smells and sounds of the horses away from the house and guests.

A chill radiated through his body when he first noticed the building, like an electrical shock, as though he had never seen the building before. Shaking off the feeling he walked toward the carriage house but his pace slowed as he neared it. He didn't know why, but for some reason he didn't wish to go near it. Something seemed to be telling him to stay away. When he reached the carriage house he found the doors spiked shut, all of them. He was thankful for the spikes; he had a legitimate reason for not entering the building, a manly way out. Placing a hand on one of the spikes, he said, "Good old Darrell. Always did things right. It'd take one hell-of-a determined thief to break in there."

A breeze began to sway the treetops and a fast moving bank of clouds rolled in covering the face of the sun. Looking up he remembered Caroline's prediction, *sailor take warning*. Turned quickly he left the carriage house, back out the tree-canopied roadway to his car, back to the city and away from old memories.

By the time he reached the gate at the property line the breeze had turned to wind and the trees were thrashing violently over his head. The first raindrops were smacking against the ground.

The roadway leading down to the summerhouse was really an extension of the unused county road, the same road that passed in front of the Lutheran Church, a dead-end road that terminated at the locked gate to the Duncan property. As he started driving back out the road he noticed wheel tracks leading into the cemetery. While he was down at the summerhouse someone had driven into the cemetery, the vehicle's wheels crushing the vegetation down creating two walking paths through the tangle of weeds and vines.

Shawn stopped the car, pulled his coat collar up to ward off the thickening rain, and followed the tracks. They terminated in the furthest corner of the cemetery. Obviously the gravedigger had been there and gone. In the very back corner of the cemetery, almost like it wasn't even part of the cemetery, someone had spray-painted an orange rectangle on trampled down vegetation, the place where his mother's grave would be dug. Along the other side of the cemetery, close to the church, two lines of grave markers jutted above the tall growth, but for some reason his mother would be buried off by herself, in the furthest corner, away from the others. *Why? Dominic Fraser said the plot had been paid for back in 1961. Why would she pick such a place? Why?* he kept asking himself as he stood there in wonderment while the rain pelted him in relentless waves. *Why?*

Chapter 11

SHAWN DUNCAN ARRIVED BACK at Portage Lake a little before eight o'clock the Monday morning of his mother's internment. Frost had whitened the landscape to a thickness resembling a dusting of snow. The sun had not yet climbed above the giant pines bordering the small cemetery and when he stepped from the warmth of his car he was holding a single yellow rose. Only squawking blue jays disturbed the quiet of the setting. Walking solemnly to the grave site, now easily accessible with the vegetation trampled down by the coming and going of the machine that had dug the grave, he peered down into the pocket of newly excavated red sand; at the bottom sat a recently installed concrete vault. A shiny lowering device sat over the top of the open grave ready to perform its grim duty. The reality of the situation pressed the air from his lungs so that he needed to dig deep and find the strength to hold back tears.

Turning away from the troubling sight he noticed the first rays of the sun piercing through the treetops and illuminating the weathered cross atop the church steeple. Going to the church he forced the door open, went inside and sat on one of the pews. Not being a religious man, he only went to church for weddings and funerals, but it seemed to give him a measure of peace just by being there. He wanted to weep, felt that he should, but the tranquility of the humble structure had a settling effect. In a strange way the little church had put his mind at rest, its gothic windows, plain white walls, arched ceilings, so simplistic, and yet so powerful.

Lost in his thoughts, he didn't hear the pickup truck stopping on the road outside, nor did he hear the footsteps coming toward the church. "Hello Shawn," came a voice from behind him.

"Caroline! You didn't have to come to this," he said, trying to smile.

"Yes I did. No one should be alone at a time like this."

She looked different from their last meeting. She had coloured her hair and the splotch of white was gone, and with the help of a little makeup she looked quite lovely. They sat on the pew together with their fingers entwined. Suddenly it was no longer cold. He could feel the radiation of her warmth and it reminded him of another time when he held that same hand in that very same church.

"Do you remember the last time we were together in this church?" she whispered.

He smiled. "The lightning storm. I was the brave guy protecting you, and I think I was more afraid than you were."

"And do you remember when your mother came looking for us and how mad she was, the both of us looking like drowned rats?"

Shawn nodded his head and smiled. "Boy, but did she give us the hell." He then paused a moment. "Isn't it strange how certain little memories will stick with you for the rest of your life while most of our lives go by without a second thought?"

"I suppose they stick because they were very important," she answered.

They sat quietly for the longest moment with their hands joined, and only came out of it when they heard an approaching vehicle. Stepping outside they could see a backhoe sitting a discreet distance down the road and they could hear the gravel on the road crunching under the wheels of the approaching hearse. Shawn checked his wristwatch: 9:30. On the shoulder of the road, opposite the backhoe, an older car pulled up and stopped. The two men in the car didn't get out, they just sat and watched with the engine running, its exhaust rolling up in a white fog. Shawn was right when he thought, *a couple nosey locals.*

The hearse stopped in front of the cemetery, and in one smooth motion it backed in close to the gravesite. Caroline took Shawn's hand and the two walked toward the cemetery, frosted grass and weeds crunching underfoot, thorns of berry vines picking at their pant legs.

"Mother was thinking of coming but I told her not too," said Caroline. "I told her you would understand."

Shawn nodded agreement.

Dominic Fraser was not with the hearse, but he did send two young employees, a male and a female. The young man looked a great deal like Fraser. P*robably his son apprenticing the undertaking business.* A second vehicle with two men had followed the hearse; *extra hands to help with a heavy lift, no doubt.* In one smooth well choreograph move the casket was rolled out of the hearse, placed on the lowering device, and then the four people stepped back from the grave and stood at attention for a moment with their heads slightly bowed.

The one resembling Fraser approached Shawn and offered his hand. "Are you Mister Duncan?" Shawn nodded. "I'm sorry for your loss, sir." He then faced Caroline. "Sorry for your loss, ma'am. Is there anything either of you would like to say----or do?"

Shawn shook his head while he struggled with his emotions. He then took the single yellow rose, Constance Duncan's favorite, and placed it on the coffin. Pressing the palm of one hand flat on the coffin, he whispered, "I love you, Mom. Goodbye." He then stepped back, turned his back to the grave and quickly walked away.

Caroline hooked her arm through his and went with him. She could feel his body trembling. "Come back to my place, Shawn," she said, after they had reached his car. "You need something warm in your stomach. We both do."

"Thank you so much, Caroline. You're so very kind, but I want to go to the old place for a while. Right now I have to be alone. I hope you can understand?"

Between the chill of the morning and the emotion of the moment, she could see his eyes filling. "Fine. You take your time and do what you must, but please, come back to the house for a while? Don't be alone for too long."

He pinched a brave smile. "Thanks."

"Okay, then. I'll see you later."

He waited while Caroline backed her company pickup onto the road, a new black Chev with the name of her marina on the door. It made him feel good to see his childhood friend had done so well for herself.

Leaving his car at the church Shawn walked down the road toward the summerhouse, stepped around the gate and continued on down the roadway. When he came to the house he went inside and sat on the old loveseat in the family room in front of the long dormant fireplace. Staring blankly at the fireplace he heard voices from the past; Harriet Colburn; his mother; Caroline's bubbly little laughter like a twittering bird. Smells of everyday life were suddenly there; smoke from the fireplace, Harriet's cooking, the lake, wild flowers, cedar trees. But the interlude was brief and he was again alone in a dilapidated place that was once full of joy. There, in the bleak quiet of the house he broke down and cried for people and a time that had passed on forever. An hour later he stood on rubbery legs and walked back to his car at the church. Before getting into his vehicle he paused a moment and watched as the backhoe swung back-and-forth filling in the grave. He then turned and stared coldly at the two gawkers, stared until they drove away. At that moment he needed warmth and companionship and he knew it was waiting for him at Caroline Colburn's home.

Chapter 12

Caroline was waiting for him at the door. After stepping inside she took his coat and hung it in the hall closet but when she turned around and faced him, without warning he put his arms around her and drew her near holding her tightly for a long moment.

"I'm---I'm sorry Caroline. I---I just..." he mumbled after releasing her.

"You just needed that, Shawn Duncan. We all do sometime in our lives." She too felt some of what he was going through, the sorrow of the situation causing her eyes to water. She returned the embrace but for a longer time, held him until the need was satisfied.

"Thank you so much, Caroline. Thanks for being here for me."

"Come on," she said, taking him by the hand. "Sit down in front of the fire and I'll fix you a coffee.

The family room, kitchen, and dining room of the modest home was constructed in the open fashion, and

Shawn watched Caroline as she busied herself in the kitchen. In fact, for some reason he couldn't help but watch her, wanted to watch her, couldn't take his eyes off her. He remembered her when she was young, when she and her mother would travel down to the city for a weekend to Christmas shop. They were only teenagers, two young people wondering about life, intrigued with the feelings and desires of youth.

When Caroline brought the coffee and bent down to set it on the table in front of him, he instantly became aware of a fragrance. She wore no heavy perfume or cologne, and yet, the hint of something very feminine lingered when she returned to the kitchen, a clean and fresh scent, a scent that reminded him of the lightning storm and the church when he held her in his arms. He was so young, and yet he still remembered holding her.

After finishing his coffee he went and stood at the patio doors. The brilliant autumn sun was high in the sky and the frost on the trees had melted leaving the leaves wet and shimmering. The Colburn home sat on a rise of land about a quarter mile back from Portage Lake, high enough up so one could view the entire lake. On the south shore, white like a marble rock outcropping, stood the Duncan summerhouse, his summerhouse, the only building on the shore of the entire lake. He tried to imagine what it would look like after he sold it to a developer. Would there be a multi-story hotel poking up into a tranquil forest, or trailers parked in neat rows with hordes of screaming children splashing in the lake, or vast numbers of trees cut for a golf course? And with that would come powerboats pulling water-skiers, and jet boats with their high-pitched whine? Mercifully, his thoughts were interrupted.

"Okay, Shawn. I guess we're ready."

"Looks Good," he said with a smile.

"Just omelets. I hope it'll do."

"And what, pray tell, is wrong with omelets? I love them."

When breakfast was finished Caroline made a second pot of coffee and they sat in front of the fire and talked for an hour, recalling the days of their youth, happy times, times that didn't seem all that long ago. They never mentioned the day's occurrences or speculated as to what lay ahead; they had enough sadness for one day. Childhood memories held far more joy.

"Caroline, I hope you won't take this the wrong way," said Shawn, "but I was wondering if you'd care to join me for dinner this evening? I don't mean as a date or anything like that, just sort of a way for me to say thanks for being such a good friend. I'm sure we could drive somewhere and find a decent place to eat. Just a thought, that's all. I want very much to do that for you."

"I would never consider it, if it's a payback you're offering, but if it's just two old friends going out for dinner, then I'd love too."

"Great!" He then sighed, "You know Caroline, it's really so good to see you again. The circumstances may not be the best, but it's *so damn good* to see you again."

"Like you said, the circumstances aren't great, but it's good to have you here, too."

That afternoon the two walked down a winding path that led to a quiet bay on Portage Lake. Sitting together on an old driftwood log they watched as migrating ducks skimmed into the calm bay. There was sharpness in the air, an invigorating chill. And as they sat quietly remembering the way things were, they could only recall the good. When the chill had worked its way through their clothing and it was time to returned to the house, Shawn held Caroline's hand as they plodded up the pathway. He loved the feel of his old friend's hand in his, didn't seem to want to let it go.

Not being familiar with the area, Shawn suggested Caroline choose a place to eat. She chose a hotel named The Islands, which was just a few miles south of her marina. The hotel had a breath-taking view of a few of the ten thousand islands of Georgian Bay. It was 3:30 in the afternoon when they began the forty-five minute drive west to the hotel. Too early to eat, so they put in some time and built an appetite by strolled along a footpath at the water's edge.

"I take it you've been here before?" said Shawn.

"Just once. It was a wedding dinner of a friend. One of the few times Peter and I ever had a good time." She instantly caught herself, refusing to go into unpleasant discussion. "I hope the food's still good," she added quickly, getting off the subject.

Shawn didn't miss the significance of her statement. "Caroline, if you find it difficult coming here----if it brings back old memories of Peter, I'm sure we can find someplace else? It's not like we're in a hurry."

"Oh, don't be silly. It was a long time ago. There are no ghosts in my life. I live for the present and future. The past is the past."

Shawn was amazed at the strength in her remark. "I think you're made of better stuff than I am, Caroline. My problem is I have trouble leaving the past alone."

Caroline stopped abruptly and looked at him. "Shawn, I have the feeling you think I'm cold-hearted, but that's not the case. Peter and I worked. That's what we did. We never took time out to go on holidays, to relax, or even to have children. We were together so much we were sometimes like strangers. I know that's a bit of an oxymoron, but it's true. I missed him at the marina after he was gone; missed his company; missed a lot of things about him, but we met at high school, went steady for three years, got married on a Saturday and went back to work on Monday. I know there were times when we were sick of each other's company because we were never apart. We kept telling ourselves we were working for a good future, but looking back I now believe our futures only held more work. I never allow myself to think of what may have been because it would only cause more pain, and I've had enough of that. I can't change the past so I leave it alone."

They continued their walk in an uncomfortable silence. After returning to the hotel Caroline stopped before entering the hotel lobby and faced him. "I'm sorry for that outburst, Shawn. I've never said that to another person before. You've just had about the worst day of your life and then I go and unload that on you. I'm sorry."

He drew her near and hugged her. "That's okay. It was your turn, anyway" he whispered in her ear. He then kissed her on the lips; it just happened, and it was not a light kiss.

Because of the lateness of the season the dining room was not busy and there were plenty of seats facing the water. And the food was great, the atmosphere peaceful. There was no more talk on gloomy subjects.

"I was wondering----on my drive back to the city last Thursday," said Shawn, after the meal was finished and he was sipping at his second cup of coffee, "what would ever have become of you and I if we had stayed in touch?"

Caroline's face crinkled with amusement. "Probably ended up getting married----or killing each other."

Shawn lips pinched into a warm smile. "You know, looking back, we did seem to fight a lot----but we always made up."

She nodded. "We had too. There were no other kids up here to play with."

"But remember all the great summers we had," said Shawn. "Remember all the times we went swimming in the little bay?"

She thought for a moment. "You know, I've never been back swimming there since that last summer I was there with you."

He gazed off across the water as he recalled the time. How could he ever forget it? At the very eastern extreme of the Duncan property a long narrow stretch of shallow water knifes into the forest, and in that secluded bay the water was always very warm, the bottom sandy and flecked with mica flakes. When they were little they collected the mica and pretended it was gold and diamonds.

"My God, but we spent a lot of wonderful times there, didn't we?"

"Every time one of our parents would take us," said Caroline, nostalgically. "One of the good memories I like to hold on to."

Shawn suddenly began to laugh.

"What is it?"

"I just remembered something. Do you remember the time you and I snuck away and went swimming by ourselves?"

Caroline paused, thought for a moment, then laughed. "Oh God, yes. We stripped off all our clothes and went swimming, and mother came and caught us."

"I can still feel the sting of that slap she gave me on my bare butt," he laughed.

"Me too," said Caroline. "Boy, she was mad."

"How old were we then, Caroline----five----six?"

"About that, I guess."

Shawn picked up his coffee cup and clicked it to hers. "A toast; to swimming in the nude." Caroline repeated the salutation with a grin.

Caroline, only for the purpose of conversation, and without thinking, asked a question she knew to be inappropriate the moment she asked it. "Shawn, how come you didn't marry?"

He shrugged casually. "Wasn't meant to be, I guess."

Caroline noticed a slight hurt on his face. "I'm sorry, Shawn. That's none of my business. Sorry I asked."

"Oh, that's all right. But like I told you before, I was engaged to a wonderful woman----at least I thought she was wonderful. Her name was Victoria Picklow----Vicki. We became engaged one night, and...." he paused for a moment and thought back to that time, "and I never saw her again. A couple days later I got a small package in the mail with my engagement ring and a letter that said 'I don't love you. I'm sorry'." He shrugged his shoulders and tried to smile. "And that, my dear Caroline, is the story of my love-life. That was as good as it got."

They finished their coffees in silence before beginning the drive back to Portage Lake.

It was dark when they arriving back at Caroline's house. The first quarter of a new moon was hanging like a silver hook in the purple vastness of the northern sky.

She asked before getting out of the car, "You weren't planning to drive back to the city tonight, were you?"

"I was, actually."

"Why? Is there anything going on there that won't wait until tomorrow?"

"It's not that. I just think I've imposed enough on you already."

She grinned. "Your *boudoir* awaits you, sir."

Once inside the house Caroline lit the fire, poured two glasses of wine, put on an easy-listening CD, tuned down the lights and the two sat together on the sofa. Through the patio doors the moon's reflection mirrored on the lake surface below while the flickering of the fire dappled the room in golden warmth. On the southern shore of the lake the old Duncan summerhouse seemed to be watching them, white and ghostly in the moon's glow, a mythological god protecting the lake from intruders.

The two moved closer together, entwined fingers, and remained that way until bedtime.

After Shawn was finished in the bathroom and was walking past Caroline's open bedroom door, he paused. "Thanks for everything, Caroline. It may have been a terrible morning, but it was a wonderful afternoon and evening."

In the soft light that filtered into her bedroom he could see her outline on the bed. Without saying a word she was speaking to him. He could see her outline move to the far side of the bed as she flung the covers back on the side nearest him. He went to her, lay down beside her and drew the covers. In the still of a quiet house near the shore of a lake that was so dear to both, the two people who remembered a childhood filled with happiness, became one before drifting off to sleep in each other's arms.

Shawn was awake before Caroline, awakened by the cold rain ticking against the bedroom window. When she did open her eyes he was on his elbows looking down on her.

"Good morning," he whispered.

"Good morning," she answered with an embarrassed smile, tucking the covers tight to her chin.

A quiet time followed before Shawn said, "Who's going to say something first?"

"About…?"

"About us being in this bed together." He smiled. "*Again.*"

She blushed. "It was certainly different this time, wasn't it?"

"It sure was. It was wonderful."

"Oh God, Shawn, I hope you don't think I'm a terrible person for inviting you into my bed? Believe me, I don't do things like this. It's the first time I've been with a man since Peter…"

"Caroline. My dear, dear Caroline. Don't talk like that. We both knew it was going to happen. We just didn't know when or where. How could I ever think you're terrible?"

"It's just that----it was so soon after----you know?"

"After mother's funeral?"

"Yes. And I suppose I should feel some guilt about it, but I don't."

"Did you ever think that maybe you had enough feeling bad and needed something to feel good about? Mother passed away almost a week ago. I miss her terribly but life must go on. And speaking of life going on----what about us?"

"How do you mean?"

He shrugged. "You know! Last night was wonderful, so I was wondering if perhaps there's a future for us----together?"

"I'd love to find out," she answered, "but I don't see how that could happen with you down in the city and me up here in the boonies."

Shawn expression turned serious. "Caroline, after you fell asleep last night, I got up and sat by the patio door for a long time. I studied the old place across the lake----before it clouded over and began to rain----and I remembered all the good times I once had there. And almost without exception those good times involved you. I don't know why mother and I stopped coming up here, and I don't remember much good happening in my life after that, but times were always good here at the lake, especially when you and I were together. I know we were only kids, but I was wondering, why can't they be good again?"

She smiled at him. "I'd sure like to find out the answer to that myself."

Shawn fell back onto his pillow. "Why'd we never come back here? I've been asking myself that question many times since mother died, and I can't find the answer."

"No, you never did, did you? And if memory serves me, the last time we saw each other was the year mother and I went to visit you and your mother in the city. Do you remember that?"

Shawn rose up onto his elbows again and looked down at Caroline. "I sure do?"

Caroline continued. "Those Christmas shopping visits were the highlight of my life. A girl from the country spending a whole weekend in the big city. Boy, but did I brag to my friends at school about that."

"But think about it, Caroline; even after all the time we were apart we instantly had a great time together."

"Didn't we, though?" mussed Caroline. "I remember you taking me downtown on the streetcar to the big Eaton's and Simpson's stores. I just couldn't believe all the Christmas decorations. It was great. How old were we then? Twelve----thirteen?"

"How old were you when you started developing boobs?"

"*What?*"

Shawn laughed. "You tell me how old you were when you started developing boobs, and I'll tell you when it was, because that was the first thing I noticed about you. You had begun to develop breasts. I was at the age when I was very interested in things like that. I remember us sitting up half the night watching TV, eating chips, drinking gallons of Coke, smooching on the couch, and I kept accidentally touching your little boobs."

She gave him a playful poke. "You took advantage of me. The worldly city kid dazzled the country bumpkin." She then laughed. "I went back to school and told my friends that my boyfriend lived in *Toronto*, and we were probably going to get married someday."

"Really!" said Shawn. "So even back then you were setting me up?"

"I sure was." She then paused and her mood turned somber. "But few plans ever work out the way the way they're supposed to, do they?"

"And that was the last time we saw each other. Do you remember what happened that night, Caroline?"

"How could I forget it? We were asleep on the couch and we were awakened by the big fight our parents were having."

"That's right. And I never found out what they were fighting about."

"Whatever it was," said Caroline, frowning, "I know that was the time when our parents stopped being friends. They were never the same after that night. Very strange! But what does it matter?" she said, throwing off the memory. "You can't get the past back, but we're here now, together again, so let's take it from here."

"Let's," said Shawn. "So that's what we'll do."

"And?"

"And, I'm going to come back here to stay----for good," said Shawn.

Caroline sat up in bed and stared at him. "You're what?"

"I'm selling out in the city and moving up here. I decided that last night when I was sitting by the patio door."

"You're joking----aren't you?"

"Nope. I can do whatever I want now. I have no ties to anything, or any place. When I go back I'm putting my studio up for sale, storing my things in mother's house for the time being, and I'm eventually going to move back here----to the old summerhouse."

Caroline was dumbfounded. "Shawn, you *are* joking----right?"

"Not at all."

"Well you'd better be, because this can be a pretty lonely place at times----especially in the winter. And did you just say, 'to the old summerhouse'?"

Shawn laughed. "I did. Caroline, I live in the loneliest place on earth. I live shoulder to shoulder with millions of people, and yet it's the loneliest place on the planet. All the people who ever meant anything to me are gone now, so what's there to fear. If it doesn't work out then I'll do something else." He then looked at Caroline's bare chest. "And there's two lovely reasons for me to come back."

Caroline instantly dropped back down on the bed and pulled the sheet up to her chin. "But, you did say, *to the old summerhouse*?"

"That's right. I'm going to move back here, and that's final. I'm going to look up an architect and revitalize the old place----like they do on those home improvement programs on TV. The building is still structurally sound, so I'm just going to have it gutted and bring it back to its old glory----with a few modern twists added, of course."

"Shawn, you can't be serious?"

"I've never been more serious in my life. Caroline, I don't know how to describe what I feel right now, but when I came back up here it was the first time in years that I've felt free. Free of everything. I just feel good again. I feel like living again. Maybe I'm acting like a child wanting my past back, but maybe that's not all bad?"

"But Shawn, refurbishing that old place would cost a fortune."

"So what? If I sell the building my studio is in; that alone would more than take care of it. And the family home is worth enough to retire on. And the Duncans weren't exactly suffering financially to begin with."

She looked at him solemnly. "Shawn, I really believe you should give this more thought."

"So, you don't really want me back here, do you?"

"Of course I do. But what you just told me is a pretty serious step, and I just think you shouldn't rush into this."

"I've given it all the thought I'm going to give it. I'm forty-three years old and I've been doing the same thing all my life. It's time for a change. I've made up my mind, and that's final."

"But what would you do with all your spare time?"

"That's just the point; I would have spare time, something I never seem to have any more. And I want to get back doing actual artwork."

"Yes, I remember you were good at it, too," she said warmly. "You used to paint and sketch all the time."

"Did you know that I studied art in university?"

"No, I didn't."

"I've spent my entire adult life buying and selling other people's artwork, and I made some serious money doing it, but it took up all my time and I had no time to keep up my own skills. I miss it, and I want it back. And I've been thinking about my age as of late and I feel that time's running out. It really hit home after mother died. I need a change. I need to have something to look forward to, not just another day. And…"

"And what?"

"And while you were asleep I watched you, and something very important occurred to me."

She reached up and placed her hand on his shoulder. "And what was that?"

"That I'm in love with you. I've probably loved you since you were a little girl, but I didn't understand what love was."

"Shawn…" she said, her eyes watering, like she believed his words but at the same time was afraid to believe them. "I don't know how to describe what I feel at this moment, but it feels like the most natural thing I've ever done in my lifetime. I'll call it love, because I don't know what else it could be."

He took her in his arms and kissed her, kept on kissing her until they again made love, kissed her all through their lovemaking.

Later that morning they ate breakfast in their pajamas, drank coffee in front of the fireplace, and through the patio doors watched the autumn leaves being stripped from the trees by the wind and the driving cold rain. Shawn stayed another night before returning home. When he got back to the city he immediately put his studio up for sale and a week later it sold. His mind was set and things happened fast; he never gave his actions a second thought. The final prints for the renovations on the summerhouse were completed in early January, a contractor was hired and the gutting of the old summerhouse began that February on a bitterly cold day.

Shawn and Caroline spent much of that November and December together their relationship growing stronger with each passing day. They discussed things openly and came to a solid conclusion; their feelings were not that of children, but of adults, exciting and fresh. By Christmastime they were together at every opportunity and Caroline suggested that Shawn move in with her to avoid the long commute back and forth to the city. He thought it would be a splendid idea. Harriet Colburn was mortified by her daughter's decision and she made her feelings crystal clear without saying a word; she refused to speak to either of them.

They spent New Years together in the little Colburn house, drank Champagne and ate shrimp while watching the arrival of 1999 from Times Square. No two people had ever found such happiness, experienced such passion, and so late in life.

In May of that year they were married aboard a large yacht offered for the occasion by a patron of Caroline's marina. The ceremony took place in a quiet cove on Georgian Bay. A United Church minister performed the nuptials. Two of Caroline's friends, and a friend of Shawn's were there as witnesses. The only low point in the marriage was Harriet's refusal to attend. She gave no reason and offered no congratulations.

Their four-week honeymoon was spent in Europe. Happiness and the world was theirs, and after the marriage they continued living in Caroline's house. The renovations to the old summerhouse were massive in scope and would not be completed until the following spring at the earliest. They spent their first married New Year's Eve snuggled down in their pajamas on the bulky old sofa in front of a flickering fire eating chips and dip and drinking Champagne. As they sat and watched the arrival of The New Millennium on TV, they made plans for a long life together. They toyed with the idea for a mid-winter getaway to South America, but discarded the idea. Nothing could ever go wrong again in their lives. The dreaded Millennium scare fizzled to nothing and life was sound. Stripping off they made love on the sofa in front of the fireplace, the dying embers casting a bronze refection through the glass doors and dappling their bodies with golden beads of perspiration, like mica flakes.

It was past 2:00 am when they called it a night, Caroline retiring to the bedroom first. Just before Shawn turned out the family room light to follow her, he paused to study their wedding picture, which was perched on a shelf above the sofa. His chest expanded with pride when he looked at the beautiful woman he had married. Taking the picture down from the shelf, and as he admired it closer, the photo seemed to change before his eyes. His bride was a little girl again clinging to him in the old church with thunder in the background. Then she was a teenager, the one he had kissed all night long when she came to visit him in the city. As those images gave way to reality he was again gazing at the woman he had just made love to and he thought of how lucky he was.

But the moment he set the wedding picture back on the shelf another thought leaked into his mind. *Where were mother's wedding pictures? I've never seen a picture of my parent's wedding. Why? Where had they gone?* Throughout the previous year he had sorted through all of his mother's belongings, and yet he had never seen a single picture of their wedding, or a picture of the two of them together. Not one. He knew that every woman kept a picture of herself in a wedding dress, but he had found none. As he thought, he wondered, *what was their marriage like? Where are their wedding pictures? What's more important in a woman's life than her wedding day?*

"Something the matter, Shawn?" Caroline called out from the bedroom.

"No. I'm coming right in."

He turned out the lights and joined his wife in the darkness of their bedroom. Caroline wished him "A Happy New Year", and fell into a deep sleep. Shawn lay awake for a time with a troubled thought haunting him, *what was their married life like? Who were my parents?*

Chapter 13

THE MARRIAGE OF CONSTANCE Louise Lawson to Cyrus Archibald Duncan, took place during a spring snowstorm. It was April 2, 1951, a most miserable time of the year for any celebration let alone a wedding. A mixture of snow, fog and rain greeted the couple when they exited the church to a sea of umbrellas. Two hired boys worked feverously trying to keep the slush from the sidewalks until the happy couple and guests could get to their cars.

"Why in the name of God didn't he wait until May or June?" a guest whispered to her friend.

"Of course. When you can count on the weather. He waited all these years, so what was his big hurry all of a sudden?"

"I'll tell you this much; if old Muriel was still alive he wouldn't be getting married in March or any other month."

"And do you think he'll know what to do when he's alone with her tonight?"

"Well if he does, it won't be because his mother told him."

But it was a grand wedding to say the least with Connie's parents up from Cape Breton for the occasion, along with two of her younger siblings. Cyrus gladly paid the shot. None of Cyrus' relatives attended the ceremony; what remained of the Duncan clan was still on the other side of the Atlantic. But there were plenty of old acquaintances and the church was about half full. Helen Borden held down a prominent position in one of the front pews. Cyrus had no real friends, so he invited just about everyone he happened to know, mostly business acquaintances. And for the most part, all the invitees came; what else was there to do on a damp Saturday one day after April Fool's Day?

The wedding dinner seated almost two hundred guests. Speeches droned on for over an hour and the stern faced Scots and English even managed to crack a few smiles. For the stiff occasion that it was, the day was summed up in the newspapers as "a joyful event with the newlyweds boarding a train later in the day to honeymoon in New York City, The Carolinas, and Florida".

The first night of marriage was spent in a berth as the train rattled along over the Niagara Gorge Bridge on its way to New York City. Connie expected the consummation to happen that very night, but it didn't, and she believed she understood why; on a shaking train and both extremely tired. It was understandable. They kissed, said good night, and fell asleep to the sway of the sleeper car.

The second night was spent in New York City in the honeymoon suite at the Waldorf Astoria; only the best for his young bride, and Cyrus Duncan could afford the best. Connie chose a sleek blue silk nightgown with a low cut neckline for the occasion, and spotted herself with a perfume she knew Cyrus was fond of. Slipping under the sheets she waited with heart pounding anticipation for the coming consummation of the vows she had sworn to just the day before.

Cyrus seemed to take forever to get out of the bathroom, and when he did slide under the covers beside his lovely young bride he merely kissed her cheek and asked if they could start their married life the following day, perhaps in the morning. He claimed to be dreadfully tired and he wanted it to be special. What he didn't tell her was that he had spent long minutes in the bathroom with a good smear of her facial cream on his limp penis trying to get him to stand up, but he couldn't achieve an erection.

After the internal frustration of failure had eased and sleep overtook him, he was totally convinced the failure of his sexual prowess was the result of the day's exhaustion and excitement, nothing more. However, a ghost was lurking in the back of his mind, one he thought would vanish at the first contact he had with his lovely young bride's body. However, he hadn't required relief through masturbation in quite some time, not in a long time in fact. No woman on earth held the power to reverse what age had taken away. The last few grains of sand had already passed through the orifice of his genetic hourglass.

They slept late the next morning, but Cyrus made sure he got out of bed and dressed before Connie awoke, before she had a chance to tempt him with her charms. And charms she had in abundance, firm breast standing proud even when she was laying flat on her back, her nipples tenting the fabric of her nightgown. After he was dressed he stood for a time by the bed and watched her sleep, her chest rising and falling gracefully, her beautiful features tempting him in a maddening way, his frustration ripping at his insides. He wanted so badly to undress again and take her but was too terrified to attempt it. Tiptoeing into the bathroom he opened the front of his pants and began stroking. The desire was certainly there but nothing happened. His touch felt pleasurable enough, the lanolin from the previous nights attempts giving smoothness to his action, but try as he might nothing happened. He would need firmness to penetrate a virgin, but the best his manhood could achieve was a slight rise followed by total collapse. Nothing. He was hopelessly impotent.

They spent three days in New York City, saw the sights, ate in the finest dining rooms and took in a play on Broadway before moving on down the coast to The Carolinas. Then it was on to the sunshine of Florida. Constance Duncan was wed a virgin, went on her honeymoon a virgin, and returned to Toronto a virgin. Although she was not a woman of the world she certainly knew what should have taken place between husband and wife. Something was terribly wrong.

The day after returning from her honeymoon, while seated at the breakfast table, she asked, "What's wrong with me, Cy?"

He was reading a newspaper. "What do you mean?"

"We've been married for almost a month, and you hardly ever touch me. And we haven't even----you know…"

"All in good time, Connie. All in good time."

Connie was at the point of tears. "You told me before we married that you wanted a namesake----a child----two or three you said. So why are we not trying?"

He didn't answer or look over the paper.

"Look at me, Cy. What's wrong? Do you find something repulsive about me? If so, I'm still a virgin and we could have the marriage annulled."

The paper snapped down and he glared at her. "There is nothing wrong. We are husband and wife and will be *until death do us part*. Is that clear?"

Tears streamed down her face. "Well, there's certainly something wrong, and I know there is nothing wrong with me. It's like you're afraid of me."

He again picked up his paper to hide behind. "There is nothing wrong," he mumbled.

She reached across the table and pulled the paper down. "Cy, if there's a problem, perhaps you could see a doctor?"

Cyrus Duncan exploded out of the chair, stepped around the table and clamped his hand onto his wife's arm. "There is nothing wrong with me," he shouted. "And don't you ever mention a word about this to anyone----ever. Do you hear me?" It was the first time she had witnessed the other Cyrus Duncan, a stranger she would become well acquainted with in the coming years. After releasing his grip on the terrified woman, he stormed out of the house and went to his office.

That evening he informed her that he would sleep in another room. He never slept with his wife again. For the following two years they were man and wife in name only. They attended church together, went to public functions, had guests over to their house, the perfect couple, but they may as well been living on different continents. The atmosphere around the home was that of a daughter caring for her father.

It was during the bleakest time of the winter of 1953 when Cyrus announced to his surprised wife that he would like to hang her portrait over the fireplace. "A very good artist has been recommended to me. He has a studio down on Front Street." He handed Connie the artist's business card. "Your first sitting will be this Monday at one o'clock." It was not a request, it was an order.

She read the artist's name on the card. "Jeremy Kane."

Chapter 14

CYRUS DUNCAN DID NOT ask his young wife if she wanted her portrait painted, he ordered it done, and since she and Cyrus practically never spoke, and never shared an intimate moment, she could not understand why. But at least it would get her out of the house.

Jeremy Kane had a smile that came easy, like the fishermen from Cape Breton Island. She could easily visualize him hauling nets over the side of a boat. When he laughed the corners of his mouth curled up into a happy face showing perfect white teeth. Not overly tall, standing just shy of six feet, he was solidly built and lean. There was lightness in his step, sort of an effortless lope when he walked. His thick light brown hair hid a reddish glint, a glint which showed itself when the light was just right, but his handsomeness came more from a combination of his spirit, his charm, his ruggedness. He wore a plain blue shirt with no undershirt, a pipe stem jutting out of the pocket, the sleeves rolled to his elbows.

A sturdy belt cinched his slim waist, and the thing she noticed first about the man, he was wearing moccasins. U*nusual footwear* thought Connie, *but somehow fitting.*

"Jerry," he insisted, when they first met. "Please call me, Jerry?"

"And you can call me, Conni*e*. I hate, *Missus Duncan.*"

When she sat on the stool to pose, and when he gently touch her cheek to angle her head just so, a tingle shot through her body. The scent of his pipe tobacco was more sensual than expensive cologne.

"You can smoke if you wish," she told him. "I love the smell of a pipe." And when he would lean over her she wanted badly to reach up and touch him, draw him to her and never let go. Through the hours of the sittings they talked, laughed, and when they took a break and sat across from each other at a small table their knees sometimes lightly touch. If something funny was said she instinctively reached over and placed her hand on his arm.

On the day of the third sitting, before she even entered Jerry Kane's studio, she knew it was going to happen and she couldn't wait. He helped her off with her coat and when she turned around and faced him they just fell together. With his lips still pressed to hers, he backed over to the door of the studio, flipped the sign to "Closed" and slid the deadbolt. He then led Connie Duncan into his small apartment at the back of the studio where a blinding flurry of removing clothes occurred. Finally, she experienced what she so long craved. They made love on his narrow bed, tears of happiness streaming down her cheeks. Jerry Kane was a man in all the ways her husband was not. Even though a throb of guilt came with the adulterous action, she couldn't stop herself, refused to even try. Throughout the remaining months of that winter they came together at every opportunity.

After their marriage, Cyrus Duncan refused to let Connie work outside the home and he hired a replacement for her at the office. "You don't need the money and I won't have it," he told her. So while he spent the days at his office the opportunities for her and Jeremy Kane to be together were many. The portrait was completed by the end of April but their rendezvous continued. Winter melted away, spring blossomed, and Connie Duncan was madly in love.

Shortly after their marriage, Cyrus drove Connie north to see his holdings on Portage Lake, the place his parents had loved so dearly. She too fell in love with the summerhouse and the lake. Cyrus detested country living and had no use for the place, so just out of the blue he told her, "You can have it. It'll be your wedding gift." He even went so far as to sign over the deed. Afterwards Connie went to Portage Lake at every opportunity and Cyrus seemed glad to be away from her.

The year following their marriage Connie suggested that she move up to the summerhouse for the entire summer. Cyrus shrugged and said, "Fine". To her amazement he actually insisted that she do exactly that. "Your leaving the city for the summer would be good for both of us." The very day she made the move to Portage Lake was the same day Jeremy Kane closed his little studio on Front Street and took up residence in a little trapper's cabin just across the lake from the Duncan summerhouse.

Chapter 15

On a warm April day, Shawn and Caroline moved into the newly renovated summerhouse. After more than a year of construction and several hundreds of thousands of dollars, the transformation was spectacular. Better Homes and Gardens would be proud to run a piece on it; in fact, the architect suggested just that, but the Duncans declined. They didn't wish to share their piece of paradise with the outside world. Tastefully furnished with reproductions, antiques taken from his mother's house, and with keepsakes from Caroline's residence, the home was a showplace. A great deal of landscaping remained to be done but the house itself was complete.

But the move left Caroline with a dilemma. After walking through her empty house she was hit with a jolt of nostalgia. The day before the move she was very much in favour of selling the little bungalow, but when she saw it sitting empty her heart sank. She just could not part with it. But what to do with the empty house? To have a perfectly good home sitting vacant made no sense at all. To sell it was out of the question. To find the right people to rent it to would be difficult. What to do? And as the month of April slipped by, another problem began to show itself, one she had already anticipated. Shawn was becoming bored, very bored. He had led a very active life in the city, but now he had far too much spare time on his hands. He was back doing artwork and his hand was improving rapidly, but he couldn't do the same thing every day. He knew nothing of gardening and was useless with tools. He did, however, purchase a boat and motor and buzzed around the lake on hot days, but he was still left with a great deal of spare time. The previous year had been incredibly hectic dealing with the architect, the builders, traveling back and forth to the city looking about selling his mother's house, sorting through what to keep and what must be sold off, but that was all behind him. It was done.

Caroline, being a practical woman, put the two problems together and she had her solution; the little bungalow would become Shawn's new art studio, a downsized version of what he once owned in the city. He would just be moving his art-dealing talents from the city to cottage country, and he'd be busy again. She would broach the idea with him at the appropriate time, but the time was not yet right. She'd wait until he was bored stiff, wait until he couldn't stand it any longer, wait until the quiet of the north country was driving him mad.

And it didn't take long for her intuitions to prove correct. Two months after moving into their newly renovated home he was pacing the floors. He had gone from a nonstop existence to an almost dead stop. He was back doing watercolours, and had started dabbling in oils, but he couldn't put in eight hours a day at it. A couple of times he went with Caroline to her marina, but he knew that was too much togetherness, and he also knew Caroline didn't want it; the marina was her world, not his. He read books during the heat of the summer afternoons, something he never had time for in the past, and took long walks about the countryside. It helped alleviate some of the boredom but it wasn't enough. As Caroline watched him she knew when the time was right.

On a sweltering July evening she put her proposal to him. "So, what do you think, Shawn? The move is totally finished and you're going to need something to do with your time. In fact, I'd say you need something to do right now. And the house is just going to sit empty. So what do you think?"

He fell into a thoughtful silence for a time. "You know, it could work. The only business would be during the summer months, and on a few weekends in the autumn----when the leaf-lookers are traveling the back roads. And probably for a couple weeks before Christmas. I could keep my hand on the old business and still have plenty of free time. Yes, I believe that could work quite nicely." He smiled at her. "I knew I married you for more than your good looks and great body."

The following day, with sketchpad in hand and Caroline's blessing, he went to the empty Colburn house. Two weeks later a contractor was called in to size up the job, but work could not start before late autumn. He couldn't open his new studio until the following summer. But that too was a blessing; it would keep him busy seeing about the alterations and lining up artwork to display. He had plenty of time to get it right.

The driveway needed to be widened to accommodate half a dozen cars. Two bedroom walls would be removed and doorways stretched into arches. Four new skylights would brighten the interior section of the building and track lights would take care of the rest. He also decided to remove the patio door and have a solarium replace the shaky old sundeck. A local sign painter fabricated the prefect green, white, and gold signs, "Portage Lake Art Studio". One sign was posted on the lawn in front of the house while a second sign was placed two miles away at a junction where the county road meets the main highway. Without that sign few people would ever find his new place of business.

The contractor promised him an early October start. Shawn wanted it to happen sooner but it was not to be. He spent the following months traveling to art sales and contacting area artists to see if they would like to display pieces of their work on consignment. He would never again deal in high-end art, but if he managed to make enough to pay the property taxes and cover the operating expenses, then that would be great.

The target date for opening his new studio was the following June.

Shawn Duncan had spent his entire life under his mother's roof, and yet, less than two years after her death he seldom thought about her. Although he passed the old Lutheran cemetery every day, he rarely cast a glance toward the back corner to where she was buried, nor did he give much thought to the very strange decision she had made a long time ago. Now and again he would think about her, but only in fleeting moments. His new joys in life left little time to dwell on things that couldn't be changed.

Chapter 16

THE WINTER BLAHS HAD vanished. Nights were still chilly with morning slivers of ice on puddles, but spring's warmth was strengthening. The last thing left to be done at the summerhouse was landscaping and the landscaping contractor, Delbert Greene, owner of Greene Thumb Landscaping, was already in the yard when Shawn hurried out of the house for his morning walk. The two men bid each other a quick "good morning" as they passed.

With the first real hit of spring's warmth in the air, Shawn picked-up his pace. It was good to be alive. The new millenium was promising a wonderful life. He actually felt like running, but wisely ruled it out. Along the roadway new growth was beginning to peek above the last year's old growth. Trilliums and fiddleheads were unfurling. The last of winter's snows was trickling through culverts, birds flitted and chirped, cumulus clouds floated lazily overhead.

It was almost a perfect day, and would have been perfect if Caroline had been there to keep him company, but the boating season was drawing near and she was spending longer days at her marina. "Boaters are an impatient lot when spring fever hits," he could hear her say.

He had no intention of visiting his mother's gravesite that morning, but when he came to the old Lutheran Church he felt he should stop and pay his respects. He hadn't been in the little cemetery for so long that he felt a bit guilty, so he decided to stop for a moment to say a silent hello to his mother. Wandering into the graveyard he made his way to where Connie Duncan was resting in her little corner of the world. Since her death he came to accept her decision and was at peace with it, and he had to admit there was certain tranquility about the place she had chosen. With a light heart of acceptance he approached the gravesite.

It had been a very heavy winter with several feet of snow on the ground for most of the season, and when the snow melted all the dead grasses and vines of the previous year's growth were flattened down tight to the ground. Whether it was the angle of the sunlight or just the angle he happened to approach the grave, Shawn noticed something he never noticed before. There was a depression in the ground right beside his mother's grave. In fact, it was directly beside her grave with no space between the two, like a giant's footprint. He crouched for a moment and stared at the depression as he slowly realized what he was looking at. Going to the depression he knelt down and traced the hollow with his hand.

There was no doubt about it; another grave was directly beside his mother's----or was there?

Carefully scanning the area looking for more depressions, he saw none. All other graves were in two straight rows along the west side of the cemetery, close to the church. His mother and another mysterious person were the only two buried on the east side of the cemetery.

Literally running back to the summerhouse he borrowed a hoe and rake from Delbert Greene and then hurried back to the cemetery. Using the hoe in a chopping motion he scuffed the vegetation from the depression in the ground and then raked the mulch away. He again got down on all fours and studied the place. There was no mistake; Constance Louise Duncan was not alone in her little forgotten corner of the world. He knew that in olden times people were buried in wooden boxes not in the newer concrete vaults, and when the wood rotted the graves collapsed. He again traced the outline of the depression with his hands. *Someone was certainly buried beside mother, but who? Not another grave was anywhere nearby. Why would that be?*

His wonderful day ended with a single question: *Who's buried beside mother?*

Hurrying back to the summerhouse he found Delbert Greene spray-painting lines on the ground and driving elevation markers about the yard. Shawn asked him, "Del, would you happen to know how I could find out the names of people who are buried in a local cemetery?"

"Joff Pedigrew," Delbert said, without giving the question a second thought.

"Pardon?"

"Joff Pedigrew. He digs most of the grave around here; has for as long as I can remember. He'd know if anyone would."

Chapter 17

A LARGE BLACK DOG bounded out of the garage when Shawn pulled into Joff Pedigrew's driveway, its teeth showing, the hackles standing on its neck. A man's head popped up from behind a bulldozer and shouted at the dog. "Lay down and shut up, you damn fool." When Shawn got out of his car he was very aware of the dog sniffing the back of his leg. The old man reminded the dog of who was boss. "Get and lay down before I break your goddamn neck." The dog's head drooped, but before sauntering back to the garage it lifted its leg and marked a wheel on Shawn's car.

"Mister Pedigrew, my name is Shawn Duncan, and I understood that it was you who dug a grave in the old Lutheran churchyard----about two years ago? My mother's grave, in fact."

"That's right. Something wrong with it?" he said defensively.

"Oh no! I'd just like to ask you a question----about the location of the grave."

"Ask away."

"Well, I just came from the cemetery and I noticed that directly beside where mother's buried, there's another grave. I was wondering if perhaps you could tell me who's buried there?"

Without saying a word Joff Pedigrew turned and began walking toward the garage. Pulling a grease-smeared rag from his back pocket he wiped his hands as he walked signaling Shawn to follow him. As Shawn trailed the old man he couldn't help but think of him as a human crab, his body bent and twisted from too many years of hard work. His trunk-like legs were slightly bowed, his back and shoulders rolled forward into a stoop, his skin badly weathered, his large ears sticking out past a filthy CAT cap, the cap pulled down tight on his head, a wide set of suspenders over his shoulders.

There was nothing clean or orderly about the place; stacks of worn-out tires were piled beside the garage; bits and pieces of various machinery parts scattered about the yard. The driveway was lined with two dump trucks, a backhoe and a bulldozer, the gravel beneath the machines glistening black from spilled oil. A neat brick house was situated beside, but well away from the garage. Shawn guessed it was under a woman's control. The lawns surrounding the house were raked and neat with flowerbeds circling the house and lining the walkway. The veranda had been recently painted and streak-free windows sparkled in the sunlight.

Tucked away in one corner of the garage was a small office. Joff entered the office, flicked on a glaring florescent light and beckoned Shawn inside. Being careful to avoid contact with the walls or anything else inside the little office---- Joff Pedigrew's environment followed him wherever he went----Shawn stood and watched as the old man removed a stack of maps from a filing cabinet. After sorting through them he picked out one in particular and returned the remaining maps to the cabinet. Unfolding the map on a cluttered desk he pointed at it with his finger.

"That the one you're talking about?"

Shawn checked the map, a map surveyed in 1884 showing a grid of burial plots.

"Yes. That looks like it."

"The names of the people who own them should be marked on the plots. If there's a body in them it'll be marked with an 'O'----for occupied."

Shawn put his face down close to the map and studied the grid lines, the task being difficult because of the dirty smudges on the paper. In the very southeast corner of the grid plan was the name "J. Kane" Beside his name, "'O' 1953".

"Jeremy Kane," whispered Shawn Duncan. And beside Kane's grave, recently penned in, was written "C. Duncan, 'O' 1998". *My God, is mother buried beside thee Jeremy Kane?*

Without counting the number of plots on the map he guessed there were at least three hundred in total, but less than three dozen were occupied. The entire center section of the cemetery was vacant. Constance Duncan and a J. Kane were the only two in the entire eastern side, and they were lying at rest with no gap between them.

"But why would this Kane have been buried away from the others?" asked Shawn. "Why would these two graves be off by themselves?"

"Probably because they're singles."

"Huh?"

"Because they're singles. The plots on the western side are all family plots. As you can see, they're large and some can hold up to a dozen bodies. I'm just guessing of course, but if you want to find out for sure you'll have to consult The Cemetery Board. There's a branch of the Government that looks after those things."

"But someone must have made that decision back in 1953," said Shawn. "Why all of a sudden did they start burying people over in the far corner?"

"Well, as it so happens," said Joff, "I'm a bit familiar with the Kane grave."

"You are?"

"Yup!" Joff readjusted his cap. "Kane's death was big news around here back then." He thought a moment before continuing. "Yeah, I remember burying him all right. No backhoes then, either. I used to help my dad dig graves by hand." He squinted at the map. "Says 1953 he was buried." He rubbed his chin as he gave it more thought. "That'd be about right----1953. He fell off the high bluff up at Portage Lake and ended up in the lake." He then looked at Shawn. "Do you know the bluff I'm talking about?"

"Yes. I own a house on the opposite shore. We can see it from our place."

" Of course! And I've been told you fixed the old place up like new and you're living there now. And you married Harriet Colburn's daughter?"

"That's right! So you know Harriet?"

"Not well, but yes I do know her. I remember when she married Darrell Colburn. They lived for years in the little house above Portage Lake."

"That's right", answered Shawn.

"And ain't it strange?" Joff said. "All those years went by and Kane's name was never mentioned and suddenly you're the second person in the last little while who came around asking about the man.

"Someone else has made inquiries about him?" said Shawn.

"Yes. About three----maybe four years ago. I can't remember his name, but he said he was writing a book about the man. Something to do with art. Apparently this Kane was an artist."

Shawn then knew for certain that his mother was indeed buried beside *thee* Jeremy Kane.

"Why is it?" Shawn asked after a long minute's silence, "that except for this Kane, no one has been buried in that cemetery since 1913? That is of course until my mother was buried there."

"Because it was around that time that everyone started moving away. You see, there was actually a town named Portage Lake and the old church is all that's left of it. Once people moved away they'd get buried someplace else. As for Kane, I believe it all came down to money. You see, that old cemetery is not kept up and the county had to come good for the funeral expenses----no family member claimed the body----and burying was cheap at that particular graveyard. And you gotta remember, no one really knew much about him----his religion or anything like that. But I think it was just a matter of getting the poor fellow under the ground."

"So, anyone can be buried there?" said Shawn.

"I suppose they could----if they really wanted too. A body could be buried in a hell-of-a-lot worse place. It's peaceful enough with all those tall pines and a view of the lake----not that anyone sees it when you're under the ground."

"Yes, I suppose it is," said Shawn Duncan with a painful frown. "My mother chose it and I'll be damned if I can figure out why."

The older man could see the hurt on Duncan's face. "She must have had a good reason or she wouldn't have requested it. Maybe she just liked the idea of the place being so quiet and peaceful."

Shawn forced a tight smile and shook Joff's hand. "Well, Mister Pedigrew, I'm very grateful for your help, and I think I've taken up enough of your time."

Joff smiled. "I quit worrying about time long ago," he said as he followed Shawn back to his car. "I'd better stay with you; you never know about that damn dog."

"Just one more question," said Shawn, while opening his car door. "By chance, would you happen to know of anyone around these parts who could tell me more about this Jeremy Kane?"

Joff thought a moment and then shook his head.

"Okay, then" said Shawn, getting into his car, "You've been very helpful."

"Wait a minute," said Joff Pedigrew snapping his finger, "I've just remembered something. About two weeks ago, me and a couple other lads were discussing a family named Doweling. A big tribe of them once lived over on County Road Ten. They had a small farm just north of the lake. Anyways, one of the lads said that Tommy Doweling was still living on the old homestead, and if memory serves me, I believe Tommy was there the day that Kane's body was found. But I could be wrong about that; it was a long time ago, you understand."

Shawn Duncan thanked Joff Pedigrew one more time and closed the door. The door window was down and before Shawn could start the engine, Joff said, "Have you asked your mother-in–law about it?"

"Harriet?"

"Yes. She was there the day they buried him. I can't remember where I laid a wrench down two minutes after I do it, but I can remember things that happened forty years ago. She was there the day Kane was buried."

Shawn got back out of the car. "Joff, are you sure?"

Joff closed his eyes, hooked his thumbs on his suspenders, and threw his head back as he thought. "Yup! She was there all right. I remember there was a preacher, too. A middle aged man. Can't remember his name or what religion he was, but the only mourner there was Harriet Colburn."

"Did you say----mourner?"

"I don't know if that's the proper word or not, but she brought flowers with her. I remember it well, because after my father and I finished filling in the grave we placed the flowers on top of it. Not a fancy wreath like you'd buy at a flower shop, just flowers from her own garden." Joff readjusted his cap and added. "Ain't it funny how some little things stick in your mind for so long? Oh yes, she was there all right."

Shawn Duncan thanked Joff Pedigrew for the final time and drove away.

Chapter 18

The Doweling farm hadn't been worked in years. What remained of the barn and outbuildings had just about completed their journey to the ground. Saplings and briers had already claimed the land that was once a barnyard. However, the century old brick farmhouse was well preserved, kept neat and up to date, the lawns mowed, the driveway paved, the shrubs and fruit trees around it neatly pruned.

A golden retriever came out to meet Shawn Duncan when he pulled into the driveway, its tail wagging, happy to befriend anyone who came along. The man standing on the porch wore slippers, a Harley Davidson T shirt, and badly faded blue jeans. Except for a fringe of side hair he was totally bald, six-foot-plus in statue, overweight with a paunch, a warm smile, and a friendly way of saying "hello".

"Tommy Doweling?"

"Tom," said the man.

"Tom, my name is Shawn Duncan. I own the house on the other side of Portage Lake."

Tom Doweling nodded. "Yes, I know the place. The Duncan Summerhouse?"

"That's right. I wonder if I might ask you a few questions about something that happened a long time ago?"

"And I'll just bet it's about that artist who fell off the bluff?"

"Why yes. As a matter-of-fact it is."

"You're the second one that's come along and asked about him. A couple years back a writer fella came by and asked me about him; said he was doing a story about the man."

"Really?" said Shawn, remembering Joff Pedigrew had said the same thing.

"Can't remember his name though, but he had a pile of notes on the man. Had a couple photos of his artwork with him, too."

"I know the artist's name was Jeremy Kane, but that's about all I know. But I understand you were there the day his body was retrieved from the lake?"

"True enough," Tom Doweling answered. He motioned Shawn up onto the porch. "Come on inside. The wife's away for the day and I was just making myself a cup of coffee. Would you like a cup?"

"Sounds great," said Shawn.

Once inside, Tom poured two cups of coffee and the two men sat at a large kitchen table. The dog followed them into the house and plopped down on a mat by the door. From the dimensions of the kitchen Shawn could only imagine the size of the family that once lived there.

"Was Kane a relative?" asked Tom.

"No. Never met the man. I wasn't even born when he died."

"I figured as much," smiled Tom. "I'm retired now and I was just a boy when it happened. 1953 it was. How I happened to be there that day, I saw the police car go tearing past the house so I jumped on my bike and followed it." Tom laughed. "We didn't have much to entertain us back then."

"What I'm really interested in, though, is to know who he was and what he was like? And why was he here at Portage Lake in the first place?"

Tom ran his hand over his puffy jowls. "Well sir, I remember there was a great interest in the man at the time. His death was big news around these parts. Now, of course, nothing shocks people." Tom made a clicking sound with his tongue. "But boy-o-boy, back then that was something to talk about."

"Tom, I'm an art dealer and I used to own a studio in Toronto, so you can see where the interest is coming from?"

"Yes, I know," said Tom, " and you married Caroline Colburn?" Tom obviously knew everything that went on around the country, made it his business to know.

"That's right," smiled Shawn with pride.

"Hell-of-a fine woman you got yourself there. Sure is a hard worker."

"Too, hard," added Shawn.

Tom jumped to his feet. "Just a minute. I've got something upstairs you'd probably like to see; you being in the art business and all." He left the kitchen and in a short time he was back carrying a picture frame. "He drew this of me. Didn't take him more than fifteen, maybe twenty minutes."

It was a charcoal of a young smiling boy, a tuff of hair falling on his forehead, freckles dotting his face, a missing front tooth, a twinkle in the boy's eyes. It was signed, J. Kane. Shawn took the drawing from Tom and turned it over; the date of completion was on the back: August 17, 1953, a tick across the seven. There was no doubt about it; Constance Louise Duncan was buried beside the artist, Jeremy Kane. Until that day Shawn only knew that Kane had died in an accident somewhere in the north country. He never for a moment imagined that it happened at Portage Lake.

"He was good," said Shawn, after a long study of the sketch.

"He sure was," agreed Tom.

"Would you consider selling it?"

Tom shook his head vigorously. "Never."

"Can't blame you," said Shawn Duncan. "Tom, I don't know if you're aware of it or not, but since this Jeremy Kane is a dead artist his work has been increasing in value. And there isn't a lot of it around. He's not well known outside the art world----yet----but that little sketch of you is probably worth a couple thousand dollars. Maybe more. And it'll only become more valuable with time, so be careful with it. And make sure it's on the list of household items with your insurance company----you know, if you ever had a fire, or if someone broke in and stole it."

"You know," said Tom, "I never thought of that. I'll be sure and do that. Thanks for the advice."

He set the picture down gently on the table and leaned back so his chair was balancing on its two back legs. "I was probably one of the last people to ever see that man alive. I only met him once. It was up top the bluff across the lake from your place. That's where he drew this."

Tom suddenly cut the story off. He couldn't reveal that Jeremy Kane was having a picnic with a woman, and he knew who the woman was. How could he ever forget that day and what had happened? He had walked onto them at a very bad time. The woman was sitting on a blanket near the edge of the bluff, the wind blowing her long hair about her face. It was probably the noise of the wind in the trees that blocked out the sound of his approach. The man was sitting on a small fold-up seat with an easel in front of him concentrating on his work of drawing the woman. Tom came to a sudden stop the moment he saw them. Not knowing what to do, he just stood there for several seconds and stared. Then the woman noticed him. The front of her dress was open and one of her breasts was totally exposed. It was the first time young Tom Doweling ever saw a woman's breast. She quickly turned away to button up, and that's when Jeremy Kane raised his head and noticed the boy.

"Hello there," he said with a smile.

Tom nodded his head nervously and returned the greeting. "Hello."

After the woman had buttoned her dress she turned and asked, "Would you like a sandwich?" Tom hesitated so she picked a sandwich from the basket and handed it to the boy. "I've never known a boy who wasn't hungry," she said warmly. "Go on and take it. We're finished and if you don't eat it, it'll just get thrown out."

Tom Doweling took the sandwich and devoured it. It was his first tuna fish sandwich and he had never before eaten a sandwich that tasted so good. Then she gave him a banana, something the Doweling children only received on special occasions.

"Would you like me to draw your picture?" asked Kane? Tom didn't know what to say. "Here," said the man changing the sheet of paper on the easel, "sit on the blanket?" Tom did as he was told and Jeremy Kane began sketching. As Tom sat he never once looked at the woman, but he couldn't help but sense her presence beside him, could smell the fragrance that wafted from her body, could feel warmth radiating from her. He would never forget those few minutes of his life.

After Kane was finished he handed young Tom his likeness. "There you go."

Tommy looked at the portrait and was amazed. After admiring it for a time he handed it back.

"You can keep it if you want," said Kane.

"You mean I can have it?"

The artist smiled warmly. "Sure, as long as you let me draw another one of you."

Beaming a wide grin the boy sat patiently while Jeremy Kane sketched. After the second sketch was completed Tom Doweling jumped to his feet and hurried home to show off his prize.

Sadness settled over Tom's gentle face. "I asked him where he was from and he told me Manitoba. We chatted for a while----you know, where I lived, and that sort of thing----then he asked me if I wanted my portrait drawn.

Of course I said yes, and that's how I come to have this. He actually drew two of me that day; one for me and one for himself. Yes sir, he was a heck of a nice guy."

"And you never saw him again?"

"Nope," answered Tom. "Not alive, anyway."

And Tom never mentioned what had happened when he got home and showed his likeness to his parents. There was no TV to keep peoples minds off other people's business in those times. The Doweling farm didn't even have electricity. The children did their homework by the light of coal oil lamps. A good part of a week's entertainment was going to church on Sunday and then gossiping for an hour afterwards on the church steps. That's the way it was. And during that summer of 1953 there was plenty of gossip. An artist from the city was carrying on with another man's wife and everyone knew who the young woman was.

That day, when young Tom got home and showed his portrait to his parents, brothers and sisters, and told them about the tuna fish sandwich and the banana, his parents were shocked. His brothers and sister were jealous but his parents were mortified and he couldn't understand why. He was told in no uncertain terms, "If you ever meet up with *those two* again, you just keep on walking". But they never explained why. Later that night Tom asked his oldest sister and she explained the situation as best she could.

"I understand that his body was found in the lake?" said Shawn.

"Well," said Tom Doweling, after rubbing his chin for a spell----Tom rubbed his chin frequently as he thought----"he was, but he never did drown. The postmortem said he died from a sever blow to the head. Probably from the fall off the bluff. The poor guy actually fell from the bluff, landed on the rock ledge below, and bounced into the lake. At least that was the final report on it. The police figured that he must have landed on his head----or on his face----because he wasn't recognizable when he was taken from the water." Tom pinched his lips together and twisted his face into a frown. "Poor man. He practically had no face left. Been in the water for some time and they figure the turtles and fish----you know? It wasn't a pretty sight."

"And where was he living at the time, Tom?"

"In an old trapper's cabin on the east end of the lake. Not much left of it now, just some pieces of rusted roofing steel and the collapsed skeleton of the building. I was told he kept a small studio in Toronto for the winter months, but I couldn't say for sure." He paused and thought a moment. "Funny thing, though."

"What's that?" said Shawn.

"When the police went to the cabin, practically everything was gone from it. The only thing they found that belonged to him was his cedar-strip canoe and his old car. The canoe was pulled up on the beach near the bluff and the paddle was under it. But practically everything in the cabin was gone----except his bedding and dishes. His clothes, art supplies, everything else was gone. And no one could figure it out. Like someone visited the place after he was dead and stole his personal stuff."

"Really?" said Shawn Duncan.

"Yup! His stuff just seemed to have disappeared, and it wouldn't have been worth a hell-of-a-lot. If memory serves me there were a few unanswered questions surrounding the man's death, but it was a long time ago. Today the scientists could tell you exactly what happened, but back then it was mostly guesswork. I don't think there ever was a completely satisfactory answer to his death."

Tom and Shawn chatted for a while longer and Shawn invited Tom over for a visit. Tom said he and his wife would take him up on it someday, but Shawn knew they wouldn't. Tom Doweling was a man content with his life and visiting a stranger might put things out of order. On his way out the door Shawn patted the dog's head and the dog gave him a parting lick on the hand.

Dog and master followed Shawn out onto the porch. They shook hands, said goodbye one last time, and as Tom Doweling watched the visitor get into his car and drive away he leaned on a veranda post and allowed his thoughts to slip back to another time and place. Once again he was meeting Jeremy Kane and his woman friend atop the high bluff. And he remembered that early autumn morning when Kane's body was brought in from the lake. Tom shuddered as he recalled the condition of the faceless man, felt saddened even after all those years, remembered the kindness of the artist, remembered too much.

Chapter 19

CORPORAL WALTER HASS SAT petrified in the stern of the small rowboat, his sweaty hands locked to the gunnels, his eyes glued on the old man working the oars. As the morning sun rose higher into the sky a light chop began ruffling the surface of the lake; the further from shore the more the chop turned into wave conditions.

"You seem a bit nervous?" said the old man.

The policeman tried to smile but he was looking down at his heavy boots, very conscious of his gun belt and holster, wishing he'd left them behind in the cruiser. *If this thing tips I'll go straight to the bottom. Less than two years from my pension and I could end up at the bottom of a lake in the middle of nowhere and some old toothless son of a bitch laughing at me as I go down.* Then to his horror he noticed something else. *Where are the lifejackets?*

"Did you ever hear of an invention called a lifejacket?" he asked, his voice tense, angry with himself for being so careless as not to notice the missing jackets before he even got into the boat.

The old man shrugged. "Got 'em at home hanging on a hook. All they're any good for is gettin' your fish hooks caught in."

"And what are you suppose to do if the boat gets swamped, or you upset?"

"Swim to shore. Wouldn't be the first time."

The policeman shook his head at the idiotic response. "How much further?"

"See that high rock bluff straight ahead?"

"Yeah, I see it."

"He's right at the bottom of it."

Several minutes of silence followed as the old man took long steady pulls on the oars, Corporal Walter Hass trying to remain calm and steady as the little craft worked its way across the open stretch of water. When the boat neared the leeward side of the high bluff the water smoothed out somewhat. "You ever think of getting a motor for this thing?" he asked sarcastically, feeling a little more secure in the calmer waters.

"Got one, but it's just a damn nuisance. Never wants to start and then you gotta lug it to and from the boat. Besides, the oars never run out of gas and I've got all the time in the world."

The two men were quiet again with only the oarlocks squeaking rhythmically their chirps echoing off the high rocky shoreline. Sensing he was nearing the bluff the old man stopped rowing and glanced over his left shoulder, judged the distance and then gave two more strong pulls on the oars. As he neared the shoreline he swung around on the seat shifting his weight and causing the little boat to rock heavily.

The policeman gasped, "Jesus! Can't you be more careful about moving around? You damn near upset the boat."

The old man kept his smiling face turned away from the big cop. He knew Walter Hass was terrified and he was enjoying the moment. "There he is," he said, pointing toward a smudge of colour in the brackish water.

"Pull a little closer," ordered the policeman. The old man gave a single easy pull on the oars. "Good. Hold'er right there."

The side of the boat was touching the corpse causing it to bob about as though it was performing an underwater dance, like it was made of jelly. It was face down, swollen, and obviously had been in the water for a considerable length of time.

"Any idea who this might be?"

The old man shrugged. "Nope."

"Do you think you could use one of the oars to push the body a little closer to shore?" said Corporal Hass.

The old man slid an oar under the body and gently floated it along toward the shoreline. "You should be able to reach it from shore now," he said after a couple gentle shoves.

Hass stared at the old man for a moment. "I forgot. What's your name again?"

"Charlie Plaxton."

"And what were you doing when you found this body, Charlie?" the policeman asked, sensing he was once again safe from a dark wet demise.

Charlie pointed to his fishing pole. "Plugging for bass along the shore."

"You seem awfully calm about this, Charlie. How come?"

"I've seen a hell-of-a-lot worse."

"Oh?" said Walter Hass.

"You ever see what's left of a man when he's hit by a mortar or an eight inch shell?"

"So, you were in the war?"

"Yup. The first one. Three long years in the trenches."

"You ever been in trouble with the law before, Charlie?"

"Couple times."

"For what?"

"Bootleggin', mostly. Did six months once."

"Hum," said Walter Hass. "And you have absolutely no idea who this man is?"

"Nope. But maybe I can answer that better when I get a look at his face?"

Charlie pushed the body one last time and it gently rolled over and floated face up. The entire one side of the cadaver's face was gone with a grayish substance oozing from a hole in the side of the skull.

"Looks like the turtles and fish have been feeding on him," said Charlie Plaxton.

Walter Hass quickly looked away. A weak stomach had always been his Achille's Heel.

"You get yourself on shore," instructed Charlie, as though he had suddenly taken over the investigation from the sickly Hass, "I'll give you a hand to pull this guy out of the water."

The rock and boulder strewn shoreline made it quite difficult getting the body from the water, but once it was out Hass took a notebook from his pocket and began writing. "And today is…?" He asked, looking at Charlie Plaxton.

"Saturday, September 24," said Charlie Plaxton.

The business of examining the remains and documenting details began. The body was turned several times and every little detail was documented. When Walter Hass was only a rookie he was made a fool of on his first court appearance, all because of poor record keeping. He never made that mistake again. From that day on he documented everything. A wallet bulged in the cadaver's back pocket, the swollen body inside the pants highlighting its shape. But the bloated condition on the body made reaching into the pocket impossible. Hass took out a pocketknife, split the pocket, and the wallet popped out. From a driver's license he read the man's name aloud, "Jeremy Kane." He put the wallet into his jacket pocket, stepped away from the body and puked.

Charlie Plaxton looked on indifferently. "How do you plan on getting this fella out of here?"

Hass thought a moment. "I think we should roll the body into your boat and you can row it back to the beach?"

"And how're plannin' to get yourself back?" asked Charlie, "'cause the boat sure-as-ole-hell won't hold all three of us."

"Well I know one thing for certain; I'm not going back with you." Hass pointed up the steep shoreline. "What's up there?"

"The old logging road you drove in on. 'Bout two, maybe three hundred feet back from the top of the ledge. Once you come to the road, turn right. It's about a quarter mile back to the beach"

"Good," said the officer. "That's the route I'm taking."

Hass held the boat steady against the shoreline while Charlie rolled the body on board, face down. After Charlie began his long row back to the beach, Walter Hass began his laborious climb to the top of the boulder and tree littered hillside.

Four men and a boy were there when Charlie Plaxton eased the boat onto the beach. That morning, after Charlie had found Kane's body, he had used the phone at Macdonald's Country Store to call the police and word traveled fast. The men gathered around the boat, took a quick look at the remains and then backed away.

Shortly afterwards Corporal Hass came plodding down the road. When he reached the beach he paused to catch his breath, his jacket draped over his arm, his shirt soaked with sweat.

"Anybody know who this is?" he asked, pointing at the body.

All the men shook their heads, but not the boy. "I think I know who it is."

"Who?" asked Walter Hass.

"That artist fella." The boy pointed to a canoe that was pulled up on the beach. "That's his canoe." He then turned to one of the men. "You know, Mister Macdonald, the guy who comes into your store."

"You could be right, Tommy," said Collin Macdonald. "That red and black checked shirt sure looks familiar. Maybe if I could see his face…"

"Aint got any," said Charlie Plaxton.

"Huh?" said another man.

"Aint got any," repeated Charlie. "Looks like the turtles and fish were feeding on him."

"Sweet Jesus," said another man.

"What's your name, son?" asked Walter Hass, turning his attention back to the boy.

"Tommy Doweling, sir."

"Tommy, do you have any idea where this man lived, or who his family might be?"

"I only talked to him once," said the boy, "and he told me he came from Manitoba, but he never mentioned family. Said he was spending the summer in the old trapper's cabin." The boy pointed. "It's over in that direction. Just follow the old logging road and you'll come to it. It's the only building on the lake----except for the Duncan place on the far shore."

"What about a vehicle?" asked Walter Hass. "How'd he get around?"

"By canoe mostly," said Tommy. "But there's a car parked over by the cabin and I think it's his. But I never saw him drivin' it, though."

"And when was the last time you were talking to him?" asked Walter Hass.

"Two weeks ago. About noon, it was. Up top the bluff. He was drawing pictures."

"You sure about that----about the day you last saw him alive?"

"Yes. Two weeks ago today it was. I had to help my dad pile wood last Saturday so it'd be the Saturday before. It was Saturday or I'd've been in school. I'm not allowed out on Sundays. I remember because I was late getting home for lunch and mom gave me the devil. That was exactly two weeks ago today."

"Two weeks ago," said Hass. Stepping over to the boat he studied the condition of the body for a time. *I'd say at least ten days in the water----probably more. This is the twenty-forth of September, so he was alive on the tenth of September.*

Collin Macdonald spoke up. "If that is that artist, he used to come into my store for supplies----coffee, sugar, pipe tobacco and the like. But he never told me his name, and I never asked."

"I believe I know his name," said Walter Hass. "I have his wallet." He then turned his attention back to the boy. "Tommy, do you think you could take me back to where you last saw this man?"

"I could," said the boy, "but I gotta get home. But you can almost drive to it." He pointed up the logging road. "You passed it on the way in here. You should be able to find it without any trouble."

Tommy was about to get on his bicycle when the policeman took hold of the handlebars. "One minute, son. I need you to show me exactly where you last saw the dead man----alive."

Walter Hass then turned to the men. "Would a couple of you boys mind staying here with the body until it gets picked up? Since the road doesn't come right down to the beach, the guy who comes for the body will probably need a hand carrying it out."

Two of the men volunteered.

Hass then directed his next question to Collin Macdonald. "And would you, sir, mind going back to your store and call a local undertaker parlor? Have them come and take away the remains?"

Collin Macdonald nodded. "Sure thing."

"Tell them to just hold it until I get back to them. The coroner will probably order a postmortem, so I don't want it embalmed----not just yet."

The officer then got into his car. Young Tommy Doweling peddled his bike back up the road and the officer followed behind in his cruiser.

"It's only in here a short ways," said Tommy Doweling when he came to a crown in the road.

A slight trace of a pathway was outlined in the carpet of dead pine needles. *Obviously a popular spot,* thought the policeman. The path terminated on a flat cliff-top overlooking Portage Lake. Hass quickly estimated the cliff-top to be less than two hundred feet across at the widest point. It jutted out of the steep hillside like the remains of an old bridge abutment. Hass could see why people would go there; the view from the top of the cliff was spectacular. *An artist's dream,* he thought.

Tommy hurried to a precise spot and pointed at his feet. "He was sitting right here. He was sitting on a small fold-up seat, and he had a three legged affair with a piece of paper fixed onto it."

"An easel," said Hass.

"Huh?"

"It's called an easel."

"Oh," replied Tommy. "Anyway, he was drawing with a piece of charcoal."

"And did he say anything to you?"

"Not much. He asked me my name and I asked him where he was from. I just watched him for a couple minutes and then he asked me if I wanted to have my picture drawn. I said sure. It only took him about fifteen, maybe twenty minutes at most. And it looks just like me, too. I have it pinned up on my bedroom wall."

"And you never saw him again?"

"Not until today," answered Tommy, then added sadly, "but boy, he could really draw good. He seemed like a nice man, too."

Then the boy asked, "Can I go home now?"

"In a minute, Tommy." After Walter Hass checked the top of the bluff and found nothing of interest, he worked his way cautiously to the edge of the overhang. Leaning ahead slightly he looked down to the water. He was standing just above where the body was found in the lake. He quickly estimated that it was at least forty, probably fifty feet straight down to a ledge of rock and shale below. He guessed the lake was another ten or fifteen feet below that. Looking across the lake he could see a large white building on the far shore, *probably two miles away,* he estimated, the only visible structure for miles.

"Whose place is that over there, Tommy?"

"That's the Duncan summerhouse. They're from Toronto. They spend the summer months here. But I suspect they're probably gone back to the city by now because it's starting to get pretty cool at night."

"But I see smoke coming from the chimney."

"That's probably the caretaker."

"Tommy, are there many people living near the lake?"

"Nope. Just the Duncans. The government owns the rest of the lakeshore and no one can buy it."

Again the officer cautiously worked his way back to the edge of the cliff. He would look down and then step back and think for a moment. He did this several times. "I wonder if you could do me a favor, son?"

"Sure," said Tommy.

"I'm going to work my way down around the side of the cliff, and once I'm down below I want you to drop a rock over the edge."

Tommy picked up a stone about the size of a baseball. "Will this do?"

"Yes. That's good. Now I don't want you to throw it, just drop it straight down."

The boy started toward the cliff edge. "Be careful, now," cautioned the police officer. "Don't get too close to the edge."

"Don't worry," said the boy smartly. "I've been here hundreds of times."

It took Walter Hass about fifteen minutes to skirt around the cliff edge, working his way down from tree to tree, rock to rock. When he reached the ledge below the cliff-face he stood off to one side and shouted up to the boy. "Okay, Tommy. Drop the stone----and be careful."

Looking up he saw the boy's hand extend clear of the ledge and then followed the progress of the falling rock. It stuck the surface of the rock-shelf very close to the cliff face.

"Okay Tommy," he shouted up. "That's good."

Tommy shouted down. "Do you need me any more, because I gotta get home?"

"No, that's fine, Tommy. But I might want to talk to you again."

The officer stood quietly for a spell studying the area, and then went to where Tommy's stone had impacted. A chalky spot marked the place. Looking up the cliff face Hass visualized the flight of a falling man. *If a man accidentally fell from the cliff, then his body should have landed close to the cliff face, close to where the stone hit, but Kane was in the lake?* Studying the ledge he guessed it to be approximately twenty, perhaps twenty-five feet wide. Except for a few hardy junipers that had taken root in the rock crevices, the ledge was devoid of vegetation. After mentally dividing the ledge into a grid pattern he began slowly pacing it off, walking around in an ever-widening circle, working his way to the outer limits of the ledge, always careful with each footstep because the ledge was littered with loose shale.

Close to where the ledge dropped off into the lake he noticed a small cluster of shale fragments that appeared to have been impacted. Kneeling down by the spot he could see that something had definitely landed there, something heavy and large. Looking closer, he found strands of hair ground into the edge of a piece of shale. Removing his cap he put his face close to get a better look. There were red coloured fibers mixed in with tuffs of hair with pieces of flesh holding the tuffs together. On one of the lighter coloured stones he noticed a brown stain. He rightly guessed it to be blood.

Hass got back on his feet and walked back to the cliff face. From where Tommy's stone had struck, to the place where he found the hair and fibers, he paced off five and a half steps, *about sixteen, maybe seventeen feet.* Taking his cap off he cocked his head back and looked up. "Well," he said in a low voice, "if that guy fell, he sure as ol' hell landed a long ways out from the cliff face."

Again he tried to visualize a man floating through the air on his way down to certain death. He could easily imagine how a body would crash onto the shale ledge, take a single bounce and keep on going into the lake----if of course it landed where he suspected it did. *That could certainly happen.* The entire ledge was slightly sloped toward the lake. *Could've landed on his face? Maybe that's why he's only got one side left? Could've landed on the side of his head and a stone drove in the side of his skull? That's certainly possible.*

Walter Hass again looked up the cliff face. "Yes sir," he said, scratching his head, "he sure hit a long ways out on the ledge, almost like he jumped."

He returned to the point of impact and carefully removed the fiber and tuffs of hair from the shale then wrapped them in his handkerchief.

The entire rocky ledge was no more than a hundred and fifty feet in length and about twenty feet wide. Hass was positioned roughly at mid point. It was while he was in the crouched position retrieving the hairs and fibers that he noticed a sheet of paper a ways off snagged in a clump of juniper bushes. After carefully wrapping the hairs and fibers in the handkerchief he walked over to the paper. It was artist's paper.

Also with the paper he discovered an easel, a folding chair, a box of charcoal sticks and a roll of sketching paper. Hass was stymied. *The art gear is close to the cliff face, a good forty feet from where the body hit.* Again he removed his cap and looked up the cliff face. *How can that be? If that guy was carrying this gear when he fell from the cliff, then the gear should've been near where the body landed----or in the lake.*

He knelt and unrolled the sketching paper and slowly studied the artwork. *Like Tommy said, he sure could draw.* He then retrieved the single piece of white paper that was fluttering in the Junipers. On it was the sketch of a woman sitting on a blanket, a picnic basket and a bottle of wine beside her, the front of her dress open showing the sides of her breasts, a sunhat hiding her face. But it was just a sketch. *I wonder if she was real or just someone from his imagination.*

Hass remained on the rock ledge for the better part of an hour pacing off distances, taking down notes, drawing little maps, trying to piece together what had happened. But regardless how many mental scenarios he came up with he couldn't construct one that made total sense. *No,* he concluded, *when that guy went off the cliff his gear should have landed close to him. Either he threw the gear and then jumped, or someone pushed him and then threw the gear off the cliff afterwards----someone in a hurry----someone scared. His canoe is over on the beach, so he must've walked up the old logging road to the top of the bluff. That would make sense; he sure as ol'hell couldn't climb up the side of the cliff carrying his gear.*

On his drive back to his office he mentally went over the days investigation. *Jeremy Kane's canoe was on the beach, so he didn't fall out of a boat. He had to have fallen off the cliff? Something smashed in the side of his face and put a hole in his skull. A fall from that height could certainly do it. And the boy, Tommy Doweling, was the only one who ever talked to the man, and he was in a hell of a hurry to get home. Something tells me he knows more than he's letting on. What's that kid not telling me?*

Walter Hass would return to Portage Lake again the next day.

Chapter 20

Maple, beech, basswood, birch, ironwoods, trees of every species lined the edges of the old logging road. They hadn't yet put on their finest autumn display but preparations for the performance were well under way that late September morning. Walter Hass was in a hurry but he couldn't help but slow his pace a little as he walked toward the trapper's cabin Jeremy Kane once called home. Shafts of brilliant sunlight speared through treetops and danced on the ground in front of him. The setting took him back to his boyhood, to another time and place, before he became a cop, before he began dealing with life's meanness.

Fifteen minutes into his walk Hass found Jeremy Kane's 1936 Ford car parked about a quarter mile from the lake. There were no fresh tire tracks so he knew the vehicle had been parked in the same location for some time. Following a path through the trees he came to the old trapper's cabin where young Tommy Doweling said it would be.

Tucked under overhanging hemlocks, the cabin seemed to be hiding from the world, like it never wanted to be found. In front of it a small dock jutted out into the sandy bay. Small in size, the structure provided the bare minimum in shelter. Built of raw lumber it had never been painted its walls a muted shade of weather-streaked gray. The unpainted metal roof bled rust, a red stain of it ringing the ground around the cabin. Leaning slightly toward the lake, the building looked as though it wanted to lie down and rest. Its single door was at the rear of the building and its only window faced the lake. The door was shut but not locked, as though the occupant intended on coming right back.

A coffeepot sat on the stove, washed and ready for its next fresh brew. Dishes were washed and stacked neatly on a shelf above the sink. Cans, mostly soups and beans, were on another shelf. A small cot in one corner was made up with gray blankets the kind the military use, the bedding neatly tucked with an extra blanket folded across the bottom. A coal oil lamp sat on the table its chimney sparkling clean, the wick trimmed. Two unused candles in holders sat on the table beside the lamp.

Hass sat on one of the two kitchen chairs for a time and studied the place. *So clean and orderly for a man's cabin.* T*oo clean, like the owner knew he wasn't coming back and wanted to leave a good impression of himself.* He ran a finger across the plastic tablecloth. *Clean as a whistle. Not a speck of dirt. Not a single crumb.* Glancing down at the floor he noticed something else; not only had it been swept, but it also appeared to have been damp mopped. He checked the cabin and found a broom, but no mop.

Hass went to the cot, picked up the pillow and sniffed it. *Perfume. Mister Jeremy Kane had entertained a woman here. I wonder who she was?* The perfume's scent was very distinctive, pleasant and not overpowering. And there was another smell that couldn't be missed, that of pipe smoke.

Remembering checking Kane's car, he recalled that inside the car was also rich with the smell of pipe tobacco. His father had smoked a pipe all his life and kept a spare pipe in his car as well as several in the house. The smell of pipe tobacco was very familiar to Hass, and each time he got a whiff of that particular scent he could see his father with a pipe stem locked between his teeth, could remember his smile, missed him, remembered how good a man he was.

Looking around the cabin he found no pipe, no pouch of tobacco, and he remembered there was none in the car either. And there was none on Jeremy Kane's body. *But it could have flown out of his pocket when he went off the cliff. It could be at the bottom of the lake. The deceased was a pipe smoker, and yet he had no smoking supplies with him, and none in his cabin or car.* Examining an ashtray on the windowsill he found it spotless, and beside the ashtray was a box of matches. *Jeremy Kane used to sit by the window and smoke his pipe, but there are no smoking supplies anywhere.*

Then, the biggest question of all, *Where were his art supplies?* Hass could find none of an artist's trade: no paper, no charcoal, no brushes, no paint. Nothing. The floor had no tiny drips of colours on it either, nothing to indicate that artwork had been done in the cabin. *Very strange! He was an artist, so where did he do his work?*

It was past noon before Hass had completed his notes and trudged back out the logging road to his cruiser. He was famished. He drove into Meedsville to a restaurant he had frequented in the past. He ordered his usual hamburger and Coke and thought as he ate. After finishing the hamburger he ordered a cup of coffee, lit a cigarette and mentally went over the entire death scenario of Jeremy Kane. *Who was the woman Jeremy Kane was seeing in that little cabin. Why had no one reported him missing. How could a man fall from a cliff in broad daylight? It had to be daytime when he went over the edge for he certainly wouldn't be there with art supplies in the dark. And why did his body hit so far from the cliff face? Why was his art gear so far away from where his body impacted? Who was the woman in his drawing? Why was that boy in such a hurry to get home?* He'd go back to Portage Lake again the next day and have another talk with the lad. But he was tired and wanted to get to the office and finish his paperwork. When that was done he'd go straight home to his wife of thirty-one years, to the little house on the shore of Bell Lake, the one he purchased for retirement, the place where he planned to grow old.

Chapter 21

AT EXACTLY TWELVE O'CLOCK a rumbling sound erupted from within the walls of the little schoolhouse and a minute later the front doors exploded open. Fifteen students bolted out into the autumn sunlight, the boys pushing and jostling, the girls following behind them in a somewhat more dignified order. Suddenly, like a well-choreographed performance they all stopped dead in their strides. A big cop was standing cross-armed at the bottom of the steps looking up at them.

"Good morning, boys and girls," he said with a smile, "or should I say good afternoon?" Corporal Walter Hass recalled his boyhood days in just such a schoolhouse, an even smaller version of the one that he was then looking at. He could still see the faces of the nine other students who attended his school, remembered their names, wondered whatever became of them. He remembered it as a good time in his life, before he became a cop.

"Hello again, Tommy," he said to the freckle-faced lad.

The boy's face flushed as he responded with a nod of his head.

"Tommy, I'd like to talk to you for a minute." The officer turned and looked around the schoolyard for a quiet place. He pointed to a large tree in the furthest corner of the schoolyard. "What do you say we go and sit down over there and have a little chat?"

The boy followed the officer across the schoolyard, his head bowed, not wanting to look at the other students, ashamed to be singled out by the law. He sat on the grass beneath the tree with his legs crossed. The officer squatting in front him. The other students stayed well off in the distance, but couldn't take their eyes off the unusual spectacle of a fellow student sitting beneath a tree with a big policeman, all wondering if Tommy Doweling was on his way to prison.

"How old are you, Tommy?"

"Twelve, sir."

"You're old enough to know the truth, then?"

"Yes, sir."

"Tommy, the last time I spoke to you I got the feeling you didn't tell me everything you knew about Jeremy Kane----the dead man."

The boy didn't look at the policeman; he kept his head down and plucked nervously at the grass.

"What did you not tell me, Tommy?"

Silence.

"Tommy? I'm asking you a question," said the officer with sternness in his voice.

Tommy Doweling slowly raised his head. "Am I in a lot trouble?"

"Only liars get into trouble, Tommy. Tell the truth and you'll be fine."

"I didn't tell you about the woman who was with him," answered the boy.

The officer nodded his head several times while he gave the answer serious thought. "Do you know who she was?"

Tommy shook his head, then added, "I might know who she is, though."

"Well then who might she be?"

"I think she was the same woman I saw him with once before. But it was the first time I ever saw her up close----if that's who it was?" answered the boy.

"And you say you saw them together one other time?"

"Yes, Sir. I saw them in a powerboat on Portage Lake----from the top of the bluff. At least I think it was the same woman. She drove the boat over to the trapper's cabin, picked him up, and then they'd scoot around the lake together."

"When you saw her the second time, did you speak to her?"

"Yes, sir.

"But she never told you her name?"

Again the boy shook his head. "No, sir."

"And it was the same day you met Jeremy Kane on top of the bluff? She was with him that day, is that correct?"

"Yes, sir."

"And why didn't you tell me this before?"

The boy shrugged and again cast his stare downward renewing his plucking of the grass.

"Were they doing something that embarrassed you, Tommy? Something that was hard to talk about in front of the men back on the beach? Is that why you didn't tell me this sooner?"

Tommy nodded his head but refused to look up.

"Did they have their clothes off, Tommy?"

"She did----sort of."

"Sort of?" asked Walter Hass.

"Well---ah----the front of her dress was open and he was drawing her like that. She buttoned up as soon as she saw me though. I think they were having a picnic. She gave me a sandwich and a banana. I ate the sandwich while he drew my picture."

"The picture you said you have at home hanging on your bedroom wall?"

"Yes, sir."

Walter Hass remembered the charcoal sketches at the bottom of the bluff; a woman with her dress open and a picnic basket on a blanket. "And you're positive she never said her name?"

"No sir, and I never asked her."

"Any idea how old she was?"

"She was pretty old," said the boy.

"How old, Tommy?"

Again the boy shrugged. "I don't really know."

"As old as your mother?"

"Not that old. About as old as my oldest sister."

"And how old is your sister?"

"Twenty-two----I think."

The officer smiled. "Oh, that old!"

There was a quiet time as Walter Hass took down notes. "Tommy, do you have any idea where the woman lives?"

"At the Duncan summerhouse. That's where the powerboat came from, and it's the only one on the lake. I just figure she must live there."

"That's the big house on the south shore of the lake you're talking about?"

"Yes, sir."

"Hum. Interesting," mumbled Walter Hass. After a silent spell the policeman said, "Well Tommy, I guess that about takes care of it----unless you have something else to tell me?"

Tommy Doweling assured the big cop that he did not.

When the policeman stood up he noticed the other students were huddled together in the middle of the schoolyard and whispering. The teacher was also standing on the schoolhouse steps, and she too was staring. He knew that Tommy was embarrassed by all the attention, and he knew the lad would have many questions to answer after he left. He had to try and put the boy in a good light.

Walter Hass walked over to the children and said, "How are you today, boys and girls?" Two of the older student responded, but the younger ones backed away in silence. "If you're wondering what this is about, I just needed Tommy's help with a matter." The officer shook Tommy Doweling's hand. "Thanks for the help, Tommy. Much appreciated." The boy was the instant star of the schoolyard and Walter Hass came away with another piece of his puzzle. *Jeremy Kane had a woman friend, and she lives in the big white house on the south shore of the lake.*

Chapter 22

Walter Hass stepped out of his cruiser and stood for a moment admiring the Duncan summerhouse, a house design not common to the area. He didn't know the name of the style but it was indeed impressive, the kind of structure a man erected to make a statement. No doubt the owners had money. The entire building was painted white with no accent colours. Two stories high with a large stone chimney towering up one side, a lazy twist of smoke rose from the chimney. Numerous multi-paned windows encircled the building, some flat, some boxed out, one oval window high up in a gable end. Surrounded by massive white birch and pine trees, the house seemed to belong there, like the area would appear artificial without the house.

About four hundred feet back behind the house, barely visible in a grove of cedars was a carriage house, put there when the horse was the sole means of travel, put well-away from the house and genteel nostrils.

On the high ground behind the house Hass could see a man splitting firewood and piling the sticks neatly, each one the exact same length. He walked over to the man. "Hello. Is your name Duncan?"

The man shook his head. "No, I'm the caretaker, Darrell Colburn."

Of medium stature, Darrell Colburn was built solidly, a man accustomed to hard work. His eyes were quite dark, his eyebrows thick, his cheekbones high, a bull-like neck, his waist slim, his legs and hips powerful, his arms roped with bulging veins, his hands callused.

"Well Darrell, I don't know if you've heard or not, but a body was found in the lake two days ago. I'm looking for people who might have known the man----a Jeremy Kane."

Darrell kept his eyes on the ground only peeking up occasional at the policeman. "I heard about it, all right. It's been on the radio all yesterday and today. But I can't say I knew him."

"You've seen him then?"

"Oh, yes. Lots of times. He used to paddle his canoe all over the lake. When he was close to the shore he'd say, 'hello. Nice day'. That sort of thing. But I never really talked to the man."

"There didn't happen to be a woman with him?" asked Walter Hass.

"A woman?" replied Darrell jerking his head up with a surprised look on his face.

"Yes, a woman. I have reason to believe he had a female companion."

Darrell shrugged. "He was alone anytime I saw him."

Hass remembered young Tommy Doweling's story. He was about to question the man further but decided to let it go for the time being. Perhaps he could use Tommy's information later to trip someone up.

As Hass watched the man he couldn't help but notice how he fidgeted. He was absentmindedly toying with a twig like he needed something for his hands to do. "Is there something you'd like to tell me, Darrell?" Hass said quickly.

"No sir, there ain't,"

"Then why are you so nervous?"

Colburn still didn't look up. "It's just my nature I guess----you being a policeman and all. My wife, Harriet, she tells me I'm too damn shy for my own good."

The officer smiled. "Is your wife around?"

Colburn nodded in the direction of the house. "She's in the house. We both work for the Duncans. We're closing the place up for the winter. I can go get her if you want?"

Hass paused a moment, thought about it, and then said, "No. You go on with your work and I'll talk to her? Maybe she saw something she hasn't told you about."

Hass found Harriet Colburn wrapping dishes in newspaper and stacking them away neatly in the kitchen cupboards.

"Hello," said Walter Hass, through the screen door. The startled woman almost dropped a plate. "Sorry if I startled you, ma'am, but I'd like to ask you a few questions?"

When the woman caught her breath she opened the door and Walter Hass stepped inside. They sat at the kitchen table and Hass took out his note pad. He mentally noted her appearance: *Slim waist, pretty face, well-formed body, shiny dark brown hair, quite a lovely young thing.*

"As you probably know," began the big cop, "a man's body was found across the lake and I'm wondering if perhaps you knew the man, or had the opportunity to talk to him?"

"I've seen him in his canoe on the lake a few times, but I've never spoken to him."

"Did you happen to notice whether or not he ever had a woman with him?"

"A woman! No. Never."

Hass noticed the strong emphases of the denial. "Do you think the Duncans would know anything about him?"

"I can't see how," she answered. "Missus Duncan was up for a while this summer, but her husband seldom comes up here at all. He's a very busy man."

"I see. And how old are the Duncans?"

"Well," said Harriet Colburn, "Mister Duncan would be probably in his mid fifties, and Missus Duncan's a bit younger."

Walter Hass wrote it down, snapped his note pad shut and glared at Harriet Colburn. As he held his stare on the woman her agitation increased. After a minute or so the cop went to the kitchen door and closed it gently. He again sat at the kitchen table directly across from the woman.

"Missus Colburn, I'm going to tell you what I know, and when I'm finished talking I want you to fill in the blanks. Okay?"

She nodded nervously.

"To begin with, I know that an artist by the name of Jeremy Kane spent a good part of the summer around Portage Lake, and that he had a female friend, a young pretty woman. Young Tommy Doweling saw them together at different times, and one of those times he met them together on top of the bluff. He told me 'they were having a picnic'. And it would have been about the time the man died----two weeks ago. In fact, it was about the same length of time the body was in the water. And young Tommy told me the front of her dress was open. Kane was drawing her with the front of her dress open. I found the sketch of her at the bottom of the bluff, so I know they were more than just friends. And yet, no woman ever phoned and inquired about him being missing, like the young woman had something to hide----like a marriage."

Harriet Colburn hung her head and her trembling intensified.

"I went over to the old trapper's cabin where he stayed, and I know that a woman had shared his bed. I also know the cabin was cleaned out in an effort to hide all traces of someone other than Jeremy Kane being there. I know that a young pretty woman used to take a speedboat over to the cabin and the two of them spent time zipping around the lake together. And that speedboat, I'll just bet, is down there in the boathouse." Hass pointed toward the lake, then paused a moment for effect.

"Harriet," said the officer in a soothing voice, "were you and Jeremy Kane having an affair? I know of no other woman that fits the description. Everything points to you; a young pretty woman who stayed here at this house?"

Harriet Colburn covered her face with her hands and dropped her head on the table.

Walter Hass placed a comforting hand on her arm. "It was you, wasn't it, Missus Colburn? I see that your husband is much older than you, and I can understand, but tell the truth. If you had nothing to do with his death then don't complicate things."

After a time she slowly raised her head, her eyes pouring. "Are you going to tell Darrell?"

"Not if I don't have to. Not if you tell me everything, and if I can see that no foul play was involved in Kane's death."

"Sometimes," she began slowly, "Darrell has to go into the city and do work at the Duncans' house. When he's away I stay here alone. I met Jerry the last time Darrell was away, and----you know---- we got to be friends. I was here alone all that week and we went on a picnic. That's when the boy saw us together."

"Tommy Doweling?"

"Yes," said Harriet. "Later that day, long after the boy had left, we finished off a second bottle of wine and we were acting silly. I began chasing him around, trying to tickle him----childish things----and he kept backing away from me. The both of us were laughing our fool heads off. He was practically running backwards when it happened."

She stopped and breathed deeply. "He ran backwards off the cliff. It was like slow motion, and I couldn't do a thing to save him. He just seemed to float out into space. I was so shocked I couldn't scream or shout----nothing.

I just froze and watched him disappear over the edge. It seemed to take forever before I heard the splash. After a time I looked over the edge and all I could see was a big ring in the water. He never came up."

"If that's how his life ended, Missus Colburn, then how did his art gear end up on the rock ledge below the cliff?"

Harriet Colburn sat quietly for a moment sobbing. "I don't know how long I stood there looking down at the water hoping for Jerry to surface, but when it became evident that he never would, I began to panic. What if Darrell found out? I sat on the ground and tried to calm down, and eventually I could reason a little. I knew I had to get out of there and hide my tracks. I picked up his art gear and dropped it over the edge. I couldn't take it with me and chance Darrell seeing it. Then I packed the picnic basket and took it back to the speedboat at the beach and got back across the lake."

"And was that you who cleaned his cabin out?" asked Hass.

Harriet nodded. "Later that evening----when it was dark enough so no one could see me----I took the speedboat over to the cabin, cleaned it all up, brought his stuff back here and burned it all in the incinerator." Harriet Colburn lowered her head and began bawling.

The policeman took a folded piece of paper from his pocket and showed it to her. "Is this you?" he asked. It was the sketch of a woman sitting on a blanket with a picnic basket and a bottle of wine, a sun hat hiding the face, one of the sketches he had recovered from the bottom of the cliff.

She inhaled deeply before whimpering, "Yes."

"Excuse me for saying this, Missus Colburn, but you seem to have shown little concern for the dead man."

She looked coldly at the big cop. "Officer, I know what I did was wrong, and I'm not proud of it, but I do love my husband regardless of what you may think. Jerry Kane wandered in and out of lots of women's lives, and I was just one of many. I know what that makes me, but that's the truth. I had a cheap fling with him. I didn't love him." She then turned away and stared out the window for a time, the kitchen dead with silence, and only the sound of Darrell Colburn's axe striking wood off in the distance.

It was a time for reflection for both Harriet Colburn and Walter Hass. Stretching back in the chair he crossed his feet under the table as he thought of another time when he was just a rookie. He had pulled over the swaying car that late night on a lonely country road, a car driven by a beautiful thirty-year-old woman, a drunken married thirty-year-old woman. He was only twenty-two at the time, and the woman suggested a compromise in the back seat of her car. He would never admit it, but he was still a virgin back then while the state of purity was long behind the woman. He could still smell her alcohol-stinking breath. She didn't go to jail or loose her right to drive, and less than a year later the same woman, again drunk, struck a child on a bicycle and almost killed him. He never forgave himself for what he had done, and he didn't feel he had the right to judge young Harriet Colburn for her sins either.

Walter Hass raised his head, folded the sketch, and put it and his notepad back in his pocket. Reaching across the table he gently patted Harriet's arm. "Well, that's it then. I'll have the coroner's report sometime today, and if it confirms your story then your secret is safe, Missus Colburn. And you'll not be seeing me again----provided of course that you've told me everything."

She looked up with a wet face. "That's what happened. I swear."

"Okay. So that's the end of it," he assured her.

"And you won't tell Darrell?" she whispered.

The cop shook his head and smiled. "No need too----if you told the truth."

Hass left the kitchen and walked back up the hill to make small talk with Darrell Colburn. "Well Darrell, your good wife had little to offer, so I guess I'll be going." He then paused and looked around for a moment. "It's a real nice place here."

"It is that," agreed Darrell. "That's our job, keeping it that way."

"Well, I'd have to say you're both doing a good job of it."

Walter Hass had what he came for. He was satisfied that the death of Jeremy Kane was accidental, and if the coroner's report added nothing new he could see no reason to question Darrell or Harriet Colburn any further. Getting back into the cruiser he drove away, his brain no longer swimming with unanswered questions.

Later that day when he got back to his office the coroner's report was waiting for him. It said the man did not drown, but had died from a stone puncture to the temple; a shard of pointed shale was actually still lodged in the wound, a stone matching the skull puncture perfectly. The dead man's shoulder was also broken from the fall. Walter Hass was not a detective, and was never trained in the art of investigating a complicated crime scene, but he felt justifiably proud of the job he had done. He had all the answers. Over the years he had seen many dead men and women, was sick of seeing the dead, their bodies disfigured from drownings, house-fires, road accidents, and one from murder.

He was only in the force a year when he and a senior officer investigated that case, and there was no doubt that it was a murder. A butcher knife had been driven into the victim's chest and the knife was still embedded. The murder was the final chapter of two decades of feuding between old enemies. The murderer, drunk at the time of the crime, was eventually hanged and Walter Hass never totally got over it. He slept very little the week leading up to the execution, and he never believed the man should have been hanged, feeling one man was as guilty as the other. He always looked on capital punishment as an abomination, remembered puking after hearing that the execution had been carried out. He never wanted to go through it again.

Jeremy Kane's death was the first time he ever had reason to question a possible murder on his own. He knew there were inconsistencies, but he didn't possess the expertise, or desire to sort them out. He thought about calling in people who were trained in investigative work, but then how would that make him look? And, if there was a reason to open an in-depth investigation, and if someone was charged with Jeremy Kane's death, it could drag on for years. He could even be called back to court after his retirement. And what if there was another hanging? If someone were found guilty of murder that could very well be the end result. He knew such an occurrence would haunt him to his grave, might even speed up his demise. And what about Harriet Colburn's marriage? What good would it do to destroy her reputation and marriage? Her confession was good enough and she'd probably never stray again. He felt confident Jeremy Kane was not murdered. Harriet Colburn was just a foolish young woman.

Hass hated his job, was sick of wrestling with drunks, of writing out tickets, of trying to calm domestic disputes. He only wanted to retire. *Two more years to go so don't go and complicate things. The guy was fucking around with another man's wife, got pissed and fell off a cliff. End of story. You did your job, now leave it alone.*

Back at his office he finished up the loose ends in his report, filed it, and went home to his wife's home cooked dinner. Later that evening he sauntered out to his workshop and spent two hours working on a purple martin birdhouse. He loved working with wood. He was one day closer to his retirement. *Rest in peace, Jeremy Kane----whoever the hell you were? And in the end, who really gives a shit?*

Walter Hass retired two years later with the Jeremy Kane case stuffed away on file, later to be stored on microfiche. The death was attributed to an accidental fall from a cliff on the shore of Portage Lake. And that was the end of it.

After the policeman left the Duncan summerhouse, Harriet went out to Darrell.

"What did you tell him?" asked Darrell.

"Basically what we had rehearsed," she said, her voice still a little shaky. "I didn't have any choice. Apparently a kid saw Kane and Connie together over on the bluff---they were having a picnic. I told him it was me. I told him I saw Kane fall off the cliff and that we were both drunk on wine."

"Do you think he bought it?"

"Let's hope so. But yes, I think he did."

Darrell looked up at his wife with a smear of disgust on his face. "I'm sorry you had to attach your good name to this, Harriet. You should never have to do something like this. You should've married a smarter man."

Going to him she placed a hand on his shoulder, and whispered, "I love you Darrell. You're a better man than I deserve."

Three days later Jeremy Kane's remains were buried in the old Lutheran cemetery above Portage Lake.

Chapter 23

AFTER LEAVING TOM DOWELING's house Shawn drove straight to his mother-in-law's apartment. "You and I are going to have a talk, Harriet," he said, the moment she opened the door. He didn't wait to be invited in; he stepped past her, walked into her living room and plopped down on the sofa.

Following behind him Harriet sat daintily on a chair opposite him.

He tried to be calm but it was difficult. "The last time I asked you about why mother chose to be buried up here, you lied. You knew that Jeremy Kane is buried beside her. Joff Pedigrew, the gravedigger, a man who knows you, told me you were there the day they buried him. He said you even put flowers on his grave. So I had to ask myself this; why would Harriet Colburn place flowers on Jeremy Kane's grave and then tell me she knew nothing about mother's wishes?"

Harriet remained silent for a time refusing to look at her son-in-law.

"Damn you, Harriet, answer me?"

She raised her head sharply. "Why didn't you stay in Toronto where you belong? Why did you have to come back here and start digging around? People like you don't belong up in this country."

Shawn sprang to his feet and stepped over to Harriet. "Well I'm here and I have no intentions of leaving." Then her words 'Digging around' struck him. "Digging around? Digging around for what, Harriet? What am I going to find if *I dig around?"*

"Nothing!" she answered defiantly. "Absolutely nothing."

"You're lying, Harriet. I know you are. You know something and I'm not leaving until you tell me."

She glared at him with icy eyes. "So you want to know, do you? So you really want to know? Well sit down and I'll tell you." She straightened her posture, drew her shoulders back and seemed to brace herself. "I'm sick of this entire affair, so let's put an end to it----right now."

Shawn glared back at her. "Yes! Why don't we do just that?"

"I first met Connie Duncan shortly after she married Cyrus Duncan," Harriet began stoically. "She befriended me, and to this day I have no idea why. But probably it was because she never felt threatened by me. She was a commoner living in an upper-class world, and I suppose that could be very scary. I was her personal servant, and I came from even lower beginnings than she had. But I was happy working for her and I was glad to have the job. I picked up after her, did her laundry, cooked her meals, and yet we remained good friends.

"You see, Shawn Duncan, I never had a privileged life like you did. I was the eldest of eleven children, and I left home early so my siblings would have it a little better. In fact, when I turned sixteen I was told by my father I was leaving. I had no choice in the matter. I'm not going into it, but my parents were not the best of people. Life was damned hard for me and my brothers and sisters.

"Anyway, my first year away from home----if one could ever call it a home----I got a summer job cleaning cabins at a resort for rich kids----a place about a half-hour north of here. They fed me three meals a day, I had my own room, and they paid me three dollars a week. That's where I met Darrell. At the time, he was working for your parents, and he also operated a little maintenance business on the side. He owned an old beat-up truck and he used it to haul away garbage and deliver firewood to the camp. He was a kind man, winter was coming, and I was alone with no place to go. Looking back, I guess one could say he became my protector----or maybe even my father. When the summer ended and my job was finished, I married Darrell. I had just turned seventeen."

"So you married him for security?"

"That's right," snapped Harriet. "Like I just said, we weren't privileged the way you were. My parents practically kicked me out. I wasn't driven around in pretty clothes with people to care for me. Lots of kids had miserable childhoods, but then you wouldn't know about that, would you?"

"Look, Harriet, I----I didn't mean it the way it sounded."

"Of course you did. Don't patronize me. I'm just poor, not stupid. Your kind always look down on people like me. And you can think what you want, but I loved my husband very much. So keep your mouth shut and let me finish," she snapped fiercely.

"For the next five years," she continued, "I stayed home and Darrell kept doing what he knew best; he worked hard every day and we got along. We rented an old farmhouse with no central heating, no hydro, and no running water, but we never complained. I had a home, someone who truly loved me, and for that I was thankful.

"In the spring of 1952 Darrell came home and asked me if I'd like a job at the Duncans' place? He said that Cyrus had gotten married and he was looking for a servant for his new bride. That's how I met your mother.

"Connie spent the entire summer up here, but Cyrus only came up to the lake to see her about three times that first year. He'd spend two, maybe three days, and then he'd go back to the city leaving Connie behind. He hated country life and made no bones about it. But Connie loved it at the lake, and she was certainly happier when your father was no where around." Harriet paused a moment before saying "And they slept in separate beds. I know, because I changed the bedding. They slept in separate beds in different rooms, both in the city and up here."

Shawn began to fidget and rubbing his hands together. The topic was unpleasant.

Harriet glared at him, "If you want to hear this, well it only gets worse. Now, do you want me to stop, or continue?"

He threw his shoulders back, "I need to know it all," he said grimly.

"The second year I worked for your parents was the year that Connie spent the entire summer at the lake----alone. Cyrus Duncan didn't come up here once that summer. Not once! And it was the year she met Jeremy Kane----Jerry she called him. He was paddling his canoe along the shoreline. That's how they met."

Shawn raised his hand. "Harriet, I believe this story is heading in a direction I don't particularly want to hear about."

"Too damned bad," said Harriet. "Your mother and Jeremy Kane formed a close relationship that summer. That's where this story is heading. Your mother is buried beside the man I believe she loved. There's no easy way to say this, Shawn Duncan. I refuse to go into details, but that's the truth. I know that for a fact. They met here that summer and became extremely close. She was young, lonely, and needed male companionship, and she sure wasn't getting any from your father."

A heavy silence filled the little apartment as he thought about the revelation. Finally he asked, "Harriet, could it be possible…?" He paused, almost like the question was too frightful to ask, "Could it be possible that Jeremy Kane was…?"

"Your father?" she said for him.

"Yes?"

"I don't see how. They met in mid-June and you were born seven months later. A bouncing eight pound boy. Connie was pregnant before her and Kane met."

Shawn Duncan exhaled with relief.

"Jeremy Kane died that year and was buried in the old Lutheran Cemetery," continued Harriet. "I can't remember the exact date, but it was in the early autumn."

"And you were there the day he was buried, and you brought flowers? Was mother also there?"

"No. Once Jerry's body was found she went back to the city. She was in a frightful state. I brought flowers just because I thought someone should do something to show respect. That's all it was; a show of respect for the dead. I just thought that someone should do something."

"And that's what mother never wanted me to know?"

"Well could you blame her?"

"Yes," he practically shouted. "She still should have told me."

Harriet let the outburst pass. "Looking back, it all seems so simple now, but your mother had one unbelievable year. She was married to an older man that was practically useless to her; met and befriended a drifter artist who ended up falling of a cliff and killing himself, and if that wasn't enough, it was also the summer her mother----your grandmother----died down in Cape Breton. She had to go down East for the funeral. I don't think she was worrying too much about telling her unborn child about her love-life."

Harriet paused a moment and then added, "And there's something else I want you to think about, Shawn Duncan. Now that Jeremy Kane's work is becoming valuable, what if their relationship ever became public knowledge? The papers would have a field day with it, and you'd pay the price. You, me, and Caroline, we all would. Think about it? You're mother, the wife of a prominent businessman, buried beside a little-known artist in an obscure graveyard. Can't you just read the sensational headlines? The speculation? The questions?"

Shawn fell silent for a long minute and thought. "Harriet, who was Jeremy Kane?"

"All I know about him was that he was born on a wheat farm in central Manitoba and was raised by his father. He was an only child and his mother died young. A lot of women died young back then. His father lost the farm when The Depression hit and they moved into Winnipeg. Connie said he didn't like to talk about his father. She said that after Jerry left Winnipeg he never contacted his father again, so I guess things must have been tough. Anyway," continued Harriet, "he joined the Air Force in 1942. He was a navigator on bombers throughout his stint in the Europe. When the war ended he came back to Canada and opened a small art studio in Toronto. During the summer months he would roam the North Country sketching and painting. Other than that, there's little more I can tell you about him."

"But Harriet, Jeremy Kane was an unknown when mother purchased her burial plot. His paintings and drawings are valuable now only because he's been dead for a time. In dealer's circles he's just now becoming well known, and he only produced a limited amount of work. I don't understand mother's need for secrecy. I don't understand why mother couldn't have just explained it to me when she was alive? I'm not a kid. I could've handled it."

"Shawn Duncan handle life's meanness? Don't make me laugh," Harriet mocked him. "You were the most shielded kid I've ever known in my life. Look at yourself for chrissake: middle-aged and just married for the first time. You had to wait until your mother died before you were allowed to marry."

Shawn jumped to his feet. "Just you back off, Harriet Colburn. My mother didn't control me."

Harriet flicked her hand rejecting the preposterous. "Think whatever makes you happy."

"Okay Harriet, enough is enough. Let's have it out. For some reason you hate my guts and I haven't the foggiest idea why, so let's have it? What did I ever do to make you hate me this much? What? Was it because of Caroline?"

Harriet's shook her head and her tone softened. "You personally did nothing wrong. It's just that when you came back here you opened up old wounds, things that had taken a lifetime to heal."

"What wounds, Harriet? What wounds?"

"Shawn, there are things that your mother never told you, and there are things I'll never tell you, so don't ask. People have secrets they don't wish to share, and I'm sure you have some of your own." She then took a deep breath, got to her feet, and said, "And I believe it's time for you to leave." She was rude and meant to be.

Walking to the front door, she held it open. Shawn followed her, but just before he stepped outside she asked a strange question. "What are you planning to do with the old carriage house?"

Shawn was taken aback by the question. "Pardon?"

"I said, what are you planning to do with the old carriage house?"

"The old carriage house?" He shrugged. "I don't know. Probably have it torn down. Why do you ask?"

"Have you been in it lately? Are the doors still nailed shut?"

"As a matter-of-fact, they are. Now that I think of it, I haven't been in the building since I was a kid."

"Well I strongly suggest that before you do anything with it, you go through the loft and clean it out. It wouldn't be wise to have strangers rummaging through it."

"Why? What's up there?"

"Lives!"

"Huh?"

"Just do as I tell you and everything will be self-explanatory. It may just help explain who your mother really was, the part of her she always hid from you."

He looked at her with a puzzled expression. "What are you saying, Harriet?"

"Just go," she ordered.

Shawn Duncan stepped outside and Harriet immediately slammed the door shut behind him.

Standing by her front window she watched her son-in-law drive away, her mind adrift in yesterdays. *Shawn Duncan, if you only knew the half of it.*

Chapter 24

When Caroline entered the house that evening Shawn was sitting in front of the fireplace with a drink in his hand. She took one look at him and knew it had not been a normal day.

"What is it, Shawn?"

He told her everything; about the sunken grave; about Jeremy Kane; about Joff Pedigrew; about his visit to Harriet and what she had told him.

"My God," was all Caroline could say after he finished talking.

The following morning, after a pot of strong coffee, Shawn and Caroline stood in front of the old carriage house and momentarily studied it, Shawn with a wrecking bar in his hand.

"Well, here goes nothing," he said, with noticeable tightness in his voice.

Three large double doors filled most of the front wall of the building, doors designed for horse and buggy days. All were spiked shut. It took Shawn several hard pulls on the wrecking bar to open the center set of doors. When finally its resistance ceased and the door groaned open the two were met by a blizzard of dust and chaff. Quickly stepped back, they waited until the air settled out. While waiting for the air to clear a strange haunting feeling came over Shawn, and somewhere deep in his psychic he heard a scream, his mother's scream. He knew the mental intrusion was asinine but it seemed so real. And when he stepped into the gloom of the building he was suddenly overcome with an urge to back away. He scolded himself for being so foolish.

Caroline couldn't help but notice his uneasiness. "What wrong, Shawn?"

He tried to smile. "Nothing. It was just a weird feeling that came over me. It's gone now."

The inside of the building was like a scene from a bad horror movie with dust webs ballooning down from the ceiling like fuzzy hammocks, gray webs heavy with dust ready to take flight with the slightest disturbance. Light bulbs hung from receptacles overhead, but the power had been disconnected years previous. In the 1920s the plank floor of the carriage house was ripped out and a concrete one installed; automobiles had replaced the horse and automobiles didn't need wooden floors beneath them.

The lower level of the building had little of value left in it; an assortment of garden tools, a couple tires hanging from hooks on a wall, a rusted gas can, a horse-drawn buggy pushed well back into a corner, oil and paint cans stacked on a shelf, a stash of assorted lumber piled high in another corner. At one end of the building a set of steep stairs led to the loft above. Shawn used a garden rake to knock down the blanket of cobwebs draped over the stairwell. Filth fell from above like volcanic ash.

Two dormer windows on the front side of the roof allowed enough light into the loft for the two to investigate the contents stored there, and they were amazed at how much was stacked into the forgotten area, most of it from a bygone era. Tables, chairs, wicker furniture, porcelain pieces, horse harnesses, books, and a complete horse drawn buggy, a landau. It had been disassembled, hauled up to the loft and covered with a dustsheet. Horse harnesses were stored with such care that it seemed the owners were not certain of the automobile's durability and perhaps someday the horse would be king again. And everything there was in wonderful condition, like stepping back in time. The bulk of it was stacked against the back wall, which left the front part of loft open and uncluttered.

Against the back wall, half hidden by the mountain of the fore-mentioned sat an armoire. It was an extra large piece of furniture and it would take a great deal of moving to get to it, but they both suspected that what they were looking for was either in, or behind the armoire. Giving up on staying clean the two dove into the work; in no time at all a path was cleared to the armoire.

Shawn took a deep breath and yanked the armoire doors open.

It was like looking into a miniature art studio. There was an easel, hardened tubes of paint, brushes, a stack of blank artist's paper, two men's shirts, a wide brimmed hat, three pipes and a can of pipe tobacco, a pair of hiking boots, moccasins, a heavy wool sweater spotted with paint. At the top of the armoire were two shelves, and on the selves, held flat with boards, rested a stack of artwork, mostly watercolours and charcoal sketches, but also several oils. Carefully removing the boards, Shawn took the stack of art to the clear area of the loft. Spreading out the art on the loft floor, the two got down on their knees and began studying the work.

"My God," said Caroline, "would you just look at all his work? And it's all signed."

Shawn turned one piece over. "And dated."

Caroline shook her head in disbelief. "I know little about art, but I know this is good----very good."

They spent the next hour on their hands and knees going over the work. Much of the art was landscapes, but some were of people; a woman standing with her back to a tree, another of the same woman sitting on a blanket looking out over Portage Lake with the wind blowing her hair. And there were two charcoals of the same woman, nude and sitting on a blanket with a sunhat hiding her face. They both knew who the woman was.

After gathering up the sheets of art and sorting them into piles as per size, Caroline noticed there was one more painting still in the very back of the armoire, a large canvas covered with a cloth. It was a stunning piece of work, an oil painting of Connie Duncan on a recliner with muted light showing her perfect youthful body. She was totally nude. Renaissance art showed a nude's breasts only with the pubic areas of females always shaded out; in the painting of Connie Duncan nothing was left out. Nothing.

Shawn glanced at the painting. "My god!" he whispered, then quickly looked away.

"It's a beautiful piece of work," Caroline said after a time, "if only it had of been of a stranger."

Shawn took a deep breath and again looked at the painting. "And I always thought I knew my mother."

The loft filled with silence as the two stared at the shocking likeness of Constance Duncan.

With surprise in her voice, Caroline said, "It was painted here in this loft." She pointed toward a recliner against an end wall. "She posed on that recliner." She then slowly walked about the loft and studied the floor flicking away bits of dust and clutter with her foot. Tiny splatters of colour and bits of crumbled charcoal where everywhere. "This loft was his studio. This is where he did the painting of your mother."

Shawn threw the cover back over the painting. "Well, Harriet was right about one thing, about not letting contractors up here. And she was certainly right about everyone having secrets."

Caroline went to Shawn to comfort him.

"How does a person deal with this, Caroline? What in the name of God do I do now?"

"We take it one day at a time. The initial shock is over, and trust me; it'll get easier to deal with as time passes."

"But now we have even a bigger problem," said Shawn with a sigh.

"What's that?"

"What do we do with this artwork? It's not ours. Jeremy Kane was not married, but there must be next-of-kin. We can't just keep it."

Caroline frowned. "You're right. What are we going to do with it?"

"If we suddenly let it be known that we stumbled onto all this art, how can we explain it without opening a very messy can of worms?"

As they were gathering up all the artwork Caroline noticed an old military duffel bag peeking out from behind a trunk along the back wall. "Is that what I think it is?" She grabbed the duffel bag and pulled it out onto the floor. J. Kane and a serial number were stenciled on the side of the bag. They both stared at it without speaking, and then Caroline got down on her knees on the floor and untied the duffle. When the bag was opened she began removing the items from it, examining each piece as though they were sacred relics. Inside the bag was a complete Air Force uniform with the medals still pinned to the jacket. There was also a stiff paper tube, the kind used to store maps in. The tube was the full length of the duffle bag and about five inches in diameter. It was packed with rolled-up papers. Shawn gently pulled at the papers while Caroline held the tube. There were so many sheets in the tube that extracting them was very difficult.

After the roll of papers were out of the tube they flattened them on the loft floor, terrified they might crease the long dormant circular sheets. It was Kane's artwork from the war years; a railcar full of soldiers; ships in Halifax harbor; soldiers leaning on the railing of a ship; a pilot flying a bomber; the back of a tail gunner looking out through the tail blister; bombs falling from the bellies of planes; aircraft hangers somewhere in England, and just everyday people going about the job of making war. They had all been drawn with charcoal and were all signed, J. Kane. On the backs in the lower left-hand corner were the dates.

"My God," whispered Shawn. "It's incredible."

Caroline then looked into the empty tube. It wasn't quite empty. Reaching inside she removed the final piece of paper. It was a photograph of a young man in an Air Force uniform. She held it up for Shawn to see. "I can certainly see why a woman would fall for him," she said. "There's no doubt who that is."

"Jeremy Kane," whispered Shawn.

The two sat in the filth on the loft floor for a time and examined the smiling man in the photo, totally enthralled by the likeness of someone neither had met, and never would.

When their work was done and all the artwork was removed to the house for safekeeping, Shawn returned to the carriage house, re-spiked the door and then leaned against it for a time and tried to sort out his thoughts. "Oh God, what do I do now?"

That evening Shawn insisted on going out for dinner, both needing to get away. They drove over to Georgian Bay, had dinner at a quiet dinning room and strolled along the water afterwards. Arriving home a little past midnight the two lay quietly in the darkened bedroom holding hands as they went over the incredible day's events.

Shawn broke the silence. "I was just wondering."

"About?"

"About what may have been----you know----if Jeremy Kane had lived. I wonder how the story would have ended?"

"You mean would they have gone away together?" asked Caroline.

"Yes. Something like that."

"It just wasn't meant to be, I suppose."

"Probably not. But you know, throughout this entire ordeal my greatest fear was that Cyrus Duncan was not my father. And yet, I never knew the man. Right now I have difficulty remembering what he even looked like."

"You can't remember anything about him? Nothing at all?"

"Just his eyes. Those dark eyes of his. And now when I think back I know I had a very real fear of him. He'd look at me with those eyes and I knew I had better do as I was told."

"It's not much wonder you can't feel any loss for the man."

"And I remember so well when he died. I can see it as plain as day. I remember standing by his coffin, a big polished thing the size of a locomotive----at least it seemed that big to me back then----and I remember asking mother if father was in that box. I always called him, Father, never Dad, and she answered me in a calm voice 'Yes Shawn. He's dead'. Mother was standing there with a black veil over her face, so I don't know if she was crying or not. Strange I should suddenly remember that."

"And now that you know the truth about your mother and Jeremy Kane, what do you think?"

"A bit sad, I guess. He went through a war only to die when he fell of a cliff here in his own country."

Caroline wrapped her arms around her husband. "But at least we both know the truth, and it's not the end of the world. So let's get back to being husband and wife----lovers----old friends----Mister and Missus.

After a short silence he said, "That's all we can do. So good night, Missus Duncan, and I'll see you in the morning."

After rolling over on their sides they thought about Jeremy Kane, remembered his smiling face on the military photo, visualized him falling to his death, wondered how that could have possibly happened?

Chapter 25

On September 4, 1953, Connie Duncan's mother, Johanna Lawson, died. Her death was totally unexpected and Connie was devastated. She went to The Maritimes to attend the funeral. Darrell drove her into Toronto to catch a train for Cape Breton Island. She was away for nine long days. And since Darrell had to drive Connie into the city anyway, he found it an opportune time to perform his yearly maintenance duties on the Duncan house. He took his tool chest with him and stayed in the city until Connie got back from the East. When she returned he picked her up at the train station and drove her straight back to Portage Lake, as per her instructions.

Between the travel and the funeral she was at the point of collapse when she returned. After taking a hot bath she went straight to bed and slept the clock around not waking until late the following morning. On the other hand, Darrell Colburn, being the loyal and honest employee that he was, went straight back to work the very hour he returned from the city.

Darrell discovered the body of Jeremy Kane at about three o'clock that afternoon. He had gone into the carriage house looking for his handsaw. Earlier he had noticed Kane's canoe was in the boathouse so he guessed he was in the loft. Kane was lying face down in the middle of the loft floor with a puddle of thick black blood pooled around his head. The handle of a walking stick was imbedded in the side if his skull, the shaft of the stick standing straight up like a Martian's antenna.

After the initial shock Darrell's next instinct was to call the police, but he remembered Cyrus Duncan telling him so often, "Nothing must ever be allowed to foul the good name of the Duncans. Never. Your job depends on that, Darrell." Since Connie was still sound asleep after her exhausting trip back from attending her mother's funeral, it gave him time to think. Leaving the carriage house and locking the door behind him, he hurried over to the summerhouse and informed Harriet of his grizzly find.

After hearing the news, Harriet eased down onto one of the kitchen chair and stared blankly at her husband like she hadn't heard a word he said.

Darrell went directly to the phone, took a deep breath, and called Cyrus Duncan.

"Mister Duncan, this is Darrell Colburn."

"Yes, Darrell?"

"Something terrible has happened up here."

Duncan's tone changed instantly. "What is it, Darrell?"

"I found the body of Jerry Kane in the carriage house. He's dead, Mister Duncan. He's dead. I thought I should call you before I called the police."

"Call the police? What happened to him, Darrell?"

Darrell's voice was shaky. "It looks like someone hit him with an old walking stick; it's still stuck in the side of his head."

The line went quiet for a lengthy time as Duncan absorbed the news. "I'm glad you called me first, Darrell. That was good thinking on your part. We must protect the family's good name, mustn't we? If he was murdered, then I can't have it associated with the family in any way. You can understand that, can't you, Darrell?"

"That's what you always told me, Mister Duncan, and that's why I called you first. And I didn't know what else to do."

"Does anyone else know about this?"

"Just Harriet. Connie's still upstairs----asleep."

"Good. Darrell, I want you to listen carefully. I don't want you calling the police, and I don't want you to tell Connie."

"*What?*"

"You heard me, Darrell."

"But he's dead, Mister Duncan. Someone killed him."

"Darrell, I want you to calm down and listen to me. I've been doing some quick thinking here, and I believe I know what happened."

"Okay, Mister Duncan, I'm listening."

"Good. That's good. Now listen very carefully. As far as I'm concerned it really doesn't matter who killed him. I want you to get rid of that body and make it look like an accident. Get it as far from the summerhouse as possible. Do you understand what I just said? I can't have a murder investigation on my property."

"Oh I understand all right, Mister Duncan, but Jesus, that's illegal. I could go to jail for that."

"And I also could go to jail for telling you to do it, Darrell. But listen to me? If you do this for me I'll be more than generous with you."

"But that guy's got a hole in his skull. I know he's been murdered. I don't think I can do this, Mister Duncan. If I did that then someone will be getting away with murder, and I could go to jail for tampering with the body. If I don't call the police right away they might just blame me for it."

Darrell Colburn was probably the only man in the world whom Cyrus Duncan trusted. He always treated him like the servant he was, but he trusted him explicitly. To his knowledge Darrell had never cheated him in any way. Each year Cyrus Duncan had him travel to the big Duncan home in the city to perform repair work. He could have hired contractors in the city but he trusted Darrell to do things right. He was truly a handyman and could turn his natural talents to anything that needed fixing, and the repairs were always done well. Duncan was certain that quiet and steady Darrell Colburn could get rid of a body, and also do that well.

"Darrell, they may just blame you for it anyway. Think about it; you're the only one up there, and I can positively prove I had no hand in the man's death; I was here in the city all the time. I haven't been up there all year." Cyrus paused a moment to let his words take affect.

After a silent spell Darrell asked, "Then what should I do, Mister Duncan?"

"I once asked you what you desired most in life, and you told me 'you wanted someday to own your own home'. Well I'm offering it to you. How would you like to own your own home, Darrell? Bought and paid for by me----clear and free with no mortgage. You once told me your life's dream was to own your own home and have a family." Duncan paused a moment while Darrell mulled it over in his mind. "Do this for me and before this year is out you will own that house. I promise. And you'll always have a job looking after the summerhouse. That too, I promise. Just get the body out of there, clean up any mess and say nothing about it. Make it look like an accident."

Darrell went into deep thought and Duncan knew he was nibbling at the bait. Darrell thought about the old ramshackle farmhouse he and Harriet were renting, and he understood only too well that the future held no promise of something better. Harriet was then twenty-two years of age, Darrell thirty-eight. They had been married over five years and his prospects were looking bleaker each year. Being an orphan he never had the opportunities other children had. Poorly educated and shy by nature, his dreams for a better life had always been just that, dreams. Life had always been hard for him, and being a no-body he could well imagine the police charging him with murder. Duncan had never lied to him before and he just offered him his own home.

Other than marrying the woman he loved it was the first real break he ever had in life.

"Mister Duncan, you did say *my own house*? Do you really mean that?"

"That's correct, Darrell. Bought and paid for by Yours Truly. And a lifetime job to go along with it. Are there any houses for sale up that way that you'd be interested in?" asked Duncan casually.

Darrell suddenly had trouble breathing. "There's a nice bungalow on the other side of the lake. Its had a "For Sale" sign on it for a time now, but it's probably a bit on the pricey side. It's a newer home and…"

"It's yours, Darrell," said Duncan instantly. "Get that body away from the summerhouse and I'll contact the realtor the minute you tell me it's done. That's a promise, and you know my word is good."

Again the line went quiet and Duncan could almost read his employee's mind.

"Okay, Mister Duncan, I'll take care of it. That lake has five hundred feet of water in places. He'll never be found."

Duncan practically shouted, "No-no, Darrell! I don't want you to do that. *The body must be found.* Connie must know that Kane is dead and he's never coming back. I don't want her traipsing around the country looking for him."

"Yes sir. I understand----I guess?"

"Good. I don't care how you do it, but the body must be found. And it must look like an accident. We can't have a murder investigation going on up around there, now can we?"

"Okay, Mister Duncan, I'll take care of it."

"Good. I knew I could count on you, Darrell. Oh, and Darrell…"

"Yes, Mister Duncan?"

"I want you to go over to Kane's cabin and remove all traces of Connie ever being there."

"Yes sir."

"And Darrell, like always, I want you to keep me posted."

"Yes sir, I will."

"Good man, Darrell. Good man. I knew I could count on you."

After Darrell hung up the phone he looked at his wife and whispered, "Jesus Christ, it was Duncan who killed him. He must have been here early this morning, killed him, and then hurried back to the city."

"Killed who?" mumbled Harriet as though in a daze.

"Killed Kane! Jesus, Harriet, who do you think I'm talking about?"

"Did Duncan actually say he did it?"

"No, but he didn't have to. He knew what was going on between Kane and Connie. He's the only one I know of who had reason to kill him."

"But how could he have known that?"

"Because I told him. He knew everything. Keeping him posted is part of my job."

"So what are you going to do now?" she asked in a trembling voice.

"Turn him in----that's what. A man would have to be out of his goddamn mind to do what he wants. He wants me to get the body away from the summerhouse and make it look like an accident."

Darrell picked up the phone, but Harriet grabbed his arm. "Then maybe we should do what he wants?"

Darrell looked hard at his young wife, shook his head in disbelief, and dialed the operator.

"Number please?"

Darrell paused. He knew he should call the police, but he thought about the lovely little bungalow on the hill overlooking Portage Lake. He also though about what Duncan had said, *What if they blame me?*

"Number please?" repeated the operator.

Darrell hung up the phone. *Don't be too hasty. Take your time and think it over. I can always phone later. Anyway, there's no way they could pin it on me----can they?*

"What is it, Darrell?" asked Harriet, seemingly coming out of her fog.

"Duncan told me that if I got rid of Kane's body he'll buy us that bungalow across the lake."

Harriet tone spiked noticeably. "Did he say that? Did he *really* say that?"

"Oh he said it, all right."

"Do it then."

Darrell couldn't believe what he was hearing. "*What*?"

"You heard me. Do it and I'll help you."

"Are you crazy?"

She placed her hands on her husband's shoulders and looked him straight into his eyes. "Think about it Darrell. Take a minute and think about it. So Duncan came up here and killed Kane. So what? Kane's been up here all summer frolicking with his wife, so really, he got what he deserved. And I also know why he killed him."

"You do?"

"Yes. Connie told me she was pregnant and that she was going to leave Duncan. Could you imagine; she was going to run off with that no-good drifter. She had already told Duncan she was leaving him. I know, because she told me she had."

Another silent spell followed. "So that's it. That's why Duncan did it."

"Darrell, forget the fact that he did it, just look at the opportunity here. Our own house, bought and paid for. You know perfectly well that we'll never be able to afford a home at the rate we're going. And so what if he was murdered? If Duncan hadn't killed him, eventually someone else would've. Do you think that Connie Duncan was the first woman he ever slept with?"

"Harriet, are you sure you want me to go through with this? Are you *absolutely* sure?"

"Yes, I'm positive."

"Okay, then," he said after a time, "I'll do it tonight. I don't know how I'll manage it, but if you're certain this is what you want, then I'll do it *for you*."

"I've never been more certain of anything in my life, Darrell."

Darrell immediately returned to the carriage house and bolted the door behind him. He had a great deal of thinking and planning to do.

Two hours later Darrell was back at the summerhouse. "I think I've got it figured out," he whispered to his anxious wife. "We'll do it around eleven tonight----not too early, not too late."

Harriet didn't question his plan; she knew it would be a good plan regardless what it was. She was very familiar with her husband's inventiveness.

It was the hole in the side of Kane's head that presented the greatest dilemma. If the handle of the walking stick was removed, then something would have to be inserted in the hole, something that wouldn't look suspicious. The walking stick was made from a knurled limb of hawthorn, sanded smooth and stained dark. The handle, the part imbedded in Kane's skull, was cast of bronze in the shape of a duck's head, the duck's bill being embedded in Kane's skull. When Darrell first tried to remove it, it refused to dislodge, the skull bone locking it in place. He had to put the toe of his boot against the side of Kane's head and wiggle the stick to extract it. A gush of brain matter and clotted blood oozed from the hole. Darrell gagged at the sight

The country around Portage Lake had many outcroppings of shale rock. It was everywhere. After removing the walking stick from Kane's skull, he took it with him up behind the carriage house and searched a shale ledge until he found a shard of stone that closely matched the shape of the bronze duckbill, one that was just a bit larger. When he found the right stone he took it back to the carriage house loft. Taking a deep breath he inserted the stone into the hole in Kane's head, pushing it with his thumbs until it popped into place on the inside of the skull. It wouldn't do to have it fall out while the body was being transported. That being done, Darrell hurried down from the loft and just managed to get outside before the vomit exploded from his mouth.

At ten-thirty that night Darrell backed his old pickup up to the carriage house doors, then he and Harriet went up to the loft. It was a gut-wrenching undertaking for both, but the inside of the carriage house had stayed relatively cool and the body hadn't yet begun to smell. However, Kane's face was bloated, black in colour, and oozing. Darrell took a piece of canvas and covered Kane's head to stop the ooze from spreading across the loft floor. He then dragged the corpse to the stairs and lowered it down onto the pickup truck. Backing the truck up to the woodpile he covered the body with stove wood. Although the backcountry around Portage Lake was lonely at anytime of day or night he couldn't take a chance of transporting the body without a good cover, and a load of firewood was a very natural sighting in cottage country. While Darrell covered the body, as to Darrell's instructions, Harriet brought down some of Kane's art supplies and placed them in the truck.

To say that Darrell Colburn was afraid that September night would be an understatement. On the back roads around Portage Lake there was little traffic at the busiest of times of the year, but once the summer season had ended there was even less; after midnight the roads were deserted. But still, he would have to travel four miles down a county road with a body in the back of his truck, and there was always an outside chance of being caught. The knowledge of that, combined with the foulness of the task, soaked him in a sweat of apprehension. His gut knotted him over the steering wheel with paralyzing cramps. As he drove along the gravel roads with his silent wife beside him, the tired Chevy truck rattling and creaking, he was sure the entire country could hear it.

Reaching the crossroad on the north side of the lake near Macdonald's General Store, he turned off the headlights and the engine and coasted by the intersection. Out in that part of the country when a vehicle went by at some ungodly hour of the night folks had a habit of jumping out of bed to see who it was. He prayed no one would see his brake lights when he swung onto the old logging road that wound its way through the bush toward the high bluff on the northern shoreline of Portage Lake. Looking in the rearview mirror he could see that Macdonald's Store stayed dark. His luck was holding.

After coming to the place on the logging road he knew was directly opposite the high bluff, he pulled in under an overhanging pine. With an overload of adrenaline racing through his body his movements were frantic. He could only think of one thing: get rid of the body and get out of there. Unloading just enough firewood to get at Kane's body, he and Harriet dragged the body from the truck and didn't stop dragging until they were at the top of the bluff.

Gasping and panting, the next part of his plan was to stand the cadaver up and just before pushing it over the edge, Harriet was to remove the canvas from the head so as not to get any of the brain-ooze on top of the bluff. But when they tried to stand the body on its feet, they couldn't do it. Kane had been dead long enough that the rigor mortis phase was passing and the body was somewhat floppy. And they had expended so much energy dragging the body they were unable to make the lift and at the same time control the uncooperative corpse to get it positioned just right for the drop over the edge. Reasoning that the body must be in a standing position when it went off the cliff if it was to land on its head, Darrell knew he had to get it right the first time.

The two were forced to wait for their strength to return. While they waited for renewed energy, Harriet seemed to be in a daze while Darrell was jumpy and hyperventilating. His ears buzzed. Every little noise were footsteps coming for him, knowing full well that out in such a desolate place in the middle of the night it would be next to impossible. But the burning fear of getting caught was terrifying. He just wanted it done and get out of there.

"Let's give it another try?" he whispered to Harriet.

Grabbing the body, in a single motion they hoisted Kane to his feet. Harriet yanked the canvas off the head and Darrell gave the corpse a hard shove. A couple seconds later they heard it thump the rock ledge below the cliff, but then, not part of the plan, there was splash. In his hyper state Darrell had pushed too hard and the body bounced into the lake. His plan was to have the body stay on the rock ledge below the cliff face where eventually someone would find it----after wildlife had fed on it. In the lake was not part of the plan.

But what was done was done and he couldn't worry about it. Hurrying back to his pickup he retrieved the artist supplies and ran back to the cliff and threw them over the edge while Harriet threw the firewood back into the truck box.

Returning to the summerhouse they took the Chris Craft from the boathouse and tied Kane's canoe behind it. With Harriet sitting up front with a flashlight they towed the canoe across the lake to the gravely beach near the high bluff. Darrell pulled the canoe up onto the beach, upended it, and placed the paddle beneath it. The two then took the speedboat over to the old trapper's cabin where they spent the next hour cleaning and making sure all traces of Connie Duncan were gone. That being done it was back across the lake to the boathouse. They returned to their rented farmhouse just before the dawn.

In the morning Darrell phoned Duncan. "It's finished, Mister Duncan."

"All went well, then?"

"There was one problem." Darrell told Duncan about pushing the body too hard and of it going in the lake. "I know damn well it would have gone straight to the bottom and it might never come up."

"Is the water in the lake still warm, Darrell?"

"Well, yes it is. A person could still swim in it. Why?"

"Then don't worry about it. I know about these things and I can tell you, it'll be floating in less than two weeks. It will be found, believe me."

On hearing that Darrell relaxed somewhat.

"And where is Connie?"

"Still asleep."

"Good. And Darrell, what's the name of the real estate company on the 'For Sale' sign? When I make a deal, I stick to it. That house is yours."

Darrell gave out a heavy sigh as he told Duncan the name of the realtor. "That's great, Mister Duncan. That's really great. And is there anything else I should do?"

"No. Just keep an eye on Connie. I know she won't want to come back home until she knows for certain that *Mister Kane* will never be coming back. Then she'll have to come home because there's no place else for her to go."

"Yes Sir. I understand."

Later that morning when Connie awoke her first words to Harriet were, "Is Jerry around?"

"Now that you mention it," said Harriet casually, "I haven't seen him."

Connie smiled. "He's probably over at the cabin. Probably doesn't know I'm back."

At around midnight a frantic Connie Duncan phoned Darrell. "Darrell, I can't find Jerry. He should have been here hours ago. Something's wrong, I just know it. I want you to come over and help me look for him."

After hanging up the phone Darrell gave Harriet a look that didn't need explanation. "Let's go," he said in a calm voice, "and remember, say as little as possible. Just try and comfort her."

"It's going to be a long night," said Harriet as she dressed.

And it was a long night. Darrell took the Chris Craft around the lake and drove his truck around the shoreline, everything to give the impression of an honest search. For almost two weeks the search went on; Connie cried; Harriet fretted, and Darrell did his best to remain calm.

The search ended on September 24, when Charlie Plaxton went plugging for bass near the high cliff.

On the third day of December Darrell Colburn drove to a lawyer's office in Meedsville and picked up the deed to Cyrus Duncan's promise. A week later he and Harriet moved their meager belongings into their new home. With no rent to pay or repairs to be made, their living standards took an instant jump. The following May Darrell's dreams were complete when Harriet gave birth to a little girl. They named the child Caroline.

Chapter 26

A BODY WAS DISCOVERED in Portage Lake and word traveled like wildfire. Later the same day it was confirmed the body was one Jeremy Kane, formerly of Toronto, formerly of Winnipeg Manitoba.

Harriet Colburn was doing the noonday dishes when the news came over the radio. She held her breath as the newsman spilled out what details there were about the death. As Harriet listened to the breaking news she didn't realize Connie Duncan had just come down the stairs from taking a bath and was standing in the adjoining room. She only realized it when she heard the front door slam and heard footsteps racing along the front veranda. By the time she dried her hands and rushed outside, Connie was nowhere to be found.

Later, when Darrell walked into the kitchen, he found Harriet in a terrible fluster.

"What is it, Harriet?"

"Connie's gone."

"Gone where?"

"They found Kane's body and she heard it on the radio. She's gone somewhere and I can't find her."

"Well go and keep looking. God only knows what she might do. I'll phone Duncan and tell him."

"Hello," came the sour voice of Cyrus Duncan.

"Mister Duncan, this is Darrell."

"Yes, Darrell?"

"They found Kane's body."

"Does Connie know?" he asked, his voice sounding stimulated.

"Yes, Sir. She heard it on the radio and took off somewhere. We're trying to find her."

"Good," said Duncan sounding satisfied, "and when you find her, get her back to the city at once. Get Harriet to take Connie's car and drive her in. I'll see that Harriet gets back to Meedsville on the evening bus."

"Yes, Sir. And is there anything else you'd like me to do, Mister Duncan?"

"Well now, Darrell," Duncan practically sang, "just close the place up for the winter."

"Yes, Sir. And thank you, Mister Duncan."

Shortly after Darrell hung up the phone Harriet came back into the kitchen all out of breath.

"Any sign of her?" he asked.

"None."

He began to pace. "Dear God, I wonder where she could be?"

"I don't know, but I can only imagine what's going through her mind."

"Well, we've got to find her and you have to drive her back to Toronto. I just talked to Duncan and he told me he wanted her home."

Harriet dashed out the kitchen door and continued her search. She started out the laneway when she glanced up toward the carriage house. Something white was lying on the ground and one door was partially open. When Harriet went to the white object she found it was a terrycloth robe, the one Connie was wearing.

She called to Darrell, "I think she's in the loft."

They both hurried up to the loft and found Connie lying on a recliner curled up in the fetal position. She wasn't crying, she was all cried out. All she could manage was a periodic whimper and an occasional snuffing sound. She was totally nude.

"Ah, Jesus," whispered Darrell when he first saw her. She reminded him of a discarded doll, lifeless and without its little dress on.

Harriet went to her, sat beside her, picked up her head and rested it on her lap. "Oh Connie, I'm so sorry." She hugged and rocked her as would a mother rock a baby. "Oh you poor thing," she kept repeating.

Darrell, not knowing how to deal with the situation, and embarrassed by Connie's state, retreated down the stairs. As Harriet held her dear friend she called down to Darrell to bring up Connie's robe. When Connie was again clothed Harriet and Darrell helped her down the stairs and got her ready for her trip back to the city. Connie went along robotically, her body limp, her mind numbed by grief as though out of touch with reality.

Harriet helped Connie dress, packed her things, and got her into the car as quickly as possible. As Darrell watched the car pull out the laneway on its way back to the city he wondered about Cyrus Duncan and how he would deal with this situation, wondered what kind of a person behaved in such a fashion, had the overwhelming urge to puke.

Chapter 27

IT WAS DUSK WHEN Harriet Colburn delivered Connie Duncan back to her home in Toronto; it was nearing midnight when she arrived back in Meedsville on the bus. Because of her extreme exhaustion Connie slept late the following morning. When she awoke Cyrus was waiting patiently on a chair by the foot of her bed.

"So," he said, indifferently, "I see you've finally decided to re-enter the world of the living."

It took her a moment to clear her mind, but when she did she remembered the horror of the previous day's news and began to weep. "Oh Jerry. No!"

Cyrus Duncan's demeanor turned fierce. Stepping around the bed he took his wife's arm and yanked her into a sitting position while delivering a terrific slap across her face. "You want something to cry about, do you? Well there's plenty more of where that came from." Connie sat in stunned silence and stared at her husband. "Now, *my dear wife*," he began, his voice bitter, "I'm going to tell you the way things will be from now on. That wild creature is gone from your life forever, and he's never coming back, so there'll be no more crying about him, is that clear?" She nodded her head. "Now get out of that bed and fix yourself, you look like a prostitute."

Her movements were lethargic so he pulled her from the bed and practically dragged her to the bathroom. Once in the bathroom he grabbed her nightdress and ripped it from her body. She loved posing nude for Jerry Kane, but with Cyrus Duncan looking at her she felt like crawling behind something. "Now get in that shower and wash all trace of that beast from you filthy body." Reaching into the shower stall he turned the knobs fully open, but before the water had a chance to warm he shoved her in. With the breath knocked from her by the cold deluge, he looked on indifferently. Leaning against the vanity he watched her for a time. "Get scrubbing," he shouted, before yanking the curtain shut.

As he waited, he thought about how things would be from then on, and how they were in the past. The noise of the cascading water blanked out all the present and his thoughts drifted back to other times. Back to his school years in Scotland and to how the other boys laughed at him because he was different, back to the night in the whorehouse when the young prostitute laughed at him when he ejaculated in her hand. But most of all, he recalled conversations he overheard when he was in the bathroom at the church hall. It was on the very Sunday morning after he returned from his honeymoon. He was in one of the toilet stalls and four men of the congregation came into the washroom. They didn't know he was there.

"So, what do you think of Duncan's new bride?"

"She's a beautiful young thing," said one of the men. Cyrus knew the man by his voice. "Do you think he knows what to do with her?"

"I doubt it," said another man, another voice he recognized. There was laughter. "I'd like to have been a fly on the wall the first night when she showed him those big tits. It probably took a full box of Kleenex to wipe up the drool."

More laughter.

"But could you just imagine what he thought when she wrapped those legs around him?" The laughter turned into a roar.

"It's a wonder he's still alive. Wonder the old ticker didn't give out right there and then."

"But really," said the forth man, "do you really think he can still get it up?"

"Well if he can't I'd be more than happy to go and give him a hand. It's the least a friend could do for the old boy."

As he recalled the laughter at his expense a rage built in him. Coming back to the present he pulled back the curtain. "Hurry up and get out of there."

Yes, they laughed at me, but when she starts to swell, and when I walk up the aisle with her on my arm I'll have the last laugh. There they'll be, sitting there beside their sows and I'll be sitting beside young, pregnant, and attractive Constance Duncan. They'll drool with envy. When we have the after-service gatherings and Connie has that glow on her face I'll look right at the ugly old bitches they're married to, and then I'll really smile.

"Hurry up," he shouted, and left the bathroom.

After a short time Connie came out of the bathroom wearing a bathrobe and a towel wrapped around her wet hair.

Cyrus pointed to a chair. "Sit."

She did as she was told. While sitting she kept her legs tight together and made certain the robe covered them. She pinched the neck of the bathrobe tight to her neck.

"Well, well," he sneered. "And would you look at Miss Modesty. I'll bet you weren't that modest when you were rolling about with Kane." She remained silent and wouldn't look at him.

"Look at me when I'm talking to you."

She raised her head but wouldn't look into his eyes.

"From now on this is how it's going to be," he began.

She cut him off. "I'm leaving you, Cyrus, and there is nothing you can do about it."

Slapping her so hard she was nearly knocked from the chair, he said, "You don't seem to be very good at listening, so let me start again." She sat trembling. "This child you're carrying will be raised to be my child. It will take the family name and I'll see to it that its undisciplined instincts are educated out of it. You will stay here in this house and be a good mother, and an obedient wife." She was about to say something but thought better of it. "And if you ever try and leave me, I'll see to it that you are laid to rest beside your Mister Kane----is that clear."

She looked into his eyes and understood clearly that he was serious. Gasping for air, she said, "My God. You had something to do with it, didn't you?"

He stood silent for a moment and smiled victorious. "Why, how can you say something like that?" His voice was sweet and mocking. "I was here at home being a good husband while you were up in the wilderness carrying on like a tramp. Dozens of people can vouch for me. I hadn't been up there all summer. Out of the goodness of my heart I let you have a quiet holiday by yourself----because I trusted you----and look at what you did behind my back."

"You did have something to do with it. I know you did."

He didn't answer, but it pleasured him that she looked on him as a killer. "Like I said, from now on you'll be the perfect wife and mother. It matters not whether you despise me, but there is only one way you'll ever leave me----the same way Jerry Kane left you. Do you understand?" She understood perfectly. "That child will carry on the Duncan name, and if you ever try and do something to change that, it wouldn't be well for you----or the child."

Connie went cold. "So this is what it's all about? That's why you let me go up there alone? You knew I was with Jerry? You knew, didn't you? You knew we were lovers before I left the city? Dear God, you let it happen. You weren't man enough to do it yourself so you stood back and let someone do it for you? Didn't you?"

He wanted so badly to confirm that it was all his idea, that he got what he wanted, but he didn't. How would it make him look? She might even laugh at him, laugh about his lack of manliness. And he could just imagine the laughter if she ever told others.

His speech became more civil. "Don't be ridiculous, Connie. What man would allow such a thing to go on and not put a stop to it? I trusted you and you betrayed me. But, I decided, while you were sleeping, I'd make the best of a bad situation. You can have a good life here in this house if you just do as you're told. But I assure you, the alternative would not be good if you ever try to leave and take my child."

"Your child?" She stood and glared at him. *"Your child?"*

"Yes," he said calmly. *"My child.* You should be thankful I'm so generous after what you've done. But then what kind of a man would I be if I punished an innocent baby for the sins of its mother? And besides, what kind of life could you possibly give the child? You a single mother and all. If you really care for this child then do the right thing----the smart thing. Or just what were you planning to do; take the child back to Cape Breton Island with you and let it live on fish?"

"Don't you dare put my family down for what they do to make a living. They're good and honest people."

"Yes, and poor as church mice." He then put a stop to the conversation. "Just remember what I've told you, Connie: if you ever try to leave me, you'll be laid to rest beside your lover----and I mean it."

"Your right about one thing," she said adamantly, "someday I will lay at rest beside Jerry, and there isn't a damn thing you can do about it. I'll never be your wife----either in life, or in death."

Cyrus Duncan left her bedroom and never again set foot in it.

Connie did the smart thing for the sake of her unborn child; she decided to stay with Cyrus for security sake----and fear. She'd never have to sleep with him so the situation was tolerable. She kept all her doctor appointments throughout her pregnancy, ate well and gave birth to a healthy child, a boy named Cyrus Shawn Duncan. Shawn was the name the boy would be called. And the members of the congregation congratulated Cyrus and he never again heard a single snicker about he and his young wife. When he walked up the church aisle each Sunday he couldn't help but smile. And when Connie would see the arrogant little smirk on his face she often wanted to jump up and shout for all to hear, to say aloud what was the truth, but she did the smart thing, kept quiet and raised her son.

But often she cried for the only one she ever loved. She cried in her bedroom, alone. And when she could cry no longer she washed and repaired the damage caused by the emotional release and went about the business of being a good wife and mother.

Cyrus sold his investment business the very year Shawn was born, but he kept a small office in a storage room of one of his apartment buildings. His long-time secretary, Helen Borden, could no longer waddle to work and she retired. With his office and business gone he had plenty of free time to keep an eye on his wife and at the same time have someplace to get away from her. He was home every night for the evening meal and Connie always cooked it. Cyrus insisted on having a servant in his employment, but Connie nixed the idea. She knew what he really wanted was a spy. Connie, never a tidy housekeeper, did her best at being maid and cook in the big house. Hard work was a family trait and it became her escape from reality.

Cyrus Duncan never physically mistreated young Shawn, but he was never warm toward the boy either. He would answer the youngster's questions, as best he could, but was really quite uncomfortable around the lad. Shawn was his mother's child, and as young as he was the boy sensed Cyrus's coldness and tended to stay clear of him. With the passing of years the bond only grew stronger between mother and son.

However, the summers were relatively good. The family went up to the summerhouse on Portage Lake where there was plenty of room for all. And Cyrus also went to the lake and stayed longer than he was accustomed to, but he still spent most of his time in the city. Little Shawn loved it at the lake, and he also had a playmate for company.

Just months after Connie became pregnant, Harriet discovered she also was in the family way. Shawn was born in early winter of 1954, and little Caroline Colburn was born in the early summer of the same year. As the years passed the two youngsters became like brother and sister, and often little Caroline would sleep over at the summerhouse and share Shawn's bed. The children's summer routine lasted until 1959.

Chapter 28

LESS THAN AN HOUR after falling asleep Shawn awoke with a jolt.

"What is it, Shawn?"

"Sorry, honey. I must have been dreaming. I thought I heard a scream." He glanced at the clock on the nightstand. 4:05a.m. The last time he looked at the clock it was 2:55a.m.

"Probably a nighthawk," whispered Caroline. "I've heard them myself lately."

"You're probably right. I'm sorry if I woke you." He put his head back down on the pillow but he couldn't sleep.

Caroline pressed her warm body up against him and threw an arm over him. "You've had a hell of a last couple of days, my dear. I guess we both have. Try and get back to sleep."

After giving him an affectionate squeeze she rolled back on her side and dozed off.

A half-hour later Shawn quietly slipped from bed, put on a housecoat and slippers, and went down the stairs. Going out the front door he stood for a time on the veranda and looked off across the mirrored surface of the lake toward the high bluff. Leaving the veranda, he strolled over toward the carriage house, and in the gray light of early dawn he could see its roofline peeking above the wall of cedars like a monster coming out of its cave. The fog of his breath added eeriness to the setting. He didn't need to go near the building to feel its darkness; he sensed it from where he stood and it seemed to be telling him a dark story. *What am I going to do with that building?* The wall of cedars did a fair job of hiding the old structure, but they couldn't shield him from the gloom emanating from it. *It certainly doesn't add to the setting. It's just a damn eyesore.* He decided then-and-there, *I'll have it torn down. When the landscaping's done, it's gone. I want it gone.*

A fish hawk glided silently overhead and Shawn watched it soar along the shoreline before it dropped down on a dead pine limb. Once comfortably on its perch the bird gave out a scream of satisfaction, the high pitch of the scream sending shivers through him, or was it just the morning's chill? He went back inside, made a cup of coffee, stoked the fireplace, selected a novel from the bookshelf and struggled to pay attention to the words on the pages.

The sun was well up when Caroline awoke. The year they married Shawn had insisted she hire a manager for the marina so she no longer needed to leave for work so early. They now had time to eat breakfast together.

"Got plans for the day?" she asked, while savoring her first cup of coffee.

"Not really. I didn't get a lot of sleep last night, so later on I might catch a little shut-eye."

"Well, I can certainly understand what you're going through," said Caroline.

Shawn expanded his chest with a deep breath. "But I'm not letting it get me down," he said bravely. "Yes, it was a hell of a shock, but there isn't a damn thing I can do to change it. You and I were so happy before this came along, and that's the way it's going to be again. This *revelation* is not going to spoil my life. I won't let it."

Caroline smiled warmly at him. "I'm happy to hear that, sweetheart. You'll never know how happy I am to hear it."

She then frowned. "But regardless, it's that time of the year again, and things are really picking up at the marina. The ice just left the bay a couple weeks ago and already they're wanting their boats in the water." She sighed. "I don't know what time I'll be home tonight, so I'll give you a call later on and let you know."

When breakfast was finished they kissed and said goodbye. "I'll have supper on when you get home," he assured her. "Any special request for the chef."

"A hot dog or a hamburger would be great as long as I don't have to cook it," she said, grabbing her jacket on her way out the door.

As Shawn put the breakfast dishes into the dishwasher a recall of the previous twenty-four hours came back at him. *Ah, the hell with it. Come on, Shawn Duncan, get your ass in gear. Forget about it.* He finished cleaning the kitchen, put on a jacket and headed out the door for his morning constitutional. “Put it behind you”, he shouted as he headed out the driveway. But when he came to the old Lutheran cemetery he stopped and wondered, *What else haven't you not told me, Mother? What?*

Chapter 29

IT WAS ON A May morning 1959 when Cyrus Duncan made the announcement. "This coming August, Shawn will be leaving for Scotland to complete his education. He'll be attending the same school I attended as a boy".

Connie was seated at the kitchen island eating her breakfast when she was hit with the bolt of lightning. She dropped her cup of coffee sending the contents splashing across the counter. Slowly rising to her feet, her tone cold and determined, she said, "Never! My child will stay here in Canada with me. He was born Canadian and by God he'll be educated as one."

"You have no say in the matter," Cyrus assured her. "The decision is mine to make."

"Like hell it is. I'll see you dead, first." It was the first time she ever stood up to him. "Do you hear me? You try and take my son away and I'll see you dead."

"Really," he laughed. "And just how do you plan on doing that." He stepped toward her and raised his hand, but she stood her ground and never flinched. He was not accustomed to resistance from her. When it came to her child she was prepared to fight. It had always been so much easier for Duncan to control things when his wife and son cowered, but now her life's purpose was being threatened and she was suddenly defiant, the likes he never witnessed before.

At that moment young Shawn walked into the kitchen and Cyrus backed away. The boy took an orange from a fruit bowl and left the kitchen as quickly as he had entered it.

"That's the way it's going to be," he said calmly, after the boy was gone. "When the summer is over he'll be leaving for Scotland. The arrangements are all made----and that's final."

"You're just doing this to hurt me, aren't you? Aren't you?" she shouted. "You know that that child is everything to me."

"I don't expect someone from Cape Breton Island to understand, but I'm doing it so the lad will get the best possible education. Carrying the Duncan name is a heavy responsibility and he must be conditioned for it----the same way I was."

She sneered at him. "And look what it produced? A mama's boy who didn't have the guts to stand up to her and be a man. Had to wait until the old bitch died so he could even look at a woman. Waited so long he didn't have anything left to give a woman."

He stepped toward her. "Watch your tongue woman." His face turned scarlet. "Don't you ever defame my mother's name, or, or..."

Connie laughed. “Or what? She was a miserable old bitch and everyone knew it.”

Duncan slapped her face extremely hard. She still didn’t flinch and didn’t attempted to shield herself from the next slap he threatened her with. Seeing her courage, courage he himself lacked, he lowered his hand and stepped away.

“I’m just doing what’s good for the boy and I don’t expect you to understand,” he said, his voice tight as he fought to stay in control.

“Liar! The schools in this country are as good as any in the world. The only thing people from over there learn is arrogance. If it’s so good over there then why did your parents leave it? It’s just your way of being dirty.” She stiffened herself and added, “but then, how could I expect you to be anything but dirty? All your life you had experts teaching you the art. Your entire family were nothing but greedy, selfish, mean-spirited bastards.”

He stepped toward her again, his lower lip trembling, his insides boiling with rage, a frightening darkness on his face. Still she didn’t flinched. “If that boy wasn’t in this house I’d teach you some manners. I’d straighten out that commoner’s tongue of yours.”

She laughed cynically. “Good thing you can straighten something out, you sure as old hell couldn’t straighten out that useless thing hanging between your legs.”

Along with his lip, his left eye began twitching. He wanted so badly to silence her but her remarks had wilted him. The truth was a knife to his heart. He turned away quickly and left the kitchen.

“He leaves in late August. End of discussion,” he said as he left the kitchen. “Oh! And just in case you’re thinking of trying something foolish; when the boy is finished school I've hired someone to drive him around for the summer and to keep an eye on him----and you also."

On the day Connie Duncan submissively banked the fire in her spirit she became a subservient wife for the good of her unborn child. She allowed her husband to rule her very existence. For the sake of a peaceful environment for Shawn, she allowed him to become supreme commander of the house, and that included her very soul. For the sake of tranquility she never once challenged his authority. She endured so that the son of Jeremy Kane could be happy. Now she was going to loose her priceless gift and she would not allow that to happen. The dampened coals in her heart began to glow hot; she could stand back and remain submissive no longer. She would act.

Although Cyrus had sold off the majority of his investing company, he still owned lease properties in the city and every Thursday he was gone most of the day looking about them. That would be the day Connie would make her escape. Reasoning that Cyrus would never suspect she would pull Shawn out of school so close to the end of the year, she chose the second Thursday in June to make her escape. She would have to do it before Cyrus had his spy in place. She needed a home for herself and her son, and she knew there was always one waiting for her on Cape Breton Island where there were large numbers of Lawson's who would be more than willing to take up her cause. Cyrus had told her, without using the exact words, that if she ever tried to run off with the boy he'd kill her and the child, but she doubted his resolve to kill, and she just didn't care anymore.

However, she was never allowed a free hand in finances. Cyrus knew that without money she couldn't be free and could never make a break. But she was allowed a weekly allowance to buy the required everyday necessities, and although the money was limited, she did manage to squirrel away a little each week. When the day of escape arrived she had plenty to make it to The Maritimes. A couple tanks of gasoline were all that were required.

Her plan was simple enough; both the family cars were in Cyrus's name, a Coupe Deville Cadillac and a Biscayne Chevrolet. She was allowed the use of the Chevrolet for shopping and taking Shawn to various functions, and she was certain that if the day started out like all the rest he wouldn't suspect a thing. Shawn would go to school----like always----and she would sit at the breakfast table and make up her weekly grocery list----like always. Nothing to raise suspicion. After Cyrus left the house to make his rental rounds she would throw her prearranged clothes into a suitcase, go to the school and collect Shawn, and she would be away before he found out what had happened. If she made it to the highway without being detected there was no way he could stop her.

But she would have to make one stop before she headed east. Portage Lake. She could not possibly leave behind Jeremy Kane's artwork. At that time his artwork was of little commercial value but it was priceless to her. And over the years she came to realize there existed one painting in particular that could be used to keep the wrath of Cyrus Duncan in check. She reasoned that his fear of people seeing her nude portrait was a big enough weapon to hold Cyrus Duncan from attacking when her location was discovered. It was her ticket to safety and she would collect it, and Cyrus had given her the old summerhouse as a wedding gift. It had real value if she ever needed money in the future.

Darrell and Harriet Colburn were at the summerhouse that June day when Connie and Shawn pulled into the yard and parked the car near the carriage house.

Harriet hurried out to greet them. "What in the world are you doing up here, Connie?"

"Escaping, Harriet. Escaping. This is the first day of a new life for us both."

Harriet's hand flew to her mouth. "Oh my God, Connie, has it come to this?"

"He wants to send Shawn to school in Scotland and I can't let that happen."

"Then where are you taking him, Connie?"

"I won't tell you, Harriet, then you won't have to lie for me."

"Well then what are you doing here?"

"I'm getting Jerry's things out of the carriage house. I can't leave them behind. They're too dear to me. And there is one in particular that'll be my insurance policy against Cyrus. You know the one I'm talking about."

Darrell was performing repairs on the boathouse and Harriet went to him and told him what was happening. He shook his head in disbelief and then went straight over to the house. Harriet went back to the carriage house to see if Connie needed her help.

"Have you had anything to eat, Connie?"

"No. I'm too excited to eat."

"I'll go fix something for you and Shawn. We were just about to stop for lunch, anyway."

Harriet hurried back to the summerhouse and Connie went up to the loft and began moving the mountain of furniture, working her way to the armoire against the back wall, to the place where Harriet had told her Darrell stored Kane's belongings. It would take most of the afternoon to sort and pack what she was going to take with her, but she felt confident she had plenty of time. Cyrus couldn't possibly know what was happening. He always came back to the house for lunch, always at twelve o'clock sharp, but with an empty house he wouldn't suspect a thing. How could he? It was Thursday and his wife was out doing her shopping and Shawn would be in school. He wouldn't know what was happening before that evening when neither son nor wife showed for dinner, and by then she'd be well on her way to the East Coast. Even if he figured out she had gone to Portage Lake it would still take him over three hours to drive there. There was plenty of time.

It was three o'clock before she had everything sorted and ready to be put in the car.

Cyrus Duncan's Cadillac pulled in the driveway and stopped. He left his car in the center of the road so there was no chance of Connie escaping. Darrell walked over and met him.

"Where is she?" he asked coldly.

Darrell pointed to the carriage house.

Connie was on her knees sorting when Cyrus came up the stairs. She heard his footsteps but didn't look to see who it was; she just thought it was either Darrell or Harriet. It was not until he grabbed her by the hair and yanked her to her feet that she knew different.

"I warned you, you dirty tramp." He kept his grip on her hair as he slapped her. The pain was so great she screamed out. He then threw her on the loft floor and began kicking her. All she could do was scream, certain he was going to kill her, knowing for certain he had killed Jerry Kane.

Standing out in the yard with his head bowed and listening to her cries for help, Darrell Colburn wanting to rush up into the loft and put a stop to it. Young Shawn ran toward the carriage house with tears streaming down his cheeks. "Mommy, Mommy."

Darrell yelled to Harriet, "Grab the boy. Take him into the house so he won't hear this."

Harriet hurried the struggling child back into the house and hugged him but was unable to say anything to comfort the youngster, or to block out the screams and curses coming from the carriage house loft.

As Darrell stood outside the carriage house listening to it all, he felt his stomach begin to heave, but he didn't know what to do, wished he hadn't done his duty to keep his job, wished he'd never called Cyrus Duncan and warned him of what his wife was up too. But was that not one of the terms of his employment, to keep Cyrus tuned to his wife behaviour when he wasn't there to watch her? It wasn't the first time he had called the man and warned him of his wife's antics. Cyrus Duncan certainly knew what was going on between his lovely young wife and

Jeremy Kane because he had told him; phoned him at least three times and spelled it out for him.

"And just what are they doing, Darrell?"

"Well, Mister Duncan, this is very difficult for me to say, but I think you know what I'm talking about?"

"No, I don't, Darrell. Tell me in plain English. What are they doing?"

"Well----well, they're doing it----you know?"

"No, I don't know, Darrell. Doing what?"

"Please don't make me say the words, Mister Duncan? You know what I'm talking about."

"Have you actually seen them, *doing it*, Darrell?"

"Yes."

"Where?"

"On the beach. Down at the little sandy bay----the one on the edge of your property. They swim naked practically every day and then they lay on a blanket on the beach. They did it right out in the open on the beach. And he sleeps with her at night. Harriet has to change the sheets every day because of it. There's no doubt, Mister Duncan. No doubt at all."

"Hum. Well Darrell, thanks for telling me. You keep me posted."

Darrell had always kept Cyrus Duncan posted and never once had he reacted like any normal man. No man with any pride would sit by and let his wife frolic with another man, and yet Duncan had, and didn't seem the least bit disturbed about it. He had been as plain as possible about it; in fact, Duncan seemed to enjoy hearing vivid details about his wife adulterous behaviour, wanted Darrell to give him a colourful description. He never once did anything to put a stop to it then, so why now? Of all the past reasons he had to beat his wife and never did, so why now? And what could he do about it? Darrell never imagined such a violent reaction from the man.

As Darrell stood there tormenting about what was happening, suddenly all went quiet.

After a time Darrell cautiously walked toward the carriage house and peeked inside, his heart pounding, expecting to find Connie unconscious, or worse. Whatever had happened had taken place in the loft. Darrell cautiously climbed the stairs.

Cyrus Duncan was lying on the loft floor with blood oozing from the crown of his head and sheets of Jerry Kane's artwork scattered about his lifeless body, some spotted with blood. Connie was standing there with a whiffletree in her hand. She seemed to be in a trance staring down at her husband's lifeless body, her lip bleeding, her face bruised, her body curled over from being kicked in the stomach.

Darrell went to Duncan, knelt down beside his lifeless body and checked his pulse. He held his fingers against his neck just long enough to feel the last weakening thumps of pulsing blood. Then there was nothing.

"Dear Jesus. Now what do I do?" he whispered.

"Is he dead, Darrell?" asked Connie, her voice amazingly calm.

He looked up at her without speaking. She knew the answer.

"Good! I'm glad he's dead. He was going to burn Jerry's art and take Shawn from me. I couldn't let him do that, Darrell." She then dropped the whiffletree on the loft floor sending a rattling clunk through the building.

Darrell remained in the kneeling position beside Duncan's body. Several times he looked up at Connie's face, and then down at the remains of her husband while shaking his head in disbelief.

"I know I'll have to go to prison for this, but I don't care. At least my son will live a normal life with my family."

That statement brought Darrell out of it. "Nobody's going to jail," he said rather loudly for the quiet man he was. "Not just yet, anyway. I just gotta think this through----figure something out. You go to the house. Your son's in a terrible state and he needs you."

She was trembling as she started down the steep stairs so Darrell hurried to her and took her by the arm. "You tell Harriet to go to the school and get Caroline. It'd be good for little Shawn if he had someone to play with. The two can entertain each other. Tell Harriet to stay at our house and not come back to the summerhouse. When I figure things out I'll go see her. And you go with them." As she was walking toward the house he warned her, "And Connie, keep your mouth shut." She didn't answer so he escorted her to the house and repeated his instructions to Harriet. "And don't talk to anyone. And if the phone rings, don't answer it."

He then went back to the carriage house and closed and locked the door behind him.

Oh, sweet Jesus, why did I phone him? What am I going to do now?

Chapter 30

DARRELL REMAINED IN THE carriage house for most of the day. It was well after dark before he got back to his house. "Harriet, where's Connie and the children?" he asked, the minute he walked through the door.

"The children are asleep. Connie's lying down with them." Then she asked, "Is he…?"

"As dead as dead can be," said Darrell calmly.

"What did the police say? Are they coming for Connie?"

"I didn't call them. I will in the morning."

"You didn't call them? Then what in the world…?"

"I said I'll call them tomorrow," he snapped, his frayed nerves showing, "but right now don't ask questions. Just do as I say. If I phone the police now she's done for. Do you want that?"

Harriet shook her head.

"Okay then. I want you to get the children up and get them and Connie in her car. Then I want you to drive them back to the city----call me when you get there----and you're going to pretend that you were there all the while, that you and Caroline were visiting with Connie and Shawn for the weekend. Say that you left just after picking Caroline up at school today. And if the police pay you a visit tomorrow you're to tell them that Connie hadn't been up here since last summer. And----*this is very important*-----when the cops call tomorrow to inform you about Cyrus's death, you're to look sad and tell them you already know. Put some soap in your eyes if you have to. Tell them I already called and told you that I found Duncan's body in the carriage house. You have to coach Connie so she'll get it right. Maybe, just maybe, I can keep her out of jail." He frowned. "Hell, what am I saying? I might just keep us both out of jail."

Harriet swallowed hard.

Connie entered the kitchen bent over and holding her stomach, her lip slightly swollen, her face showing a small bruise on the left cheek. Duncan had delivered most of his punishment with blows and kicks to her stomach; a facial beating would be hard to explain. "Are they coming for me, Darrell?"

"Not yet, Connie. Not yet. And if we all do our parts maybe they won't. Your boy needs a mother. It's not good growing up without a mother."

"I'm not afraid to go to jail," she said calmly. "I'd do anything for my son."

"Listen to me, Connie? You are *not* going to jail!"

Darrell was raised in an orphanage until the age of eight. Never adopted he was sent to live with a farm family. Merely a source of free labour he was denied a proper education, was never taken in as part of the family, never knew the warmth of a mother's arms. He couldn't allow that to happen to little Shawn. And besides, he liked the lad. When Darrell was working around the summerhouse the boy often followed him about asking questions. Why was he cutting a board? Why was he turning the bolts on a motor? Why was he painting a door? Why did cement get hard? He loved to listen to the little fellow's chatter, loved to watch as he and Caroline played together. He once looked in on them one night when they slept together in the same bed, like brother and sister.

Darrell looked closely at Connie's bruises. "Harriet, get some ice and put it on her lip, and when you get back to Toronto, see if you can hide that bruise with makeup. You probably won't be contacted until tomorrow afternoon sometime, so between now and then do your best to hide that mark. And rehearse what you're going to do and say. And give Connie enough painkillers so she can stand up straight."

He then went to Connie and placed his hands on her shoulders and squeezed her with firmness. "I want you to listen to me, Connie. Listen to what I'm saying."

She looked dazed but indicated she understood.

"You were NOT----I repeat----NOT here today. Do you understand me? You never left the city."

Her response was slow so he shook her lightly. "Do you understand? We're both in a lot of trouble if they catch us, so listen carefully. You were NOT here today. Understood?"

She nodded, but he doubted it was sinking in.

He turned to Harriet. "Make her understand. Make sure she gets some sleep, and make her understand. Now,

get the kids up and get them out of here while it's dark---
-before one of the neighbours drive by and sees her car."

At ten-thirty the following morning Darrell Colburn phoned the police and put the ruse to the test. While he waited their arrival he went over the previous day's preparations for the investigation. Darrell was a quiet man so he wasn't worried about saying too much, but he had to rehearse his story to make sure he said enough. By the time he had everything ready and had sent through the call to the police, his nerves were shot. The policeman at the other end of the phone had to keep telling him to "calm down----calm down". *Just as well,* thought Darrell. *I think I sounded like a guy in a state of shock. It can only help.*

Darrell's greatest handicap was his backwardness. He was taught from an early age to keep his mouth shut and do as he was told. But he was not a stupid man, anything but stupid. He seldom missed the midday news; always read the local newspaper front to back, never left a crossword puzzle uncompleted. He loved doing crosswords and was able to complete every line. His usual Christmas gift was a book of crossword puzzles. He thought a lot in his quiet world, solved difficult problems inside his head, came to conclusions no one would ever suspect he was capable of solving; about politics, about the future, about life. He just couldn't discuss things openly with people.

But the greatest problem staring at him that morning was testing every nerve in his body. It was the crescent shaped dint in Cyrus Duncan's skull, the place where the wiffletree had struck. A whiffletree is a shaft of hardwood used to hitch a horse to a buggy, or an implement. They're about the same length but a little heavier than a baseball bat with steel collars and hooks on each end. It was one of those steel collars that put a quarter moon dint in Cyrus Duncan's head, not an easy wound to hide.

He thought about pushing Duncan's body down the loft stairs and leaving the whiffletree on the landing at the bottom, as though Duncan fell down the steps and hit his head on it. But the angle would be all wrong. He was forced to spend over two hours in the carriage house with Duncan's remains and studying the wound on his skull, a wound that kept oozing blood and an oily liquid. But stay he did, stayed until a plan began to formulate in his mind, one he believed would pass inspection. His reasoning was simple; to eliminate one wound he needed to inflict a more destructive one over top of the existing one. But how was that to be achieved?

Duncan was a heavy man and Darrell reasoned correctly, if such a heavy man fell from the loft to the concrete floor below, and landed on his head, it would do considerable damage to the skull. But there was another problem; it was the way in which the stairs had been constructed. The stairs had a landing near the bottom, a landing about two feet above the concrete floor where the steps turned ninety degrees. There was no unobstructed passage from the loft to the concrete floor below.

First he checked out the sturdiness of the landing; it had been built of thick pine lumber and measured about four-foot square. Jumping on the landing with both feet it didn't feel all that strong but he guessed it would have to do. His next problem was how to get a two hundred and fifty-pound body directly over the stairwell so it would fall straight down on its head? For Darrell, that problem was easy to solve.

Block-an-tackles were common items in olden times and Darrell owned a set. He used them to pull the Chris Craft from the water in the autumn, or to lift rocks, or to pull tree stumps; lifting Duncan's body would be easy. Taking a ladder to the loft he tied the block-an-tackle to a rafter directly over the stairwell. After putting a bag over Duncan's head----to keep the blood and ooze from dragging across the loft----he then dragged the body over to the stairwell, feet first. He thought of tying a rope around the arms to stop them from hanging down, but he reasoned they must be left loose seeing as a natural reaction for one falling was to put out their hands for protection. He then padded the cadaver's ankles with a piece of old horse blanket so as not to leave rope marks on the ankles. Then he tied a sheep shank hitch around the padding.

It was then time to lift Duncan's remains over the stairwell. Up Duncan went, as high as possible, and when the corpse's feet touched the rafter Darrell tied off the bock-an-tackle. Removing the bag from Duncan's head, he stood back to examine his work. A large prehistoric bat hanging from a rafter, a bat wearing an expensive suit was how Darrell saw Duncan. He felt no emotion for Duncan whatsoever.

Taking several deep breaths he mentally readied himself for the final act. Climbing the ladder with his pocketknife in hand, he took one more incredibly deep breath and drew the blade across the rope. There was no turning back, but no sooner had the rope parted than he remembered something very important. In that split second he realized he had calculated wrong. He had lifted the body almost twice the height he should have. If a man accidentally tripped and fell down a flight of stairs, the fall would be from the loft floor to the landing below, and Duncan's head was a good six feet above the loft floor. He had dropped the body twice too far.

When the body's weight was released from the rafter, the roof sprung skyward, and when it hit the landing below the entire building vibrated. A cloud of dust and chaff rolled up the stairwell like ash from the throat of an erupting volcano. A chorus of shattering wood and breaking bones accompanied the dust explosion.

"Jesus Christ!" Darrell hurried down the ladder. The entire carriage house filled with a fog of dust. "This is not good," he whispered. "This is not good at all."

After the dust had settled somewhat, he cautiously looked down the stairwell but could only see part of Duncan. All that was showing above the landing were his legs, his derrière, his shiny shoes, and one hand. The weight of the body falling on the arms had twisted them into broken shapes. One hand was actually resting on his crotch, like he was scratching his testicles. The kinetic energy of the falling body had turned the landing into kindling wood. The body's upper half went clean through to the concrete floor below.

Oh Jesus. This is not good.

Steeling himself, he went down the stairs to examine the results of his handiwork and to remove the horse blanket from Duncan's ankles. The top of Duncan's head was totally flattened against the concrete floor with shards of skull and wood splinters sticking out like pedals on a sunflower. The other half of Duncan's skull had been driven up between the shoulder blades with the nose hooked on the chest bone. A fresh puddle of ooze was beginning to form around the head, blood mixed in with brain matter. And there was a distinctive aroma of excrement. The sudden stop had forced the contents of Duncan's stomach out his mouth. *Well,* thought Darrell, trying to make light of the situation, *that little cut on the top of the head is certainly gone.*

After gagging a few times from the sight and smell, he returned to the loft to remove the ladder and the block-an-tackle. Luckily, Duncan had only bled onto two of Kane's scattered drawings and not onto the dry floor planks. After removing the two soiled drawings, he put the remainder of the artwork back into the armoire and pilled the loft's contents back in front of it. With everything back where it belonged, he spent another hour going over everything making sure he missed nothing. However, just before he descended the stairs for the final time he realized something very obvious; his footprints were everywhere. The dust storm caused by the impact of Duncan's fall had coated the entire loft in a gray film and his footprints were everywhere. He thought for a moment before hurrying downstairs. Scraping up a big armload of chaff and dust from the lower floor, he took it up the steps and threw it high into the air. When the dust settled out his footprints had vanished.

He could do no more in the loft, but on his way out the door he added the final piece to the puzzle; he dropped a notebook and pen on the floor near the landing.

The police car came down the driveway of the summerhouse just after 11:00 a.m. The officer was young, well over six feet tall with a slight build, clean-shaven----if there ever was anything there to shave in the first place----and acne marks pocked his cheeks. Darrell knew right away the young cop was in over his head.

"Where's the body?" he asked nervously when he stepped from the cruiser.

Darrell pointed toward the carriage house.

"Show me?"

"I'd just as soon not. I saw it once and that's enough for me. Just go inside and you'll see it easy enough."

The officer cautiously entered the building. He remained inside for about three minutes. When he did reappear he took off his cap and began fanning himself with it. Looking down and seeing Darrell's vomit on the driveway his complexion instantly turned ashen. Walking back to the cruiser he folded his arms on the roof of the car, put his head down on his arms and remained in that position for several minutes. Darrell was right when he guessed that it was the officer's first serious investigation of a death.

When the cop was steady again he took out his notepad and asked, "What is your name, sir."

"Darrell Colburn. I work for Mister Duncan. I've worked here for years."

"And the dead man's name is Duncan?"

"Yes, sir. He's the owner."

"And you were the one who found him?"

"Yes, sir. And I phoned you as soon as I did."

"Did you touch anything after you found the body?"

Darrell shook his head vigorously. “No, sir. I got out of there and stayed out.”

“And what do you suppose happened to him?”

“Oh God, I have no Idea. I just went in there to get my tools----I was going to replace a broken board on the dock----and when I saw him I got out of there quick as I could.”

“Was that you who got sick on the driveway?”

“Yeah, it was.” *Play stupid, Darrell. Act weak.* “I’m not used to seeing stuff like that. My stomach’s a bit soft at the best of times.”

“When was the last time you saw Mister Duncan alive?’

Darrell pantomimed deep thought. “I guess it was about three o’clock yesterday afternoon. I was just getting ready to knock-off for the day when he drove in the driveway.”

“Was he alone.”

“Yes, sir.”

“Did he say anything to you?”

“Just hello----when I first saw him----and goodbye when I left for the day.”

“You didn’t ask what he was doing----why he was here?”

Darrell scratched his head and looked at the officer in a peculiar way. “He owns this place. I work for him----or did. I’d never ask him his business. If I started asking him his business he might just hire someone that knows how to mind his own business. And I need this job.” Darrell went quiet for a minute and let on he was in deep thought. “I wonder if Missus Duncan will keep me on now?” It was a valid concern for him.

"He's married?"

"Yes. And has a son."

"And where do they live?"

"In Toronto. This is their summer place." He then added as the officer was writing, "She probably already knows about this."

The officer stopped writing. "Oh?"

My wife and Missus Duncan are good friends. That's where my wife and daughter are right now; they were spending a couple days with them in the city. I phoned and told Harriet----that's my missus---- right after I phoned you'. And I'd guess she's already told Missus Duncan----Connie's her name."

The officer continued writing. "Do you have any idea why he'd be in the building? It doesn't look like a place a well dressed man like him would be spending time."

"I was wondering about that myself----I mean after I phoned you----him being in there in at all. Then I remembered he had mentioning that he was planning on selling off all that junk that's piled up there in the loft. Called them antiques. Said they were worth quite a bit of money. I don't know why anyone would pay good money for that old junk."

The officer smiled and put his notebook away. Darrell guessed the cop had bought the dumb act.

"Keep away from the building until the coroner arrives," the officer instructed Darrell.

"You don't have to worry about that," Darrell assured him.

All the time the officer waited for the coroner he never once checked around the building or the property. He just sat in the cruiser and waited. Darrell saw him use the radio a couple times, but basically he just sat in his car and waited. He was new at his job and Darrell rightly guessed he just wasn't sure of what to do next.

An hour-and-a-half later the coroner, Dr. Fredrick Vanderhaden drove into the yard.

Darrell knew who the County Coroner was; he had seen his name in the local newspaper. In his mid to late sixties, Fredrick----no one ever called him Fred or Freddie-----had silver hair, a handlebar mustache, wore a tweed jacket and matching cap, beige slacks, tie, highly polished loafers, and could easily pass for a British country squire. He drove a black Lincoln Continental, and when he stepped out of the car he went into a well-rehearsed routine. Opening the trunk he took out a doormat and placed it on the ground. He then removed a pair of high rubber boots from the trunk and placed them on the mat. Stepping out of his loafers he neatly rolled his pant legs around his legs and stepped into the rubber boots. He then took a white lab coat from the trunk and put it on, making sure all the wrinkles were brushed from the coat as though someone might see him in a ruffled condition. The man dripped of superiority to the point of being comical.

The coroner didn't acknowledge Darrell's presence; he spoke to the policeman as though Darrell didn't exist. He and the police officer stood off a distance from Darrell and talked in low voices for a time, and then the policeman took a camera from the cruiser. The two men entered the carriage house. Darrell worked his way closer to the open door and listened to their conversation. There were several camera flashes as they talked and he heard them climb up the steps to the loft. More flashes bounced down the stairway from the darkened carriage house loft. Darrell stood quietly outside the door with his ear close to a crack.

"Do you see anything unusual about it?" asked the coroner.

"No. I'd say the guy was either starting down the steps and tripped, or he was up here, forgot where he was, and accidentally stepped backwards into the stairwell. If there was a hand-railing around this opening we'd know for sure, but seeing as there isn't..."

"That's about the way I see it, too," replied the coroner casually. "And he landed on his head on the landing and went straight through it."

"That would be quite a fall," said the officer, "and I suppose the boards were old and weak."

"Precisely. And those steps are quite steep, so I could see it happening quite easily," added the coroner.

The officer confided in the older man. "I have to admit I'm new at this, so I could use some guidance. I'd appreciate your help. What should I be looking for?"

Darrell could imagine the arrogant older man puffing his chest out. "Well, let's go downstairs and I'll go over the corpse with you."

Darrell heard them clumping down the stairs and he strained to listen to what they were saying.

"Look at this," said the coroner. "If you notice the tiny blood spots and the minute bits of brain tissue splattered about, that indicates a hell of a hard impact. You could just imagine the kinetic energy a heavy body like that would generate falling from that height. We're talking tons of impact weight."

Darrell again gagged recalling cutting Duncan loose and the terrific noise the body made when it hit the landing.

"Yes, I sure could," said the policeman, sounding back in control of himself.

The two again went back up the stairs.

"Will you do an postmortem on him?"

"Not unless I find something out of the ordinary," said the coroner. "It's all quite straightforward. Self-explanatory, really. Ask yourself this, how would one stage a scene like this?"

"I can't imagine it," said the cop.

The body had begun the decaying process and Coroner Dr. Fredrick Vanderhaden was not keen on cracking the skulls of people swollen and emitting gasses, or combing through two-day-old blood the consistency of liver laced with slivers of bone and wood. He didn't mind the fresh ones, the ones that had been refrigerated, but swollen and stinking bodies he didn't care for in the least. He knew by the time he would get at it, the internal organs would have begun to develop very offensive odors, and Duncan's body was already turning ripe. There was obviously pressure inside the cadaver.

"I wonder where the pencil and notebook came from?" said the coroner.

As Darrell listened he prayed, *Please buy it. God, please let them buy it?*

"The handyman told me that Duncan told him he was going to sell off all the antiques in the loft. He could have been up here taking inventory; you know, itemizing everything. Other than that, I can't see why he'd have a pencil and notepad with him----or be up here in the first place for that matter?"

"Makes sense to me," said the coroner. "Especially a man dressed like that. And, I must say, there are some fine looking pieces up here."

"By the looks of this place, and the car he was driving, I'd have to say this guy had money," the officer continued.

"Oh yes, I'd think so, too" added the older man. "I can't say I've ever heard the name Duncan before, but then I live a considerable distance from here."

"You don't have any suspicions about the handyman?" asked the coroner.

"Hell no. Did you notice the puke on the driveway? That's his." He failed to mention that he had also come very close to adding to it when he first arrived on the scene.

"He'd drop dead if he saw some of the remains I have to work on," added Dr. Fredrick Vanderhaden.

Darrell smiled nervously after hearing the two men laugh. *Yes. They bought it.*

Darrell had met Vanderhaden once before, and once was enough. He was to be Harriet's physician throughout her pregnancy with Caroline, but she took an instant dislike of the man. He talked down to her and she couldn't tolerate him. And because Darrell knew from reading the newspapers that he was the County Coroner, that knowledge was his ace-in-the-hole. A man so arrogant and self-righteous would be easy to fool. He'd fool himself.

Later that day people from a funeral parlor came and removed the body. They even borrowed some of Darrell's tools to free the cadaver from the tangled landing. When the policeman told Darrell that the investigation was complete, and after Duncan's body was removed, Darrell took a scrub brush and cleaned the blackened blood from the concrete floor. He replaced the broken landing boards and burned all traces of the grizzly scene. After one final check of the carriage house he removed his tools and took a handful of large spikes and nailed the doors shut. He never again entered the building.

When the police officer got back to his detachment he phoned the Toronto Metropolitan Police and they sent an officer to the Duncan residence. Harriet answered the door and confirmed that she knew of the death of Cyrus Duncan, that her husband had called earlier and told her about it, and of how shocked everyone was. She doubted that Missus Duncan could come to the door because a doctor had given her something for shock, and she was in a terrible state after hearing the news. The officer told Harriet "That wouldn't be necessary, and I'm very sorry for your troubles".

The funeral was an affair fit for a man of high office, prearranged by Cyrus in his will, even the eulogy. It was read in a solemn manner by a minister who repeated several times of "how great was the loss of such a peer of the community". If all the relatives and friends who attended the funeral were packed into the same seats, they wouldn't have taken up two rows.

And Constance Louise Duncan was the perfect grieving widow. Because of the stress of everything that had happened, she looked haggard and drawn, and it was only proper for her to wear a black veil, which hid the mark on her face. She certainly had the look of a woman who had lost a loved one, for indeed she had, seven years previous. She thought about Jerry Kane throughout the entire service and grieved openly for him, her tears real. Her sorrow was unquestioned.

Chapter 31

Connie kept Darrell on as caretaker of the summerhouse even though there was little for him to do. Connie and her son never spent another summer there. And because he had so little to do, Darrell began looking for winter work; he found it in a lumber camp in northern woods, hard, cold work. For the next nine years, usually during the first week following the New Year, Darrell went away to the lumber camp and returned home in early May. The Colburn's lifestyle improved greatly because of the extra money he earned, and it gave Darrell a great measure of pride to see his loved ones prospering because of his labours.

On the third day of January 1969 he left for the lumber camp for the last time. The evening before departing he and Harriet sat down for an evening of TV. Caroline stayed with her parents for a time but went to bed early so they could be alone. The consuming of alcohol was a rarity in the Colburn household, but

Darrell was in a melancholy mood that night and drank more than he should have. Alcohol was the only thing that could loosen his tongue. By the time Harriet got him to bed he was talking up a storm.

Sitting on the edge of the bed trying to undress, Harriet had a bit of a laugh as she watched him fumble about with his clothes, trying to remove his shirt before unbuttoning it.

"Here," she finally said, "let me help you." She removed his shoes and socks, pushed him back onto the bed, unbuckled his pants and tugged them off. Pulling him back up into the sitting position she unbuttoned his shirt, removed it, and then pulled his undershirt off.

"I don't know what I'd do without you, Harriet?" he mumbled. "You and Caroline are the best things that ever happened in my life."

His words were slurred but she knew they came from the heart. Darrell Colburn released his feelings reluctantly and she found his next words odd. "And I've never cheated on you, Harriet. And I never would. I hate people who cheat on their partners. Up at the camp I see it going on all the time and it makes me sick. Every Saturday night the same bunch of men take their paychecks and go into town, get drunk and then take up with some barroom floozy. Them with wives and children at home going without while they puke their money down the toilet, or give it to a whore."

Harriet watched him swaying about as he sat on the side of the bed mumbling as if to himself, probably not even aware he was speaking aloud. "That's why I always hated that Kane and Connie Duncan. The two of them rolling around like dogs in heat, and me and my dear wife having to see it. No self-respect. If old Duncan was no good to her then why didn't she just leave him? Why did she carry on the way she did?"

Harriet was stunned to hear her husband's words, and although he was drunk she knew he meant every word. She had never looked at her quiet husband as a great lover, or a great anything, but she suddenly saw him in a different light, one she admired. She was married to a man who loved and respected her and would never do anything to hurt her. But he seemed so much older as of late; he was sixteen years her senior, too old to be doing backbreaking work in lumber camps, and he was doing it because he loved her.

After helping Darrell on with his pajamas she lay down beside him and placed an arm over his chest, thinking he was ready to sleep. He wasn't.

"You know, Harriet, you and I paid a hell of a price for this little home. No people ever paid more. No sir, no one ever paid a bigger price for a place to call their own."

"We sure did," said Harriet. "We sure did."

Darrell babbled on. "Our pride, our self respect. Dear Jesus, two people never paid more."

Darrell then turned and faced Harriet. "And then the worst part of all was you having to lie to that cop and tell him it was you carrying on with Kane, *to protect the good Duncan name*. Sweet Jesus, and would someone please tell me what good was there in that name worth protecting? It was only money that made them better than us."

Harriet then said, "Darrell, wasn't it strange how that cop---Hass I think his name was---never put two-an-two together. He knew that Cyrus Duncan was in his late fifties, so he must have just presumed his wife was also middle-aged. He was looking for a young woman and I was the only one around, so he naturally thought it was me. He knew Jerry Kane was having a fling with a young married woman and he took it for granted it was me. I lied and he never questioned it."

"Because he wanted to believe it," said Darrell. "That's what they think all women are; cheats and whores. And that was the saddest part of it all, Harriet, you having to admit to something you'd never do. You had to say that you were as low as that lot, that you were screwing that piece of shit. I get sick every time I think of it."

Darrell began sobbing. "I'm sorry you couldn't have married a smarter man, Harriet. It seems there's people put on this earth to do others dirty work and you're married to one of them. When I was growing up on that farm, working for those no-good bastards, I had to do the work of a slave and take the lickings just to stay alive. Then I go and work for those cursed Duncans and put up with their dirt just to keep a roof over our heads." His agitation picked up. "And I put up with that miserable old Muriel, his mother. And if that wasn't bad enough, after she dies I had to put up with her arrogant son. Then he marries someone young enough to be his daughter and he's no good to her, so what does he do? He hires that Kane to come up and service her like a farmer hires a bull to breed the cows, and he leaves them to it. Then he has the nerve to phone me and I have to tell him where and how they're doing it. He actually liked hearing about it. Can you believe that?"

Harriet was stunned. "Is that true, Darrell?"

"True as can be."

"And poor Connie," said Harriet, after thinking about it for a minute, "she thought it all just happened, that their meeting was a fluke."

"It was no fluke, but if that's what she thinks, then leave her to it. There's been enough hurt already. No use adding any more to it."

"And," said Harriet, "Cyrus actually phoned you and asked how things were going between them?"

"It's as true as can be. And what kind of a man does that make me? What? Going along with that pig just so I can pay the bills. Harriet, if you start hating me because of it no one would ever blame you."

As she looked into his eyes she saw something she never dreamed she'd ever see; tears forming, and when they began to run down his cheeks she pulled him to her and let him weep.

"Now," he continued, his voice heavy with emotion, "I can't even look at my own daughter I'm so ashamed of myself. I love her and I can't even look her in the eye. I know I'm no good at talking to people, but at least I should be able to look into my own daughter's eyes."

Harriet lay quiet for a time and thought about his words. She remembered Darrell and Caroline's routine every Saturday night before he went away to the lumber camp; sitting together on the couch and watching the hockey games on TV. She knew Darrell loved Caroline, and now she understood the anguish he must have felt all those years as he watched her growing up, ashamed about what he had to do to make a living.

"The work at the lumber camp is hard and cold," he continued, "but it's honest work. At least I feel like a man when I'm there. I hate being away from you and Caroline, and I miss it when I can't sit with Caroline and watch the hockey games, but it's better than working for those Duncans. At least I don't feel like a pimp when I cash my cheque."

Harriet held her husband tightly in her arms, held him until he slipped into a heavy snore, found herself weeping along with him.

Darrell was up early the next morning, sick. Earlier that week travel arrangements were made with another man who was also going to work at the same lumber camp, and he would be by at ten o'clock to pick up Darrell. Harriet had Darrell's suitcase packed and sitting by the door.

"You'd better try and eat something, Darrell. It's going to be a long trip."

"Yeah. You're right. Maybe I can keep down a bowl of cereal." He managed to eat the cereal and forced down two cups of coffee.

Caroline wasn't up yet and so Harriet knew she must say something before it was too late.

"Darrell, do you remember what you told me last night----about Caroline?" Darrell couldn't look at his wife but she knew he heard her. "Well, there's something that I want you to know, and you're never to doubt it. There are two women in this house who love you very much, and I say women because Caroline is no longer a girl. She's fifteen, soon to be sixteen. Every time you leave for the lumber camp she hugs you and tells you she loves you, but you never respond. Darrell, in a few more years she's going to be grown and gone and you're going to regret it. Darrell, she needs to hear the words." Darrell sat motionless and stared into his empty cereal bowl. "And there's something else I want you to know, and this too you're never to question. I love and respect you Darrell, and you'll always be the man I love." She then breathed deeply and added, "And I'll always love you for what you did to keep us warm and safe. Don't ever be ashamed of yourself, sweetheart; we all do what we must in this world." She then walked behind his chair, put her arms around his neck and hugged him for the longest time.

Caroline came into the kitchen. "Goodbye Daddy," she said, throwing her arms around his neck and kissing his cheek.

Standing behind her daughter, Harriet made signals and mouthed words to Darrell. She pantomimed him hugging his daughter, and mouthed, "Tell her, I love you?" She then put her palms together in a pleading way and mouthed, "please?"

After a slight hesitation Darrell did put his arms around his daughter, and whispered in her ear, "I love you little girl. You look after Mommy when I'm away."

"I will Daddy," said Caroline, her eyes filling. She then left the room knowing it was a hard time for her parents.

A half-hour later Darrell's ride pulled into the driveway and tooted the horn. Harriet and Darrell hugged and fought back the tears. When they released each other, he turned, picked up his suitcase and said, "Goodbye. I'll see you in the spring".

Through a frosted windowpane Harriet waved goodbye to the man she loved. As the bitter winter wind whipped the snow across the driveway she watched with a sinking sense of foreboding as it slowly erased his footsteps, like the snow was whitening out a chapter from a book. To the end of her days every time she saw a lone set of footprints in the snow she would remember that cold January morning when she waved goodbye to her husband.

While standing there by the window watching the car distancing itself down the road, Caroline came and stood beside her mother. "I didn't mean to eavesdrop, Mom, but I heard it all last night. I wasn't asleep and you guys were talking loud."

"Oh God, you didn't?"

"It doesn't matter, Mom. He's still my dad and I still love him. I'm lucky to have a dad like him. I just know now that I'm going to have to work hard and not go through what you two were forced to do."

Harriet tried to smile. "But listen Caroline, you must never breathe a word of what you heard. Never."

"I'm not a child, Mom. I know how to keep a secret."

"That's good, and make sure of it," she warned. "And now you know, there's a lot more to your father than what people think."

After a time Caroline cocked her head to one side and looked at her mother. "So a guy named Kane is actually Shawn Duncan's father?"

Harriet looked away and didn't answer.

Then Caroline asked, "Mom, what ever happened between you and Connie Duncan. We used to always visit them in the city before Christmas, to shop. I always looked forward to it. But that last time we were there we left late at night and I never figured out why. Why were you and her fighting? What happened that night?"

Harriet shrugged. "The friendship had worn itself out, that's all. Nothing's forever. We had words over dinner and it went from bad to worse. And besides, I was sick of hearing about Jeremy Kane and how wonderful he was. I suppose I was just sick of her."

"But, why were you mad at me, too? You never spoke to me for days after that."

Harriet ignored the question. "I guess I'd better start the laundry and clean the house."

Darrell Colburn was crushed to death that February by a load of logs.

Chapter 32

SHAWN BROUGHT THE SIX Kane sketches to his new studio that morning. He was toying with the idea of having them as a drawing attraction, so he hung them on the entrance wall to see how they showed. What to do with the mountain of Kane's work from the carriage house was still troubling him, but he felt the six sketches rightly belonged to his mother. While he worked he left the studio doors open to help remove some of the new carpet and paint smells.

The man walked in unannounced. About middle-aged, of average height and build, he wore running shoes, blue jeans, a baseball cap and a white sweatshirt. There was a tourist look about him, but Shawn instinctively knew he was not a tourist.

"May I help you?" Shawn asked. He didn't know why, but he felt chilled the very moment the man walked in.

"I sure hope so," answered the stranger. He stepped over to where Shawn was standing and was about to say something when he noticed the six sketches on the wall. "My God! Kane's work. In all my life I've only seen a few of his pieces, and here I am looking at six of them, all on same wall."

"I'm sorry," said Shawn, " but the studio's not open yet. Opening day is in three weeks. If you'd care to come back then...?"

The man offered his hand, which Shawn took hesitantly. "I'm not here to buy anything, Mister Duncan. My name's Frank Everett. I'm a freelance writer and I'm researching the life and times of Jeremy Kane, and it looks like I've hit the jackpot." He pointed to the six sketches. "Within the last few years several more pieces of Kane's work came on the market, and prices are going through the roof. I strongly suggest you don't leave these unguarded. A stranger could walk out the door with them when you're busy doing something else."

"You don't have to worry about that," Shawn assured him. "I just put them up to get an idea as to how they'd show. I have no intention of leaving them here when I'm away. And I have no intention of selling them, either. I was just thinking about displaying them for the opening of the studio----a door-crasher I suppose you could say."

"Some door-crasher," mused Everett.

"If you're doing a story on Jeremy Kane, Mister…?"

"Everett."

"Yes, Mister Everett. I'm afraid you're wasting your time by coming here, because you probably know more about the artist than I do."

"Funny you should say that. A couple locals told me you'd be just the man to see. Now why do you think they would say that?"

Shawn forced a laugh. "Mister Everett, I have absolutely no idea why anyone would tell you such a thing."

Frank Everett stared at Shawn for a minute. "Mister Duncan, is this some kind of act, or has someone beaten me to the story?"

"And what story are you talking about?" said Shawn, trying hard to stay calm.

"About the life, the work, and the death of Jeremy Kane. What else?"

Shawn Duncan wanted no further discussion with Frank Everett. Although he came across as a pleasant enough man, well mannered and all, there seemed to be darkness about him, like he was a grave robber and his words were a shovel. "I'm sorry, Frank---ah, Mister Everett----but I'm afraid you've been misinformed about my knowledge of Jeremy Kane. I can't help you. I know very little about the man. In fact, practically nothing."

Everett pointed to the sketches. "Then what about these?"

"They belonged to my mother. She acquired them years ago, and if she knew anything about the artist then you're too late. She's been dead two years now."

"Yes, I know. Constance Louise Duncan----nee Lawson. She's buried beside Kane up in the little cemetery----beside the great man himself."

Shawn's voice turned defensive. "Mister Everett, I don't care what you've been told, or what you think, but those two people are buried beside each other through circumstance, and for no other reason. And don't go reading into it something that's not there. I think I can honestly say they never knew each other. They may have met at some time, but they certainly didn't *know* each other."

Everett tapped the wall beside the six sketches. "Really?'

"Like I said, Mister Everett, the studio is closed and I'm a busy man."

Everett ignored the statement. "Someone will write the story, Mister Duncan. It won't go away. Those two people are buried together for a reason. They knew each other very well in life, and you know exactly what I'm talking about."

Shawn exploded. "And you are very mistaken, Mister Everett. And like I said, I'm a very busy man, and I've told you all I know. Now, please leave?"

Instead of leaving Frank Everett followed Shawn as he walked toward the back of the studio. "Mister Duncan, I can write the story in its entirety, do it justice and be respectful to those involved, or you can put me off and I can write a lot of half-truths and gossip. I don't need your assistance to write the book. I already know where the story is heading. But it *will* be written because Jeremy Kane's work is on the world stage, whether you like it or not. He's not one of the Group of Seven, yet, but I think it's not far down the road. It's only a matter of time before the general public will recognize his name, the same way they recognize Tom Thomson, Carmichael, Harris, and A. Y. Jackson. Do you want the story filled with half-truths and hearsay, or written with respect for those involved? There's a lot of smut writers out there,

Shawn," Everett decided to take the less formal approach, "and if I don't write the story, one day one of them will. It can't be stopped, so what will it be?"

Shawn Duncan stepped toward Frank Everett in a challenging manner. "Just what is it you're looking for, *Mister Everett*?"

"The truth, Shawn. I already have my book. I'm just trying to make it exact as possible. It's called research."

"Really? You're writing a fable and you want my assistance, is that it?"

"It's not a fable and you know it. I learned one thing in university, Shawn; I learned how to research and I'm damn good at it too. I know what I have, I just want confirmation. I understand how this could be painful because I know your mother was involved with this man when she was married to Cyrus Duncan."

Shawn turned on Everett and actually pushed him back with a stiff finger. "You've got a lot of damn nerve coming into my place without being invited, and insinuating…"

"Insinuating what? That your mother and Jeremy Kane were lovers? That he did some of his finest work here at this lake in the company of another man's wife?"

Shawn began shaking. "Get out of my establishment---now?"

Everett didn't budge. "Shawn, a few years ago, when I began looking into the life of Jeremy Kane as an interest story for a magazine piece, I knew practically nothing about the man. But then I went to England to write about the upcoming celebrations for the sixtieth anniversary of The Battle of Britain----about Canadian involvement in the fight. And seeing as I knew that Jeremy Kane was a veteran, I looked into his military career while I was over there. I went into a pub in the area where he was stationed and there was one of his sketches hanging on the wall. The owner had no idea who Jeremy Kane was. I could've offered the guy a hundred pounds for the sketch and he probably would have taken it, but I don't do things like that. I told him what he had. He thanked me and gave me a free drink. Shawn, I didn't cheat the man out of his piece of art, and when I'm finished with this book I won't have cheated on his memory----or your mother's. This man's life deserves a book and I'm going ahead with it."

"Well good for you," said Shawn sarcastically. "But let me assure you, *Mister Frank Everett,* if you ever print a single word concerning my mother I'll sue you into the poorhouse. Is that clear?"

"Oh, I get your message all right, and I understand why you're saying it, but I don't see how it can be avoided. Everyone who lived around these parts at the time knew about him, and also about the woman he was involved with. I know his body was found in Portage Lake, that he fell to his death from the high bluff on the north shore," Everett pointed out the window toward the direction of the cliff, "and I know the woman he was involved with was a married woman----your mother. The police report stated that he was with Harriet Colburn when he fell off the cliff, but I know different. It was your mother he was with."

"Harriet Colburn?" Shawn Duncan tried to laugh. "You do have a wild imagination, don't you, *Mister Everett.* And are you sure you don't write for one of those gossip tabloids that are always getting sued?"

"It's not imagination, Shawn. Old police files confirmed it. A Corporal Walter Hass investigated Kane's death at the time. I've read the report. It's all stored on microfiche; you can look at it yourself if you wish. Or better still, I'll leave you a copy of the investigation and you can read it at your leisure. It seems that the late Walter Hass was a very meticulous records keeper. His notes on the death of Jeremy Kane are very precise. He stated that Jeremy Kane lived in an abandoned trapper's cabin on Portage Lake that summer, and indications showed there was a woman in that cabin, that a woman----and I quote----'had shared his bed'. And his notes also state that he talked to the handyman and his wife at the Duncan summerhouse, a Darrell and Harriet Colburn-----your in-laws I believe. And Harriet Colburn said----and again I quote----'Mister Duncan very seldom comes up to the lake, and that summer he never once came up to the summerhouse'.

"And I've talked to other people who were around at the time. Four years ago I spoke to the man who dug Kane's grave," Everett spewed out information in rapid fire, "a Joff Pedigrew, and he told me where I could find Jeremy Kane's grave. When I found it I felt bad because such a talented individual could be thought so little of. Then yesterday I went back to revisit the gravesite. I don't know why----looking for inspiration perhaps----and didn't I find a relatively fresh grave beside his. So I went back to Joff Pedigrew and he told me it was your mother's grave, and that you had also recently inquired about Kane's grave. And the pieces all began to fit together."

Then Frank Everett slowed his tongue and said in a precise positive way, "And this is where all Walter Hass's report began to fall to pieces. The report stated that Harriet Coburn admitted to Corporal Walter Hass that she had had an affair with Jeremy Kane, but strangely, it was your mother who was laid beside him over in the little cemetery. Wouldn't you have to admit that that is a bit odd, Shawn? Wouldn't you?"

Shawn Duncan stared at Frank Everett with disbelief. "Harriet said she had an affair with Jeremy Kane?"

Everett held up the report. "It's all right here."

"Show it to me," demanded Shawn.

Everett produced the well-worn documents and pointed out the paragraph. Shawn read it and then fell silent, his face blank with astonishment.

"Tom Doweling also told me there was a woman. He actually saw her with Kane, 'a beautiful woman,' that he believed to be your mother. He talked to her and she gave him a sandwich and a banana. At the time he couldn't distinguish between Harriet Colburn and Constance Duncan because he had never met either women, but his sister had told him it was *your mother.* And I had to ask myself; why would Harriet admit to such a falsehood? It didn't make any sense. Why would she take the fall for someone else? What was she hiding? And the biggest question of all; what did she get out of it? Like I said, Shawn, I'm damn good at researching, so when I checked back in the county archives I discovered that Darrell and Harriet Colburn purchased a house----this house----at about the same time Jeremy Kane was killed. And it was a cash deal. Now where would a handyman and his wife get that kind of money? And so I continued looking? And low-and-behold didn't I discover that Cyrus Duncan wrote out the check. Your mother and Jeremy Kane had an affair, and to save the Duncan name, Harriet Colburn said it was she so nothing would lead back to the prominent Duncan family of Toronto. I'm damn certain that's what happened. And I know you know, Shawn, because you also asked these same people the same questions I did. And not long ago, either."

"Shawn, I know that Jeremy Kane was your father. I've put the pieces together, and so will others."

"My----my what?"

"You heard me. Your father."

For the first time in his life Shawn rolled his hands into fists meaning to use them. "I'm only going to say this one last time, get t'hell out of here----now?"

Frank Everett watched the man's facial expression with astonishment. He caught something he hadn't noticed before and he could not believe what he was seeing. "My God! You really didn't know, did you? You weren't trying to throw me off the trail? *You really didn't know*?" he whispered. "You're hearing this for the first time, aren't you, Shawn?" Everett closed his eyes and shook his head in disbelief. "I'm sorry, Shawn. I never imagined you didn't know. I honestly thought you were just trying to throw me off the trail. How could you not have known that Jeremy Kane was your father? It was so obvious."

Shawn Duncan turned robotically and began slowly walking toward the bathroom, almost staggering.

"I'm sorry," Frank Everett repeated as he walked toward the studio door, appearing to leave. Instead, he stopped and turned. "Shawn, four years ago----when

I first started my research into this story----I talked to Harriet Colburn and her daughter----your now wife. It was right in this very building, when they lived here. I confronted her with Walter Hass's old police report and the fact that it was recorded clearly that she had admitted to having an affair with Jeremy Kane, and the fact she was with him when he fell off the cliff. She denied it and said it was another woman. She insisted the report was wrong. She said it was another woman, but she wouldn't tell me who the other woman was. I didn't believe her until yesterday when I revisited the old cemetery and saw that your mother was buried beside Kane. If your mother-in-law knew, and your wife knew, then I was certain you also knew. I'm sorry I was the one to break it to you. I *really am* sorry." He then repeated his warning. "But it won't go away, Shawn. He was too important an artist. The book will be written. I know what the problem is here, and I can see your point of view----and your fear----but it can't be hidden any longer. It's too obvious. I've looked at Jeremy Kane's date of death and your birthday. I doesn't take a mathematician to put the numbers together. Any fool could figure it out."

Shawn stopped his trek to the bathroom as Everett continued. He wouldn't face Everett, but he listened.

"Nine months back from your birthday, that puts the time of conception in early June, and the locals told me that Jeremy Kane took up residence in the old trapper's cabin in mid-May of that year. They also said that your mother was here at the same time. One of those people----Tom Doweling----is still alive and has a very good memory of the time. Four years ago, when I asked people about it, it was confirmed, and two of those people were your wife, and your mother-in-law. If you were to work with me on this, Shawn, I'd only write what's acceptable to you and your family. The fact that Kane was your father *can be deleted.* You would get to okay the final draft, and that's a promise. I'm not out to crucify anyone only to tell the story of an incredible man. A very gifted man. In fact, you should be proud of who your father was. And," Everett said as an afterthought, "it's nice to see the man's talents have continued on in his son."

Frank Everett then took a business card from his wallet and placed it on a windowsill. "Just in case you change your mind, Shawn. My number's on the card."

After Everett drove away, Shawn Duncan was still standing in stunned silence with the copy of the police report in his hand, struggling to digest what he had just learned. His life, the life of his mother, Cyrus Duncan's life, everything he had ever held sacred seemed to be floating around the room like bits of confetti. And it was about to all become public knowledge. Everyone seemed to have known the truth, the scandal, the shame. Everyone but him.

He hurried to the bathroom, and just before he dropped onto his knees in front of the bowl he stared at his refection in the mirror. He recalled the picture of Cyrus Duncan, could actually remember looking into the old man's cold eyes when he was a boy, and he knew there was no resemblance. He recalled the photo of Jeremy Kane, remembered the date of his death, the dates on the backs of his artwork, and it confirmed that Kane was at Portage Lake in May and June of 1953. He remembered the two tuffs of hair in his mother's safety box, and he remembered thinking the rusty-coloured tuff was his own, but now he knew otherwise. Nine months before he was born, the year Cyrus Duncan never once came to Portage Lake, the man that owned the rusty tuff of hair was here at Portage Lake with his mother. But the most devastating part of it all was, he also knew Harriet Colburn and her daughter----his wife, Caroline----knew all about it, and they knew it all along.

Chapter 33

HARRIET COLBURN OPENED HER apartment door and her son-in-law bolted past her physically brushing her aside. Once inside the apartment he exploded, "Is it true? Did both you and Caroline know? Did everyone in the whole goddamn country know except me."

"Shawn, calm down. What are you talking about?"

"I want someone to tell me the truth. Is it true?"

"And just what is it you're talking about, Shawn? Is *what* true?"

"You know damn well what I'm talking about. A guy named Frank Everett came to my studio and he told me everything. He said he talked to both you and Caroline four years ago, and you both knew that Jeremy Kane was my father."

"Oh dear God! Mister Frank Everett. I'd forgotten all about him," she mumbled, bowing her head.

"Yes, Frank Everett. I want you to either confirm it, or deny it; is Jeremy Kane my father?"

Raising her head slowly, she said, "We didn't lie. We just never told you what you didn't need to know."

Shawn Duncan wilted into a slump. "It's true then."

After a deep breath Harriet said, "Yes. It's true," then adding, "We were only trying to protect you, Shawn. What people don't know, won't hurt them."

"*Protect me? Protect me?* Who in hell do you think your talking to, a child?"

"Yes," said Harriet calmly. "Your mother always treated you like a child. She'd never let you grow up. And personally, I didn't think you could deal with the truth."

"Knock-it-off, Harriet. I don't want any more of your lies. Why was I the only one left out in the dark about this----this family secret?"

Harriet went quiet for a long minute and thought. "Okay. So you want to know?" she finally said. "Then come into the living room, sit down, and I'll tell you all."

Once seated in the living room, Harriet began, not taking her eyes from her son-in-law throughout the entire telling. "Connie----your mother, lived in a dream world. A man old enough to be her father swept her off her feet----or more precisely, his wealth did. She was a poor Maritime girl alone in a strange city when along comes Cyrus Duncan and gave her everything she had ever dreamed of. She married him, moved into a mansion, had servants, plenty of money, but there was one thing Cyrus Duncan's money couldn't buy. He was not a man in the way that really counted. In short, he was no good in bed. Totally useless, in fact. She was at the peak of her sexuality locked into a marriage with a man that couldn't perform. So along comes Jeremy Kane.

"They started a relationship that lasted until his death----when he fell from the bluff on Portage Lake. Connie was madly in love with him and pregnant with his baby---- you. She was going to leave Cyrus and run off with Kane, that's how serious it was, but when Kane was killed she went back with Cyrus because she had no where else to go. And Cyrus took her in and raised you as his own. What else could he do? He couldn't allow the Duncan name to be muddied by a scandal. And besides, with Connie pregnant, old useless Cyrus ended up looking like a real man.

"After Kane's death everything about him became an obsession with your mother, like he was a saint, and that's why she's buried beside him. That's why she kept everything that belonged to the man; all his artwork, his clothes, everything that you found in the loft." Harriet paused for effect. "And above all else, she kept you, her love child. And that's why she never allowed you to be a free man, because you were Jerry Kane's greatest gift to her. She wasn't about to let another woman steal you away from her."

"Harriet," said Shawn shaking his head with disgust, "you're amazing. That's the biggest lie I've ever heard. All my life I was free to do as I pleased with no strings attacked."

Harriet remained extremely calm. "Really? Well then tell me, Shawn Duncan, how is it that you never married while your mother was alive? Most men your age have at least two wives in that length of time, but not you. The very day after your mother died you came up here and latched onto my daughter like a man possessed. Your life-long protector wasn't even in the ground and you were looking for someone else to fill her place."

"Stop," he shouted, springing to his feet. "Stop right there. Over my lifetime I went with women----lots of women. I was even engaged once."

"Were you really? Well-well! I wonder how she managed to put a stop to that?"

Shawn threw up his hands in frustration. "I'm out of here."

Harriet managed to catch him by the arm before he could get out the door. "If you were engaged----like you say you were----then how come you didn't marry the woman?"

"Because Vicki called it off. It happens."

"But why did this *Vicki* call it off?"

"How should I know? She just did. She never explained."

"Called it off without an explanation! Hum. It'd certainly be interesting to know the story behind that one. I wonder how she did it?" Harriet mused.

"You wonder who did what?"

"Your mother, who else? I wonder how she got rid of the other woman in your life?"

"Harriet, you're something else. And to think you were once her friend."

Shawn was about to continue on out the door when Harriet said, "Do you remember the night when your mother and I ended our friendship? Do you remember our last night in Toronto when you were with Caroline?"

He paused for a second and thought about it. "Sure I do. You two fought about something, and you took Caroline home that very night."

"That's right. Do you want to know what the fight was all about?"

Shawn's feet locked in position..

"The row was because you and Caroline were sleeping together on the couch. Myself, I thought it was cute, but Connie went ballistic. She told me to take my daughter and get the hell out of her house and never come back. Don't you see, Shawn? Caroline was a threat to *Jerry Kane's wonderful gift.* You and Caroline had a strong attachment to each other, and she knew it."

"You're lying. Mom would never do a thing like that. I had lots of girl friends in my life and she never once tried to interfere. Like I said Harriet, you're something else."

"But you never married any of them," she continued. "Isn't that strange? But you and Caroline were different. I saw the attraction and so did your mother. And I was right, because the first chance that came along you married Caroline----once *mommy dearest* wasn't around to put a stop to it."

He stepped close to Harriet and pointed a finger in her face. He opened his mouth to say something, but instead, spun around and stormed out of the apartment.

Squealing the tires as he pulled away from Harriet's apartment, he didn't go far until he pulled over by the side of the road. Where was he going? What was he going to do? In the turmoil of his mind he kept going over Harriet words. W*as she lying again?* He couldn't accept Harriet's accusations without question, but she had certainly created a harassing doubt in his mind.

After a time he started the engine and headed south.

Chapter 34

THERE HAD ALWAYS BEEN a light left on for her but the moment Caroline walked into the darkened home she sensed something was very wrong. The ringing silence of the house chilled her like a winter's draft. As she walked from the kitchen into the living room turning on lights, she instinctively knew that nothing in her newfound happiness would ever be the same again. "Shawn, are you here?" she called, knowing the futility of her words before they were spoken.

In the living room, on the coffee table and scattered about on the floor were the six charcoal sketches which Shawn had taken to his studio just that morning, and leaning against the chesterfield was the portrait of Connie Duncan, the one that once hung in Connie Duncan's office. Its paper backing had been ripped away. Although the portrait had never been signed, it was dated on the back: February 18, 1953. It proved that the artist was Jeremy Kane, and it proved that Connie Duncan knew him long before that infamous summer. Caroline never cared to have the smiling face of her deceased mother–in-law in her home; she only accepted its presence for Shawn's sake.

Dropping her coat and purse onto the floor she picked up the copy of Walter Hass's police report and glanced through it. It didn't take her long to understand the full magnitude of what had happened. Wilting down to the floor she buried her face in her hands and wept, "Oh, please God, no. Please don't let this be happening."

"Mom, did you see Shawn today?" she asked, after finding the strength to get back on her feet and call her mother.

"I'm afraid I did," said Harriet. "He knows, Caroline. He knows everything."

"How could you have done such a terrible thing, Mother? How?"

"Caroline, do you remember a few years back when a man by the name of Frank Everett paid us a call?"

"Oh, God! I forgot all about him."

"So had I," said Harriet, "but he didn't forget about us. He's still writing his book and he visited Shawn at his studio. He was the one who told him."

"Do you have any idea where he may have gone?" asked Caroline, gasping for air.

"No I don't."

"What am I going to do?" whispered Caroline.

"If you had of listened to me in the first place you wouldn't be in this fix. I told you not to marry him."

"Oh, shut up, mother. Just shut up." Caroline slammed the phone down.

Chapter 35

RUNNING HIS FINGER ALONG the names in the phonebook, he wondered, *can that be her? Could she still be using her maiden name?* Dropping a quarter into the slot he dialed the number.

"Hello."

After all those years her voice hadn't change one iota. It *was* her. "Vicki?"

"Yes." A slight pause followed. "Who is this?"

He cleared his throat. "You'll probably find this hard to believe, but it's Shawn Duncan, and I need to speak to you."

After a short hesitation she said, "You know, I've always believed that sometime down the road you'd get in touch with me again."

"Vicki, I'm not mad, or hurt, or anything, but I need to know something. It's very important."

"Are you here in the city?" she asked calmly.

"Yes. Downtown."

After a slight pause she said, "I guess I do owe you that much. But I don't want to talk on the phone. I'd sooner be facing you. I live in a condo by the lakeshore. Can you stop by?"

"Sure. No trouble at all."

She gave him her address. "I'll buzz you in when you arrive. It's unit 906."

Threading his way through the bumper-to-bumper later afternoon traffic all he could think about was Vicki, found it unbelievable that he was going to see her again, wondering if her looks had changed as little as her voice. He first met her when she walked into his studio. With jet-black hair, wonderful large dark eyes, a great figure, bouncy exuberance, a love for life, her effervescent demeanor made her a pleasure to be near. He fell in love with her there and then, couldn't help himself.

He remembered his first words to her, "May I help you?"

"Oh, no thanks. Just looking. I love fine art but I couldn't afford any of these works, but perhaps someday." Then she laughed. "Right now my art collection comes from the galleries of Woolco." She could always make him laugh.

"Well then, seeing as you may be a future customer, let me show you what I have."

She spent almost an hour in the studio and for her youthfulness he was amazed at her solid understanding of art. He just couldn't let her walk away without finding out more about the beautiful creature. "What's your name, Miss Future Customer?"

"Victoria," she smiled, "but don't you ever dare call me that. It's Vicki. Vicki Ramsey."

"Okay, Vicki Ramsey. My name is Shawn Duncan, and I must say that you're about the youngest customer I've ever had in my studio."

She pulled back and looked at him with disbelief. "You own this place? You seem awfully young to own a place like this."

He swayed his head from side to side and smiled sheepishly. "You can do that when your family's bankrolling you. But," he continued, "you're right. I'm only twenty-eight, and normally it would take a lifetime for a man to reach this level in the art world. I was very fortunate."

"And I must say, for a young man you're very knowledgeable when it comes to art."

"It's what I do. I've been studying it all my life. I love doing art work and I love dealing in it, too."

That night he took twenty-four year old Vicki Ramsey out to dinner and it was the start of an incredible love story. But for some reason, one he couldn't even explain to himself, Shawn instinctively kept the love affair private for as long as possible. He went with Vicki for over two months before he brought her home and introduced her to his mother. He seemed to have known in advance that the greeting would not be warm, and it wasn't. Connie Duncan was polite, but seemed indifferent to the relationship. Vicki didn't pick up on it right away, and Shawn didn't want to see it. *Why didn't mother like her? Why? Vicki was a wonderful woman, smart and gorgeous.*

She was standing by her door waiting for him when he stepped off the elevator. When he walked up to her they shook hands formally and smiled awkwardly.

"Hi, Vic."

"Hi, Shawn." She stepped aside. "Come in?"

Vicki had gained thirty pounds since the last time he had seen her. Giving birth to two children and long days at a computer desk had taken a toll, but she was still quite lovely. He could tell she had prepared somewhat for the occasion, the way her hair was fixed, her perfectly applied makeup, the sent of perfume, black pantyhose, the snug-fitting black dress. He also guessed that because of her added weight she often wore black.

"How have you been, Shawn?"

"Okay I guess. And yourself?"

She tightened her lips and smiled. "No complaints," but he detected otherwise.

The condo was an older building but well maintained. The windows overlooked Lake Ontario and the view was worth a million. Financially, Vicki wasn't suffering any.

"Nice place."

"Thanks."

"Is there a Mister in your life?" he asked a little hesitantly.

"There was. Two in fact. And I have two teenaged children."

His eyebrows arched. "Really?"

"Yes, really. What about you?"

Shawn smiled. "Believe it or not I got married for the first time just last year?"

Without the slightest hesitation, Vicki said, "Then your mother's dead?"

Her statement took him off guard. "Yes. As a matter-of-fact she is. She died two years ago."

"Figures."

"What?"

"I said, it figures," she repeated sharply, "because if she was still alive you wouldn't be married. She'd of put a stop to it." Her voice was intent, almost mean. She had changed over the years and her natural softness was gone. When they dated her voice was never hurtful.

Shawn was stunned by the remark. "Vicki, what are you saying?"

"You poor man." She looked at him as a mother would look at a child who had stubbed its toe. "You still haven't figured it out, have you? That's what you're doing here right now, isn't it? Mommy's dead and now you're trying to figure things out."

In disbelief he asked, "Vicki, what's happening here? Why are you talking about mother the way you are? She never did anything to you. And neither have I----unless you consider asking you to marry me as something bad. Why the attitude?"

Vicki gave a cynical little laugh. "You think not, eh?"

He shook his head in total confusion. "No! She didn't."

Vicki drew in a very deep breath and a look of frustration shrouded her face. "Shawn, I know you can't stand hearing anything negative about you *dear sweet mother,* but I believe it's high time you did." She was struggling to keep her anger in check. "Why don't you just sit down and I'll tell you all about her, the side you refused to see----if of course you're now grown up enough to listen?"

Shawn eased down onto a sofa, straightened himself and said defiantly, "Go ahead. Tell me? What's got you so pissed off? I'm the one that should be full of bitterness, not you."

"You think so?" Vicki sat on a chair facing him. "Shawn," she began slowly, "do you remember the night we became engaged?"

"Of course I do. How could I ever forget it?"

"Neither can I. It was the most wonderful day of my life. I was the happiest woman in the world."

He jumped to his feet. "Well then...?"

She raised her hand to cut him off. "Shawn, just sit and listen----please."

He slowly sunk back down onto the sofa.

"I remember it was in a Chinese restaurant called, The Red Lantern----just off The Danforth. It's gone now. We sat in a back booth and that's when you asked me to marry you, and you put the ring on my finger. Afterwards we went back to my little apartment and danced in the nude with the lights off. Then we went to bed and made love----twice if I recall. Do you remember that, Shawn?"

"Of course I do. I'll always remember it? We were together for most of the night. It was daylight before I got home."

"That's right. And because I was so tired I slept in the next morning and didn't wake up until someone knocked on my door. It was your mother." Vicki expelled a chest-collapsing breath. "The minute I opened the door she marched right in without even saying good morning.

She had this thick envelope in her hand. She went over to my little kitchen table and dumped out the contents of the envelope. As soon as I saw what was in it I knew our relationship was over. She handed me a check for twenty-five thousand dollars and said, 'You are never to see my son again. If you do I'll show him these pictures and these statements. I'll show them to your friends and your employer. I'll ruin you. There's enough money to get you on your way, so leave and I never want you to contact Shawn again.' And then she shouted into my face, 'Never!'"

Shawn sat in stunned disbelief with his head moving slowly from side to side, rejecting what he had just heard.

"Oh, don't shake your head, Shawn. It's true. It's all true. It's natural to think one's mother was a saint, but when it came to keeping her son, she was manipulative, mean, and heartless. You were always *her* boy----and I knew that----but I also knew that you had a kind and caring heart. I just figured I could put up with your mother until we were married, and when we had children she'd focus on her grandchildren and things would be fine. Boy, was I wrong."

"What was in the envelope?" asked Shawn, his voice unsteady. "What were the pictures? What statements?"

Vicki smiled sheepishly. "We all have skeletons, Shawn. We all have'm."

"What were the pictures?" he demanded.

"Of me from my university days. As you remember me telling you, I attended McGill University in Montreal, and I didn't have a lot of money. But my roommate told me how I could make some easy money. "I became a weekend stripper. That's how I helped pay for my education. Lots of girls did it. They still do.

"When I'd put on a blond wig and layers of makeup, I'll bet even you wouldn't recognize me. But then the patrons didn't give a damn what you looked like; they were only interested in your tits and your crotch. Some of the girls made so much money they quit school and stayed at it. Some of them had sex with patrons after the show----for a good price of course. But I never did any of that. If you recall, we went together for over a month before we slept together. I was a virgin when I met you, and you know I was. When I was finished university, I left Montreal, got a job with an accounting firm here in Toronto, and then you came into my life. My stripping days were behind me and there was no harm done. No one would ever know----or so I thought.

"But then, *Constance Duncan* had other plans. There was no way she was going to let someone steal away her precious son. She hired an investigation company to check me out and it didn't take them long. They got hold of the photos of me in the nude----I used them for my résumé. A girl needs them to get work in the strip clubs. And they also tracked down a couple of the other girls who were doing the same thing, and they got statements from them. And, as they say, the rest is history."

"I don't believe you," said Shawn. "I don't believe any of it."

In a very calm voice Vicki asked, "And what part don't you believe? That I once stripped to pay for my education, or what the old bitch did to keep control over you?"

He jumped to his feet. "Don't you ever call her that again."

"Why? I've called her a hell've lot worse. And what should I call a person who destroyed my life along with her own son's life? Saint Joan of Arc? After she forced me out of your life I prayed that someone would blow her head off. I even thought of getting a gun and doing it myself."

Shawn started for the door but Vicki caught him by the arm. "Shawn, in my entire life I've only told you one lie. When I wrote you that letter and said that I didn't love you----that was a lie. I've always loved you, and in a strange sort of way I think I still do. I've married twice trying to find another man like you, and I never succeeded. That's the honest truth."

She placed her hands on his shoulders forcing him to face her. "Look at me Shawn----please?" After the initial hesitation he found the courage to do so. "I would never lie to you. That morning your mother stood over me and forced me to write that letter. She forced me to drop your ring----my ring----into that envelope with the letter. That very day I packed and went over to England and stayed a year with an old aunt of mine----Aunt Myrna. I left no forwarding address so you couldn't find me. I went through two years of absolute mental hell. I became so depressed that one-day----after I found an old bottle of sleeping pills in Myrna's medicine cabinet----I took the entire bottle.

"Fortunately----or maybe it was unfortunate----Myrna came home early and found me. They pumped my stomach and she sent me for counseling. When I moved back home I got a job with a different company, an unlisted phone number, then got married and had two children. I got divorced, remarried, and divorced again. And now, here I am, overweight, single and alone. That mother of yours destroyed me and I hate her. I'm glad she's dead. You have no idea how many times I wished her dead."

Shawn could only shake his head. "I don't believe you. I don't believe any of it. You just got cold feet and ran away."

"I can see why you want to believe that, Shawn," she continued, "so let me ask you a question? Why did you have to wait until your mother died before you married, eh?" It was the second time that day he'd been asked that same question. "And don't tell me that I was the only woman in your life. You were the best lover I ever had, and you loved our rolls in the sack. And I know that just because I was out of your life you didn't quit sex. But you never married. I was married twice and they failed, but at least I gave it a shot. Why didn't you? What normal man wouldn't want to be a father? And you'd've made a great one, too.

"Shawn, I have no idea how your life continued on after I left you, but I'll bet you anything your mother controlled every facet of it." She then paused and her voice turned gentle. "For the love of God, Shawn, tear down that monument you've built for her. She doesn't deserve one. See her for what she really was; a manipulative tyrant who destroyed your life and mine."

A heavy silence filled the room. "Shawn," Vicki continued, breaking the quiet "I want you to allow me to do one thing before you leave; I want you to let me kiss you goodbye because I never got the chance too. It's very important to me----please? I loved you more than I've ever loved another human being. You were stolen from me and I never got to say goodbye."

Slowly, putting her arms around his neck, she pressed her lips to his and the kiss was deep, passionate, and long. And when it was finished she buried her face into the crook of his neck and broke down. Wrapping his arms around her he held her tightly, held her until she was cried out, became tearful himself.

"Shawn, when you go back to your wife I want you to love her the same way you once loved me. You're a good and kind man, but please----oh please----don't resurrect that mother of yours or she'll destroy you again. Leave her buried, where she belongs."

Vicki walked Shawn back to the elevator. While waiting for the door to open, without speaking, they embraced and kissed one last time. Shawn stepped onto the elevator, gave a finger wave goodbye, and experienced a horrific sinking sensation in his gut; it wasn't the drop of the elevator that caused it.

As he absentmindedly drove his car back north through thinning evening traffic, he thought about Vicki's words and about his past loves. He remembered some of his many dates----mostly one-nighters----but he remembered Jean Zouker and the four-and-a-half year relationship he had with her. He had met Jean about three years after Vicki left him. *Strange,* he thought, *all that time I spent with Jean and I've practically forgotten all about her.* He never loved Jean but they had a great relationship. They went on holidays together, the sex was unbelievable, she was beautiful, a great traveling companion, and yet nothing ever became of it. And more than once he had brought up the topic of moving in with her, but she refused to even discuss it. *I wonder why? She worked at a menial job and I could've given her a good life, so why wouldn't she live with me?*

As he made his way through the city traffic his mind became fixed on Jean Zouker, where she lived, what she was like, how they first met, and the day she announced she had found someone new and left him. *Four-and-a-half years I spent with that woman and it all ended with an unemotional goodbye. Why? Why was the relationship never deep?* They would go to bed, always in her apartment, have great sex, and then he'd go home. He was seldom invited to stay the night. *Sure, I stayed over a couple times, but she never wanted me to get too close.*

Then, a thought suddenly hit him and he almost drove through a red light. Slamming on the brakes, the car slid to a stop just in time. *The building she lived in, 1332 Vaughn Street; where did I see that address before? What's so damn familiar about that address? What?*

A car behind him tooted the horn. The light was green. Driving through the intersection he pulled over to the curb at the first opportunity and shut the engine off. "1332 Vaughn Street". *A nice place! Jean, a single mom with a little girl who worked as a grocery checkout at an A&P, and yet she lived very well. And she owned a car, too. Now that I think of it, how could she have afforded all that?* With the advantage of hindsight, and the things that Vicki had told him still burning in his ears, he wanted to remember Jean Zouker. *And mother liked Jean. Whenever they met they were always friendly to one another----very friendly. Almost too friendly, now that I think about it. But mom was never friendly toward Vicki, and she was a far better woman than Jean. So why? Jean was a gum-snapper; great looking, but not that smart.*

Cyrus Duncan was a businessman; Connie and Shawn Duncan were not. After Cyrus's death the Cossney Law Firm setup a trust to look after all the Duncan investment properties, the only way Connie could handle things. After Connie Duncan died, Shawn was called into Milton M. Cossney's office to review the family holdings. He spent almost two full hours with the lawyer. Properties, bonds, investments, two hours of it and Shawn couldn't have cared less, couldn't keep his mind on what the lawyer was saying. His world was art so everything the lawyer said went by him in a fog. Shawn only kept the deeds to his art studio, his mother's house, and the Portage Lake property. The trust set up for his mother continued on as before, and each month there was an investment dividend deposited in his account; no muss, no fuss, no headaches.

Reaching into the glove box he found Milton M. Cossney's business card while at the same time pulled his cell-phone from his pocket. Checking call answering, he found three messages, all from Caroline. He wouldn't listen to them, he couldn't, it would be too painful.

He phoned the lawyer and his secretary answered. "This is Shawn Duncan. I wonder if I might speak to Milton?"

"One moment and I'll see if he's still in,"

Yeah, right. Like you don't know if he's in the next room.

"Yes, Shawn. Milton here." No one called Milton M. Crossney, Milt or Miltie.

"Milton, I have one question for you."

"Shoot."

"Does my Trust own a piece of property on Vaughn Street?"

After a ten second pause the lawyer said. "I believe so. An apartment if memory serves me?

"Milton, right off the top of your head, would you happen to remember the street number of that property on Vaughn Street?"

"Oh God!" A longer pause. "I'd have to look it up for you. Ten years ago I'd've remembered it right off, but right now I'm having a senior's moment."

"Tell me about it," laughed Shawn. "But does 1332 ring a bell?"

"Bingo," said the lawyer. "Once you said it, I remembered. I'm sure that's the number. Yes. It's a twelve-unit apartment building."

The line went quiet for a spell. "Well, I guess that's all I wanted to know," said Shawn.

"Nothing else I can do for you, then?"

"Nope. And thanks for your time, Milton."

"No problem at all, Shawn. Call me anytime."

Oblivious of the traffic flowing by his car, the horns, the people walking past, Shawn Duncan saw and heard none of it. He was back in another time, at a dinner party where he first met Jean Zouker, the dinner party he attended with his mother, a party he didn't wish to attend but one his mother had insisted upon him attending.

And Jean made the first move. She came up to him and introduced herself. *My God but she was beautiful. She wore a royal blue low-cut dress, matching high heels, silver necklace and earrings, her blond hair flowing down over her shoulders.* Suddenly he was able to remember every little detail about that night, every word spoken, every move made. *She made it so easy for me. We left the dinner party early and went straight to her place.* He remembered his mother saying, 'you two run along and have fun and I'll see you in the morning'. *Why wasn't she mad at me leaving her alone at the party? Less than an hour in Jean's apartment and we were in bed together. All that time together and yet we were never close. In the Jacuzzi with candles and wine, on a Caribbean cruise, dances, dinners with friends, and yet we literally remained strangers. How could that be? It was as though Jean had placed an invisible wall between us and I was never allowed on the other side.*

"Because the whole thing was a setup. That's why," he shouted, his anger growing at his naiveté. "She arranged everything? She kept her horny little son on a leash without him ever knowing it." *How did you work it out, Mom; Jean got free rent and the odd bonus as long as she kept me satisfied and single? Was that the arrangement? Jean, you keep my boy single and happy, and* I'll *make it worth your while?*

If there were any lingering doubts about what his mother had achieved one glaring recall put an end to it. It was a statement Jean had made when she finally told him goodbye, when she had found someone new and was getting married. "Don't take it hard, Shawn. It was a real slice. We both were winners. It was a great contract, but it's time I became an honest woman. Don and I love each other." *Don. The name of the guy she married. A great contract, she said. Jesus Christ! A great contract. She was telling me, and it went right over my stupid head. And after saying it, she just shook her head and smiled because she knew I didn't catch it. I must have looked like one pathetic jerk? Vicki was telling the truth. I could've been the father of her children, a husband, but oh no.* "I'm a goddamn mama's boy."

And he recalled the time he took it on himself and rented an apartment. He was going to move out of his mother's house. It was right after his thirtieth birthday.

"Well that is the silliest thing I've ever heard of," Connie told him. "Wasting good money for an apartment and leaving this big house practically empty."

"But I think it's time for me to be on my own, Mom."

"But I need you here."

Shawn laughed. "Nonsense!"

"So, now you think it's time to start laughing at your mother, do you?"

It was the start of a guilt trip he could never get past, and his mother always won out. Shawn sublet the apartment and never again brought up the subject of leaving home.

Putting his head down on the steering wheel, his entire life tumbled through his mind, a life of nothingness. He reached into his coat pocket and opened his cell-phone. As he listened to Caroline's voice weeping and pleading for him to come back, telling him she was sorry, asking for forgiveness, he could no longer hold his emotions in check.

Chapter 36

CAROLINE WANDERED LETHARGICALLY THROUGH the house her mind locked in the past. Her once happy life, was it over after such a short time? Was that it? One husband had left her through death, was her second one just walking away forever? Chimes from the grandfather clock in the foyer brought her out of it. It was 2:00 a.m. She suddenly needed to do something. Anything. She needed to get out of the house. Grabbing a jacket from the hallway closet she hurried out the door and up the driveway, past the carriage house, into the shadows of the overhanging trees her breath showing white on the cool night air. The platinum glow of the moon reflected with a mirror's clarity on the lake surface, on distant hills, on the treetops, on all things that it touched. As her sight adjusted to the shadows she picked up her pace her outline racing along the gound in front her.

When she emerged from the heavy-forested laneway into the more open country at the edge of the Duncan property, the moonlight exploded into brilliance, and ahead she saw another moon, a reflection on a car windshield. A car was parked in front of the old Lutheran church. Slowing her pace she walked cautiously toward it.

On reaching the car, a car she recognized only too well, she stood in silence on the roadway for a time and stared at the church, at its darkness, at the moon-induced halo encircling the cross atop its steeple, at the giant pines behind it, at the muted white headstones in the graveyard beside it. With unsteady footsteps she approached the church door and found it ajar. Waiting outside for a time, waiting to hear a sound, any sound, she heard only the thumping of her heart. Taking one brave step through the open door into the interior darkness of the church she said softly, "Shawn, are you in here?" Only silence. "Shawn, if you're here please talk to me?"

"I'm here," came a voice, a voice as soft as a child's whimper.

Feeling her way along the back of a pew she sensed his nearness before she could feel his body, before her hand rested on his shoulder. Working her way around the pew she came to him and sat with her body tight to his. Taking his limp hand in hers they sat in silence, sat in the muted light that penetrated the smudged windows of that forgotten house of God.

"Are you going to leave me, Shawn?" she asked, her expression defeated.

"Why would you even want to stay with a man like me?"

"Because I love you."

"I don't know what I'm going to do, but I know I love you, too."

"Since I was a little girl I've loved you, Shawn Duncan."

Another long silence followed before he said, "What are we going to do? Everything seems to be falling apart. Everything was so good, and now…"

She squeezed his hand and laid her head on his shoulder. "I'm sorry I didn't tell you, Shawn. I wanted to, but as time went by I just…"

He pressed his cheek against the top of her head. "It wasn't that. I know what you did, and why you did it. I'm just so damn hurt and angry with myself. But most of all, I'm mad at mother for doing this to me. I was just so stupid. 'Any fool could figure it out' Frank Everett said. And he was right. So why didn't I?"

"Because you had no reason to."

"Probably because I was such a mama's boy. All my life she protected me and I let her do it. When I was a kid I wanted to play football, but she wouldn't let me. Said 'it was too rough a sport'. Do you want to know a sad truth about me; every kid I ever knew got into fights----except me? I've never once been punched on the nose, or threw a punch. Never had a cut lip. Other kids used to call me, 'sissy and wimp'. She always protected me from the world, and then she goes and sets me up for this." He gave out a weak laugh. "When Everett was at the studio today I wanted so badly to punch him in the mouth, but I didn't know how. *I didn't know how to throw a punch.*"

"That's because you're a gentle person," Caroline defended, "but you know something, Shawn, being a gentle person is not a bad thing. Living with someone that's violent and loud isn't great, and I should know. I've always loved you because you are the way you are. Don't ever be ashamed of that, and please, oh please, don't ever change?"

After a short silence he said, "You must promise me one thing, Caroline; that you'll never protect me again? It's high time I faced life for what it is."

She lifted her head from his shoulder and look at his dark profile. "Shawn, there's something I've never told you, something I've never told another living soul. Something I find hard to even tell myself. It's about Peter and me."

He squeezed her hand. "You can keep your life with Peter to yourself. I don't have to know. I really don't want to know."

"But I must tell someone. You're not the only one that feels pain and betrayal, Shawn. I only gave you a tiny outline of how my marriage ended. I told you that Peter died from an accident."

"You don't have to say anything, Caroline. Keep your secrets. It's okay."

She ignored him and continued. "When I was married to Peter," she began slowly, "when we lived in the little apartment at the marina, things weren't exactly a bed of roses. To be honest, it was really hell on earth. We were heavily in debt. We did nothing but work----and fight. And I mean *fight*. Physically fight. Not only screaming and shouting, but pushes and slaps. Peter drank too much and near the end, so did I. Twice I remember going around wearing dark glasses to hide a black eye. We were up at five, or earlier each morning, so we wouldn't have to hire any help and keep the costs down. From spring 'til fall that's how we lived; up in the dark, to bed in the dark. I was determined to make it. I was determined not to be poor like my parents were. I'm ashamed to say it, but looking back, I was ashamed of my parents----at least at what they had to do to make a living.

"One night----shortly before Dad was killed----I overheard my parents talking, and I heard what they went through to make ends meet. I heard some of what you now know. I won't go on about it, but it sure shocked me. Dad was ashamed of himself for what he had endured in life, and strangely, I think some of his shame rubbed off on me. And it shouldn't've. But by God, I became determined not to go through what they did. I was going to make it and I brought that attitude into the marriage.

"The year Peter died was a year of absolute hell. It was all my idea to buy the marina and it wasn't working. But I wouldn't give up. The year he died he tried to talk me into selling the marina and the two of us getting regular jobs----so we could have time together and maybe even have a child or two. He really wanted to save our marriage. But no way. I was going to make it. I wasn't going to be like my parents. I often wondered how things would have turned out if I had listened to him. He'd probably still be alive, and I may have been a mother.

"Shawn, you just called yourself a wimp. On the other hand, Peter was a macho kind of guy. Throughout the winter months he played hockey in a bush league, drank beer *with the boys*, lost his license for drunk driving, and we fought. So much for a macho-man! Except for the few times we went out for dinner----and we always drank too much and came home miserable----there was no time for anything but work. Sex was something we did to help fall asleep at night, something that happened every time we went for two days in a row without fighting.

"One night," Caroline said courageously, "I remember it was a hot night in July, I was getting ready for bed. I saw something strange down at one of the docks. There's a window in the apartment that overlooks the docks. A cabin cruiser was tied up there----a thirty-six foot Carver. It was owned by a divorcee from Michigan, a Gertrude Flannagan. She always called herself *Miss.* Married and divorced three times, yet she was still a *Miss.* Apparently the divorce settlements were very good. She'd been coming across the lake and tying up at our marina for a couple years, sometimes alone, sometimes with a friend. She'd stay a few days before traveling on to another marina. But she'd always come back a couple times throughout the season. I never thought anything of it. She was a good paying customer and I was glad to see her.

"But that night the water in the bay was dead calm. There were no lights on in the cruiser, and yet there were ripples coming from around her boat, nice, gentle, evenly spaced ripples. I stood there by the window watching the yacht and casually wondering what was causing the ripples? What was Gertrude doing in there? I actually stood there like an idiot and wondering what was making her boat rock. I'll tell you how smart----or dumb I was; my husband and Gertrude were making waves at *my* marina, and I'm standing there in my pajamas wondering what was causing the ripples around her boat. I actually went to bed and was almost asleep when it dawned on me. How smart is that, eh? When it finally hit me I went down and walked in on them."

Shawn patted her hand and whispered, "I'm sorry."

"Oh, don't feel sorry. He was only doing with Gertrude what I didn't have time to do with him." She half-laughed, half-cried. "Then to top it all off, I had the nerve to be mad at him, like it was all his fault. I told him at the season's end I was divorcing him. For the rest of our time together we just tolerated each other. We stopped fighting because there was no more need to fight. The marriage was dead and so were my dreams."

She stopped talking for a moment, breathed deeply, and then continued. "He was in the water at the shallow end of a dock; that's where one of the boaters found his body. There was an extension cord leading from the shop to the dock, because all of the boat outlets were in use. The dock outlets have safeties on them, but the ones in the shop don't. An electric drill was plugged into the cord. He had been electrocuted. He had been drinking heavily for some time and I think it threw his judgement off because he knew better than to get into water with an electric drill. For God's sakes, he wired most of the marina. He used to give me hell for going around taps and the bathtub when a lightning storm was on. I don't know how many times he told me 'water and electricity don't mix'."

She had to struggle to say what came next. "If I only would have forgiven him and agreed to sell the marina he'd still be alive today. I killed him! So, I got rid of a dying marriage and a huge mortgage all in one shot. His life insurance paid off the mortgage. When I stood beside his grave I swore I'd never marry again. And then you came along, my first love, and then I go and screw things up again by not telling you all that I knew."

Caroline began to weep softly, but it quickly turned to a flood. Her body's shaking and sobs filled the quiet of the church and it went on for the longest time, went on until she was empty, went on like a penance. "Oh Shawn----Oh Peter. Oh God I'm sorry," she whispered, when she could again speak.

"Come on. Let's go home," said Shawn.

They left the gloom of the church and walked to the road. He left his car parked where it was; the night's chill had settled in on them and they needed the warmth of a walk. Just as they passed in front of the cemetery they stopped. Looking across to the far corner where his parents were buried, Shawn said, "Do you think they ever gave a minutes thought about the consequences of what they were doing?"

"How many young lovers have you known who ever thought it through?" said Caroline.

"I'll bet they never imagined they'd have a book written about them."

"Shawn, are you ashamed of them----of what they did?"

"No. Strangely I'm not."

"Good! And Shawn, I think that you should work with Frank Everett and write the best book possible, tell everyone just how great your family really was."

Shawn thought about her words for a moment. "Great? No, they weren't great. They were just people and now they're gone. Earlier today, Vicki, the woman that I was once engaged to, told me to leave the past buried and to give all my love to you. I'm taking her advice." He pointed toward the back corner of the cemetery and tightened his jaw with determination. "They're gone and we're still here. I don't hate them, but I'll never allow them back into my life again. Today I discovered some very shocking news; the two greatest hurts I've ever experienced in my life were both of my mother's making. You already know about Frank Everett, and someday----but not tonight----I'll tell you about Vicki Picklow and what happened to us." Looking stalwart into the back corner of the cemetery, he shouted, "Goodbye Jeremy Kane and Constance Louise Lawson. Rest in peace."

In the middle of a lonely road two people entwined as one and rocked gently, the white of their breath against the cool night air. Clinging fiercely to each other, the silver light of the moon reflecting on their faces, he whispered softly in her ear, "Come on, let's go home?"

Chapter 37

Harriet Colburn turned on the TV, stared at it for a moment, then turned it off again. Standing by her living room window she gazed vacantly at the empty street as yesterdays tumbled through her mind. For more than half a lifetime she had struggled to keep the memory of that year locked in its cage but the beast was again loose and gnawing at her insides.

On September 4, 1953, Connie Duncan's mother died suddenly. Darrell drove Connie into Toronto to catch a train to Cape Breton Island to attend the funeral; trains were the mode of travel back then----and that left only Harriet to look after the summerhouse. Darrell hated the drive into the city, hated everything about cities, but since he was required to do maintenance work on the Duncan home once a year anyway, he decided to kill two birds with one stone. Taking his tool chest with him he stayed in Toronto and worked on the Duncan house until Connie got back from the East. Both were away from Portage Lake for nine long days.

Harriet knew Connie was madly in love with Jerry Kane, and she rightly guessed it was a one-sided affair. Different times Kane had brushed up against her and she knew it was no accident; his smile said as much. Harriet had often fantasized about being alone with the man, but fantasies were safe so she allowed her mind to toy with the idea of physically being with the man. Darrell was a good and decent provider, but he was more the fatherly type and not a strong lover. However, Harriet had witnessed Kane's manliness firsthand.

It happened on a hot day that July. Harriet heard laughter coming from the direction of the little sandy bay. Darrell was in town for some reason or other and curiosity got the better of her. She hurried over to the bay and watched Connie and Jerry at play. From the shadows of the evergreens she watched them swim in the nude, watched them make love on the beach their bodies glistening wet in the bright sunlight, watched them until she could stand it no longer. Quietly returning to the summerhouse, her underwear damp from stimulation, her desires leaping inside her, she wished that just once she could experience Jeremy Kane's animal lust.

Suddenly she was confronted with the chance of making that fantasy come true; she didn't even try to fight the temptation. The very first morning after Darrell and Connie were gone, Harriet came to the summerhouse early, very early, went into the kitchen and made coffee and toast, put it on a tray and carried it over to the carriage house for Kane, something she had never done before. Wearing only a light summer dress she went up to the loft and Kane met her at the top of the stairs. Without saying a word he took the tray, set it on the floor, and then scooped her up in his arms and carried her to the recliner. Paralyzed with fear, wanting to scream and run, her desires over-ruled that fear as her skin turned to goose flesh. Before gently forcing her down on the recliner he slipped off her dress. In an instant he was out of his clothes. Coming down on top of her he entered her with the intensity of a rutting buck, each thrust firm and deep. It was the first time she had ever climaxed. Those following days were spent in one endless mating ritual; no shame, no self-respect, no holds barred. It was a golden opportunity to experience something she had always craved and she gave into it with everything she had.

Darrell's lifestyle was always predictable, his habits never varying, and he was far away from Portage Lake. He also trusted Harriet without reservation. He called home every evening at eight o'clock just to hear Harriet's voice, and she was always there to take his call. No sooner did she hang up the phone than the old pickup was heading back to the summerhouse. She would then spend the night with Kane. Over the course of those nine days they swam naked in the little sandy bay, mated openly wherever, and whenever the urge hit them, had a picnic on the high bluff across Portage Lake----where Tommy Doweling saw them together----skimmed about the lake in the Chris Craft and frolicked in the old trapper's cabin. And she posed nude for Kane, always insisted her face remained hidden.

But on the morning of the ninth day, the day when Darrell brought Connie back to the lake, everything came to an end. That morning Harriet got out of bed early----Kane, always the early riser, was already up and in the loft of the carriage house----made up the bed with fresh sheets, and looked carefully for any tell-tale signs which might betray her behavior.

She then went to the carriage house to put an official end to the affair.

"Jerry, we have to talk. It's been fun, but it's over. It's now back to being ourselves." The truth was, she was riddled with guilt and she also had had enough of Jerry Kane. She saw him for what he truly was; the picture was ugly and she was no better.

"What's over with my dear little nymphomaniac?"

"Jerry, Connie and Darrell will be back in a couple hours. It's over. It was great, but it's over. I want you to understand that. No more smiles, no more touching, and certainly no more sex."

Kane came to her and wrapped his arms around her, grabbed her buttocks firmly and slammed her hard against his groin. He laughed, "You mean no more of this?"

"Stop Jerry!" she tried pushing him away. "It's over, now stop."

"It's over when I say it's over, Harriet."

She struggled so he twisted her arm behind her back. Pulling her dress up, he tore off her underpants.

"Jerry, stop." She was in pain and couldn't pull away. "You're hurting me."

"Oh come on, Harriet. Don't start having conscience problems, not after the best time you've ever had in your entire life."

"Please, Jerry, stop?"

"Why?" he said, pushing her backward toward the recliner, "it was you who instigated all this. It was you who came up those stairs with your crotch on fire. But you know something Harriet, you're the best time I've ever had, and I've had some great ones in my time." When the backs of her legs touch the recliner he pushed her down onto her back.

"Okay. I know what it makes me, but it has to stop, here and now. What if Connie should ever find out? She's pregnant and you and her are going away together. She told me so."

"Well she told you wrong."

"What?"

Kane's expression turned sober. "She told you wrong. When I leave here it'll be by myself."

"But----but she thinks...."

"Yeah, I know what she thinks. But the truth is she's going back with her husband. That was the deal. I knock-her-up so old limp-dick Duncan can have a kid, and then I leave. Back in Toronto I had some problems. I owed money to some very nasty people. Believe me, Harriet, gambling is a terrible vice. Between the rent on my studio and my gambling debts, I was in a tight spot. Duncan owns the studio I rent, and when I went to him to try and see what could be done about holding off on the rent for a while, he offered me a deal I couldn't refuse. Basically it was this: knock the wife up for me, and I'll take care of the rent and your debts."

"You're lying," said Harriet.

He looked coldly at her. "I never lie, Harriet. Going away together was all Connie's idea. I never encouraged her and I never agreed to it. If she had just asked me if I was going away with her I would've told her the truth. I just let her think what she wanted too. Now, on the other hand, you were honest. You came up those stairs and as much as said, let's do it? I like that in a woman."

Kane then dropped his pants and drove into her with a mean energy each thrust jogging the recliner in little increments across the floor. The excitement of the rape over-excited Kane and it only lasted a couple minutes. Throughout the ordeal Harriet never took part. She only felt self-loathing, shame and disgust, like a drapery of slime had been drawn over her body and it was oozing from her pores.

The instant Kane finished, Harriet jumped to her feet. "That was rape, you pig. You got away with it that time, Kane, but I swear to God, if you ever so much as lay a finger on me again, I'll kill you."

Kane laughed as he pulled up his pants and tucked in his shirt. "Really. And after all the fun we had together." He then gave her a twisted smile. "That was exciting, wouldn't you say?"

As he walked away from her, still adjusting his shirt and pants, Harriet said, "It was rape, and if you ever tell anyone about us, or if Darrell or Connie ever find out, I *will* kill you. I know I'm a slut for doing what I did and I'm going to have to live with it, but if you ever hurt the two people I love most in life, or if you ever try that again, I swear…"

"Oh, stop the bullshit, Harriet. You loved it. And as for Connie, she brought it on herself. As for old block-headed Darrell, if he ever caught us he's so dumb he probably wouldn't know what we were doing, anyway."

For the remainder of her life Harriet would not be able to recall any of the following seconds. All she'd remember was seeing Kane lying on the floor shaking as though having an epileptic seizure, a walking stick standing straight up from the side of his skull, a circle of blood growing ever larger around his head. She just stood there and watched him until the twitching stopped, more concerned about the semen running down her legs than what she had done. Trance-like, she went down from the loft and back to the summerhouse, took a shower, washed a few dishes and waited the arrival of her husband and dearest friend. Her mind refused to acknowledge the reality of what had taken place.

Darrell and Connie returned to the lake at around one-thirty that afternoon. Darrell seemed his old self, but Connie looked terrible. Between the shock of her mother's death and the long train ride, she was at the point of collapse. Going straight upstairs, while she took a quick bath Harriet closed the drapes and turned down the bedding for her. Connie slept the clock around not waking until late the following morning.

That afternoon, Darrell, white-faced with shock, came into the kitchen and announced in a hushed voice that he had found Kane's body. It was that news which clicked Harriet's mind back to reality. She then remembered killing him and for all intents and purposes she realized her life, as she knew it, was over. While Darrell was on the phone talking to Cyrus Duncan it all came back to her. She couldn't recall pulling the old walking stick from the umbrella stand, but she knew she had. Nor did she remember swinging it at Kane, but that too she knew to be a fact. Her life, her marriage, her friendship, everything was finished.

After Darrell hung up the phone, he said, "Jesus Christ, Duncan did it". Then Darrell told Harriet about Duncan's offer of a new home if he'd get rid of the body. She instantly realized a life preserver had been thrown to her and she instinctively grabbed it. "Then do it Darrell, and I'll help you." While Connie Duncan slept the full day away, Darrell and Harriet Colburn disposed of her lover's body and became the owners of their own home. Two weeks later when the County buried Kane's remains, Harriet placed flowers on his unmarked grave, not to show respect----for she would rather have spat on it---- but to give the proper impression. She wanted to show people there was no animosity between them, and also to reassure herself that Kane was indeed dead and gone.

And she remembered that bitter cold January day when Cyrus Duncan phoned the house wanting to speak with Darrell. "I'm sorry, Mister Duncan, but Darrell is away right now. Do you want me to have him give you a call when he gets back?"

"Yes I do, Harriet. But since you're already on the phone I'd like to ask you a question."

"Yes?"

"I was just wondering; what in hell did Kane do to you that made you kill him?"

The line went silent.

"Oh come-come, Harriet. We're all in this together. Just minutes after Darrell told me Kane was dead I knew it was you who did it. I know Darrell thinks it was me, but we both know it was you."

More silence.

"You see, Harriet, I knew it wasn't Darrell because he would have just strangled Kane, got rid of his body and that would've been it. And I certainly didn't do it because I never left the city. And Connie, she was in love with him, so that only left you. So why'd you do it? You don't have to tell if you don't wish; I'm just curious, that's all."

After another silence she bleated out, "He raped me----and called Darrell a blockhead?"

"Well then, my dear, you did the right thing. And isn't it ironic? Darrell got rid of his body, made it look like an accident and fooled everyone. A blockhead could never pull that off. And Harriet," Duncan switched to a more fatherly tone, "put it behind you. You did everyone a favour and all is well. And never say a word to Darrell about killing Kane, and certainly never tell him what Kane did to you. It would crush the man if he knew how violated you were."

Duncan then changed the subject. "Oh, and by the way; Darrell told me you're in the family way. Congratulations."

"Thank you," she whispered.

Darrell and Harriet went on working for Duncans up until Darrell's death. However, after Cyrus's death, Connie and Shawn stopped coming to the lake. But Harriet and Connie stayed in touch and remained friends, and each December Harriet and Caroline went into the city and spent a few days at the Duncan home. Shawn and Caroline traveling about the city on the buses and streetcars while Connie and Harriet Christmas shopped and spent quality time together.

That tradition lasted until the two youngsters turned thirteen years of age.

The night their friendship ended, Connie and Harriet had left the children alone to watch TV while they went out for a movie and dinner. It was late when they came home and they found the teenagers asleep on the couch with their arms around each other. Harriet's face turned ashen when she saw them. Grabbing the smiling Connie by the arm she pulled her rather roughly to another room.

"Harriet, what in the world…?" gasped the startled Connie.

Harriet pointed toward the room where the children were. "That in there."

"For God's sake, Harriet. They're children. So they were necking. So what?"

Harriet glared at Connie with icy eyes but was too rankled to speak her mind.

Connie was shocked. "What's happening here, Harriet?"

Harriet suddenly announced, "We're going home----now."

"Harriet? Harriet?" said Connie. "They're only children."

Then Harriet turned on her old friend. "It's not the kids that's bothering me; I'm leaving because I'm sick of listening to you talking about that bastard of a Kane. Dear Jesus, Connie, grow up. Every time we talk or visit, you go on and on about him. I'm sick of hearing about him. He didn't love you. He told me he wasn't going away with you. He was a hired stud. He told me that when he was raping me----when you were away at your mother's funeral."

Connie's face whitened with shock. "Harriet, don't say that? You're just making this all up? Why are you doing this to me?"

"Let me put it this way, Connie; he's where he belongs, under the ground. He was hired by Cyrus Duncan to get him a child." Harriet then grabbed Connie by the shoulders and shook the stunned woman. "Accept it, Connie, he was garbage. He was a great artist, but as a human being he was pure dirt."

Harriet then went to the living room and shook her daughter. "Come on, Caroline. Wake up. We're going home."

Several times that night on the drive back to Portage Lake, Caroline, bewildered and shaken by what had taken place, asked her mother what was wrong, but she never got an answer. Shawn and Caroline would not see each other for the next thirty years. As for Connie and Harriet, it was the last time they would ever see each other. But they did talk one final time.

"Hello, Harriet. This is Connie----Connie Duncan. Please don't hang up on me?"

After a slight hesitation Harriet said, "How did you know where to find me?"

"I called your old number and Caroline told me."

"I see," said Harriet.

"Harriet," Connie began slowly, "I have to know something, and I'm begging you to tell me the truth. Everything."

"Yes?" Harriet knew the question before it was even asked.

"What you told me a long time ago----about Jerry. Was it true, or were you just mad about finding the children together? Did he really rape you?"

"Connie, I've already told you the truth and nothing has changed. I didn't make it up. Kane raped me and told me he wasn't going anywhere with you." Harriet could hear soft weeping on the other end of the line. "Connie, I know you don't want to believe it, and I don't like hurting you, but Kane was dirt. He wasn't going to go away with you. Cyrus Duncan hired him to get a child. Your relationship with him was just----well----a business deal. You wanted someone to love you; Cyrus wanted a child to make himself look like a man, and Kane needed to pay off some bills. It was that simple. I got raped, you and Cyrus got the child you both wanted, and in the end Kane got what was coming to him.

"Please don't say that, Harriet?" Connie whimpered. "He didn't deserve to die the way he did."

"Connie. Kane was dead before he went off that cliff, because Darrell and I pushed him. It was me who killed him, about one minute after he raped me. He could have gotten away with the rape, but he made the mistake of saying something terrible about Darrell, the dearest man I ever knew. I don't want to hurt you, Connie, but there's no nice way to say it. Kane did not love you."

After a lengthy silence Connie said, "I'm sorry too, Harriet. And deep down I think I've known that for some time. I just didn't want to believe it. It was easier not to believe it." Then she added, "Harriet, you were the dearest friend I ever had, and before it's too late, I'd like to..."

"Before what's too late, Connie? What are you trying to say?"

"I'm having medical problems. I don't know how much time I have left, and there are things I must do. You know me, the great procrastinator; keep putting things off. Well it's caught up to me and now I have to go up to the old summerhouse and deal with some unfinished business.

"What unfinished business, Connie?"

"Jerry's things in the carriage house. Shawn must never see any of it----one painting in particular. I used to want to tell him who his father was, but now I don't. He must never know. I don't want him thinking badly of me."

Harriet's interest twigged. "What are you planning to do, Connie?"

"Simple! I'm taking a book of matches with me."

"You're going to burn the old carriage house?"

"That's right. And everything in it. Now that I know the absolute truth I want all traces of Jerry Kane gone. I want Shawn to believe that Cyrus Duncan was his father. I don't want him to ever find out that his mother was a----you know. And I'm going to see my lawyer sometime this week and have my will changed. After Cyrus died, and I still believed Jerry was a *saint*, I bought a burial plot in the old Lutheran cemetery right beside him. I believe I told you about it at the time and you advised me against it. I put it in my will that I was going to be buried there. We were going to be together forever----and all that childish nonsense. Can you believe that? Can you believe I was that foolish? Anyway, I never got around to changing my will and I plan on doing it as soon as I can. I will be buried beside Cyrus in Pleasant Hills, and Shawn will never know the truth about me. And besides, what does it really matter where you're buried?"

"That's good, Connie. I'm glad to hear that. In fact, I'm relieved to hear that."

Anyway," continued Connie, "there is something else I would like to do while I'm up there; I'd like to be able to visit my old friend. I'd like to be able to stop by and see you again, Harriet. Would that be possible before it's too late?"

Harriet paused a moment before saying, "Sure. I'd like that, too. I'll be expecting you."

Constance Louise Duncan died one hour after hanging up the phone.

But Harriet's greatest fear came to pass. After all those years, just when she believed all was safe, Shawn and Caroline's natural draw brought them back together and there was only one way she could stop it. When the two were youngsters she encouraged them to play together, believing that if they grew up like brother and sister they would never become romantically involved. But when she found the two asleep with their arms around each other she knew the experiment was a failure. She couldn't tell them the truth, that she had been a cheat with the same man as Connie Duncan, that they had shared the same bed, so the only option left to her was to keep the two apart. For their entire married lives Harriet and Darrell never once used birth control but Caroline was her only child. After Caroline was born Harriet never again conceived. She wanted a second child so badly, but it never happened. And when she counted back to those nine disgusting days with Jeremy Kane, Caroline's birthday matched that time exactly.

But then she really didn't need to count back nine months; each time Harriet looked into her daughter's eyes she saw her sins staring back at her, and her hatred of Kane was always a barrier between her and Caroline. So in the end, there was only one way to stop Caroline from marrying Shawn Duncan; she would have to confess the truth. But that would crush Caroline's memory of Darrell and she couldn't do it. Those nine adulterous days had stretched into a lifetime of self-loathing. Her lust had produced a child with a birth defect, one only she could see.

It was past 3:00 a.m. when Harriet drew the drapes and retired to her bedroom. But in the darkness, beneath the loneliness of the sheets, her torment went on. Guilt would never let her be at peace. *But maybe it's not all bad? At their age they'll never have children so they'll never find out that their relationship is anything more than just husband and wife. Who's going to tell them? Certainly not me. At least somewhere in this damnable world there are two happy people.*

The End